"Linda Grant scored a solid success with her first Catherine Sayler novel. Her second, skillfully plotted and smoothly written, is even better."

The San Diego Union

"If [you] still can't get enough feminist private eyes, pick up a copy of Linda Grant's *Blind Trust*.... Should put Grant right up there with her best-selling colleagues... [She] is a character readers will want to get to know better."

The Denver Post

"Add to the list of new crime novel writers who have obvious talent and great promise the name Linda Grant."

St. Petersburg Times

"Grant's Catherine Sayler is a worthy addition to this special class of sleuths, and, to my mind, has the potential for becoming the best.... Sayler [is] sensitive without being know-it-all, tough without being hard and independent without being icy. Sayler is simply a great detective."

The Patriot Ledger

BLIND TRUST

Linda Grant

IVY BOOKS • NEW YORK

Ivy Books
Published by Ballantine Books
Copyright © 1990 by Linda V. Williams

Library of Congress Catalog Card Number: 90-30145

ISBN 0-8041-0791-2

This edition published by arrangement with Charles Scribner's Sons, an Imprint of Macmillan Publishing Company.

Manufactured in the United States of America

First Ballantine Books Edition: June 1991

To my mother, Charlene Ver Lee,
and to the memory of my father,
Jay Ver Lee,
with love and gratitude

Acknowledgments

I would like to thank the many people who generously shared their expertise and ideas: Mike Young, whose "have I got a story for you" provided the initial idea for the plot; Sara Battin and Travis Davison for a short course in banking; Joe Petzel and Vern Masse for background on Vietnam; Elizabeth A. Lynn for help with the aikido scenes; Carol Kelly-Thomas for medical information; George Posner, CLI, and Lynne Houghton, CLI, for their private eyes' view of the world; and Don Solomon for finding homes for my characters in Modesto. I would also like to thank Andy Williams and Barbara Dean for their helpful comments on the manuscript.

BLIND TRUST

1

MAKEUP CAN DO a lot for a woman, but it cannot cover a black eye. Thirty minutes of concentrated effort and a small fortune in cosmetics and I still looked like I'd gotten my eye shadow on upside down.

And an impressive display it was; every shade from deep purple to fuchsia decorated the area under my left eye. I was not looking forward to going out in public. "Another of those damned opportunities for personal growth," I groaned.

In twelve years as a private investigator and ten years studying the martial art of aikido, I had never gotten a black eye. It had taken my two-year-old niece to accomplish that.

I glowered at my reflection. The eye did draw attention away from the tiny wrinkles I'd noticed lately at the corners of my eyes and the fact that the roots of my blond hair were a shade darker than the rest of it. But none of that compensated for the fact that I was wearing a glaring advertisement of my own incompetence. At the dojo, I would be subjected to endless quips about "not getting out of the way." In other martial arts you blocked punches; in aikido you moved out of the path of the attack. Clearly, I had not moved fast enough.

A black eye wasn't going to do me any good at the office, either. In some circles a shiner might be considered part of the profession, but I didn't travel in those circles. My clients were large corporations. In their book it was bad enough to have to hire a private investigator, unthinkable to have one who looked the part.

I considered lying low for a few days, but this was not the

moment to take off work. For the first time in years my client list was shrinking instead of growing. The most likely cause of this unfortunate situation was Miles Clarke, the son of one of San Francisco's first families, who had decided that banking was too dull for him and had opened his own corporate security firm. He was charming and bright; he was a member of the right clubs, securely positioned in the old-boy network, and he was the right sex. In the four months since he'd announced his new endeavor to his friends and former business associates, either the crime rate had plunged, or I was losing customers.

No, holing up in my apartment was definitely not a good idea. So I resigned myself to the inevitable ribbing and headed for the office.

It's only about four blocks away, and each time I walk it, I congratulate myself on fleeing downtown San Francisco. Being able to walk to work is a luxury few people enjoy in this city, and my neighborhood is infinitely more interesting than the glass-and-steel towers of the business district.

Much of Divisadero Street is pretty seedy, but my office is just far enough up the hill to qualify as "on the edge" of Pacific Heights. The graceful Victorian house, which I refuse to tart up with a four-color paint job, is respectable enough for my corporate clients and comfortable enough for me.

When I came through the door, my secretary, Amy, gasped.

"Never ask for a discount from your plastic surgeon," I quipped.

"Oh, Catherine, what happened?"

"I've got to stop telling jokes at Republican gatherings."

At that point Jesse appeared in the hall. His presence at work at eight-thirty was a sure sign that things were not going my way. He hadn't been less than fifteen minutes late in a month, and today he was a full thirty minutes early.

Jesse had never deigned to adopt the subtle subservience appropriate to an assistant. The closest he came to acknowledging that he worked for me was the cocky "Morning, boss lady" with which he greeted me each day and an occasional reference to the trials of "working for a honky." This morning he smiled broadly and asked, "What's the other guy look like?"

"It's not true that you can't get hurt mud wrestling," I replied.

"You white people do have a funny sense of style."

"S and M eyes, want to try it? Purple'd be a good color on you."

Jesse chuckled and wandered back to the coffee machine.

My office was already occupied. McGee, the firm's gray-and-white mascot, was curled up on my chair. "Big night, I'll bet," I observed as I nudged him. He gave me one of his best bored tomcat stares and refused to move. "Down," I ordered, giving him a shove. He finally got up, but instead of jumping down, he climbed onto my desk and began to wash his paw with exaggerated indifference.

"You cocky bastard," I said with a sigh. "Did you finally drive off that big orange tom, or is there a new lady in your life?" McGee wasn't one to kiss and tell. He just continued his toilette.

He'd filled out a lot since I'd adopted him as a scraggly teenager. Nguyen Van Thanh, the owner of the Vietnamese restaurant down the street, had threatened to dispatch the noisy beggar to the pound, so I'd installed him in my office. He spent his days shedding on the furniture and his nights in search of romance.

The telephone startled McGee out of his complacence and sent him in search of a quieter place to finish his morning ablutions.

Amy informed me that Daniel Martin of First Central Bank was calling. Mr. Martin had a deep voice; his words came out as if each had been cut and polished. He wanted to see me urgently, as soon as possible.

It was always as soon as possible in this business, though I'd bet season tickets to the symphony that he'd been sitting on the situation for at least a week, hoping to find some other way to deal with it.

I told him that I could see him in forty-five minutes, and he agreed. "Do you want me to come to your office?"

"No, no. I'd prefer to meet at yours." That, too, was predictable. Sometimes I feel like the neighborhood abortionist. Everyone's glad you're there when things go wrong, but no one wants to admit to ever needing your services.

The phone rang again, and this time it was the one voice I wanted to hear: Peter's.

"Morning, babe, how's the eye?"

"It looks worse than it feels, and it doesn't feel good," I replied. "You were up unusually early this morning. I didn't even hear you leave." I'd missed our morning snuggle, but I didn't tell him that.

"You looked so comfortable, I didn't want to wake you. The guy I'm watching is a *very* early riser. No one who gets up that early can be completely honest."

"Maybe he's a stockbroker," I suggested.

"Like I said," Peter said with his usual lack of faith in the capitalist system.

"Is this the kiddy-porn king?"

"Yep. Now that I've located him, it's just a matter of tagging along till he leads me to his studio. With luck, that'll be where he stores his film and I can pick up the Carlisle reel before I tip the vice squad. Oops, here he comes now. See you tonight."

The line went dead. I was glad I wasn't spending my day following a man who dealt in child pornography. Corporate crooks aren't an exemplary lot. They cost the society considerably more than run-of-the-mill thieves, but they're rarely violent or vicious. Greed was a wholesome vice compared with the things Peter dealt with.

2

D ANIEL MARTIN ARRIVED at precisely nine-thirty. He had the look of a man who was always in a hurry. He was about my age, late thirties, which always seems a bit young for bank executives. You don't get that high that fast by being overly concerned with your fellow man or woman. Performance and the bottom line govern everything, and most of the young execs I'd known were long on smarts, short on wisdom, and a real pain to work for.

Martin gave me the impression that it was a good thing I was ready to see him at the specified time. His expression suggested a temperament in constant need of Maalox. I was prepared to explain the black eye, but he never gave me a chance. He simply shook hands and gave me the sort of look reserved for junior partners who've had too much to drink in public.

He inspected my office and seemed reassured by the expensive Baluchi carpet and teak furniture. Or maybe it was the IBM PC he liked or the small forest of plants that Amy had installed in the bay window behind my desk. Whatever it was, he relaxed enough to seat himself carefully in the chair in front of my desk.

He was the sort of man that some women find terribly attractive—lean and aggressively fit, sandy blond hair that waved just right, and piercing blue eyes. The precision in his manner showed in his appearance. His dark blue suit was about as stylish as a banker is allowed to get, and definitely expensive. His grooming was immaculate; not so much as a hair or a bit of dandruff on the dark blue of his jacket.

"Before I explain my situation to you, I'll need your guarantee of complete confidentiality," he began. The statement was more a device for opening discussion than a request for reassurance. Daniel Martin didn't need my guarantee. He wouldn't have called me unless he'd already checked me out and decided that he could count on my discretion. But I played along and gave him my version of cross-my-heart-and-hope-to-die.

He nodded. "As you are no doubt aware, banks have come to rely an increasing amount on computerized systems." He paused, and I inclined my head to show that I was aware.

"At First Central we pioneered the adoption of automated systems, believing that it would increase our ability to meet our customer needs."

Commercial time, I thought, wondering why so many of my clients seemed to need to assure me of the quality and virtue of their corporation before telling me of the evil that menaced it. I smiled sympathetically. The sympathy was genuine; it was not for the bank but for the man who sat before me. He was working hard to present a business-as-usual image, but a thin film of perspiration below his hairline and the tight, controlled quality of his voice revealed his profound discomfort. Just sitting in my office was an admission that something had gone horribly wrong, and Daniel Martin was not a man who admitted easily to mistakes.

It took Martin another five minutes to acknowledge that the much-touted computer system adopted by his bank was not quite perfect.

"Last year, the president of the bank became concerned that our computerized system might be vulnerable to some form of tampering. He assigned me to assemble a panel of experts from within the bank to examine the major components of the system and report on any potential weaknesses."

Martin was not one to use two words if five were possible. He explained in great detail the selection of the panel and the difficulty of locating individuals who not only possessed the requisite expertise but could also be trusted on such a sensitive assignment. In the end he'd selected four men.

They'd studied the bank's system for nine months and found five ways that a truly inventive thief might crack it. The first four ways involved rather minor problems, and the panel had been able to suggest appropriate remedies.

The fifth possibility, however, was basic to the way the trust programs functioned. Any effort to close the loophole would require complete restructuring of the system. Many of the computer functions would be down for weeks during the transition, and the cost of the work would be astronomical. The president and board of directors had carefully considered the report. They had calculated the likelihood of a crook discovering the vulnerable point, weighed it against the cost of eliminating the problem, and decided that it wasn't worth fixing.

"It was a calculated gamble," Martin explained. "In order to discover the weakness, an individual would have required access to complete information on the system. Only a very few people have that information, and except for the four employees who studied the system, they are all high-level bank officers. The board determined that the chance of such a thing happening simply did not justify the expense."

"How serious is this weakness?" I asked. "How much could someone steal before you caught them?"

Martin grimaced. "It's hard to say exactly, as much as five million dollars, possibly even more."

I've disciplined myself not to look shocked at anything a client tells me, and Martin's story was a real test of that discipline. The idea of a bank gambling on a vulnerable computer system was like the parish priest renting space to the local madam. The bankers I knew absolutely hated security risks.

Martin didn't look too happy, for that matter. "It was a gamble, of course," he said, "but not much of one. The chances of a thief finding the flaw in the system were very small; and within a year or two we plan gradually to convert to a new, more efficient and secure system."

"But something did go wrong," I prompted.

"We believe that may be the case."

At this rate it was going to take all day to get the full story, but I waited as patiently as I could.

"One of the men who studied the problems in the computer system is missing," Martin said. "James Mendoza did not come to work yesterday, and his wife can give no proper accounting of his whereabouts. I'm very much afraid that he's about to use his knowledge to rob First Central."

Missing work for a day hardly seemed cause to assume that a man was a thief. "Perhaps Mr. Mendoza is just taking some time off," I suggested.

"Employees in Mr. Mendoza's position do not take time off without informing their superiors. And his wife's responses to my questions were completely unsatisfactory. She either does not know or refuses to reveal where her husband has gone. We're very worried."

"Do you have any evidence that his disappearance is linked to a withdrawal of funds?" I asked.

"Not conclusive evidence. I won't know for sure for another fourteen days, and by then the damage will be done."

"And you want me to locate Mr. Mendoza before the fourteenth day," I suggested.

Martin nodded. "That is precisely what I want. He must be found before the twenty-fifth of the month. That's exactly two weeks from yesterday."

"If Mendoza's gone now, what makes you think the theft won't happen for another fourteen days?"

Martin cleared his throat. He was looking more uncomfortable by the minute. "You no doubt know of the acquisition of Carleton Industries by Jackson-Simmons."

There weren't many people in San Francisco who hadn't heard of the Carleton acquisition. Carleton was a California firm that had started out canning fruit and expanded into other food lines. Fill up a basket at your local supermarket and you'd probably have at least ten or fifteen Carleton products, most of them with different brand names. Grandfather Carleton had settled both his family and his corporate headquarters in San Francisco. He was considered a native son.

Jackson-Simmons was a Texas conglomerate that made

cigarettes, toothpaste, small appliances, and a bunch of other stuff. The fact that they owned companies that made a number of products that competed with Carleton's hadn't bothered the antitrust division, but then nothing bothered the antitrust division anymore.

"The Trust Division of First Central is handling the Carleton acquisition," Martin confided. "Jackson-Simmons has agreed to purchase each share of Carleton for one share of Jackson-Simmons plus ten dollars. We are responsible for distributing the Jackson-Simmons shares and the cash to the Carleton shareholders."

I did a little quick mental arithmetic. At ten dollars a share, investors would receive a million dollars for each hundred thousand shares they held. For institutional investors the amount could easily top five million dollars.

"This is one of the largest acquisitions we've handled. There are over thirty million Carleton shares outstanding." Martin paused, then continued, his voice so low it was almost a whisper. "The weakness in the computer system is such that someone could tamper with the transactions without our error-checking program alerting us."

"You mean there is no way at all that you can detect such tampering?"

"None."

"And someone could create a fictitious investor or alter the destination of the wire transfers?"

"Theoretically, yes. I can't be any more specific than that. I'm not hiring you to stop the theft; we've already determined that that isn't possible. I need you to catch the thief before the transfer of funds takes place."

"Fourteen days from now."

"That's right. The closing date for the Carleton acquisition is January twenty-fifth; funds for most of the large institutional holders will be wired on that day."

I considered what he'd told me for a few moments. There were a number of questions I'd have liked to ask, but I don't solicit information on cases I'm not going to take. "Mr. Martin," I said, "I don't think I can help you."

Martin looked absolutely shocked. "You mean you're refusing to take the case?"

"I'm telling you that tracking a man who intentionally disappears is usually possible, but it takes time. Often quite a long time. The chances of finding him in less than fourteen days are extremely small. I doubt very much that anyone can help you."

"I realize that you can't guarantee success, but surely that's no reason not to take a case."

"I don't take cases I don't have a reasonable chance of solving."

"But you'll be paid regardless of whether you succeed or not."

"There's a lot more than money at stake," I pointed out. "If I were to take this case and fail to locate Mendoza, I would be known as the lady who cost First Central five million dollars. That would not be good for business."

"But if you solved the case . . ." Martin suggested.

"If I solved the case, no one would ever know. You're certainly not going to announce that your bank's computer system has a hole you can drive a truck through."

Martin nodded. He was finally beginning to understand. "You're telling me that no investigator with any reputation at all would take the case."

"I can't speak for other investigators," I replied. "I can give you the names of some firms you might try." With Miles Clarke at the top of the list, I thought.

He shook his head. "I don't want another firm; I want you. How much would it be worth to you to gamble on this case?" He eyed me with a shrewdness that assumed that everything had a price.

I considered his point. What was the risk worth to me? A hundred thousand dollars? A quarter of a million? And what was it worth to him?

Six months ago I'd have turned him down flat. But six months ago we had more cases than we could handle and a healthy cash flow. I didn't expect our current difficulties to go on forever. Miles might be bright, but his experience with security work was limited, and in time his cronies would discover that experience was more important than connections. "I'll need a few hours to consider it," I replied. Martin looked relieved. "I'm not promising anything," I warned.

"No, of course not. I respect your position. I simply want to assure you that finding Mr. Mendoza quickly is our highest priority, and I'm sure we can agree on a sum that would make the case worthwhile for you."

"I'll call you today with an answer," I promised, ushering him to the door.

IT TOOK ME exactly eight minutes to weigh the pros and cons and decide that I'd be nuts to take the case. Betting on finding Mendoza in less than two weeks was as dumb as letting Dan Quayle out of the White House. But before I could call Daniel Martin, Jesse appeared at my door.

"Got a minute?"

"Sure."

"Halstead Industries filed for bankruptcy this morning."

My stomach made a little jump and came down queasy. "You're sure?"

Jesse nodded. "Guess that explains why they haven't been returning our calls."

"And why the check that was 'in the mail' two weeks ago never got here," I said.

"Sons of bitches been stringing us along. Almost a month on the case and they stiff us." His face was tight with anger. He paced, too wound up to stand still.

I'd be angry later. Right now I was sick. "I shouldn't be

surprised," I said. "The CEO was an idiot, and the men under him weren't much better."

Jesse exploded. "Shit, we saved them ten times our fee. They could have paid us out of the money we recovered."

"It doesn't work that way, I'm afraid."

"So we caught a little crook while the bigger crooks were catching us."

"You got it."

"We going to be all right?" Jesse asked.

"Oh, sure," I said a bit too quickly. "There may be a bit of a cash-flow problem, but we'll survive."

Jesse nodded and stopped pacing. "I couldn't help noticing that our usual butt-busting pace has slowed a bit lately. It's always possible that's because you've mellowed out and decided to stop abusing the help, but I was afraid there might be a more ominous reason."

"We're hurting," I said. "Business is down for the last four months. I was counting on the Halstead check to buy us some time."

"Miles Clarke?"

"That's my guess."

Jesse shook his head. "Sure. What respectable businessman would hire two broads and a spade when he could get a member of the fraternity."

"Yeah, well, class loyalty can't compete with the profit motive. All he has to do is screw up and cost some people money and they'll forget his name real fast."

"I hope the screwup comes sooner rather than later."

"Me, too. But in the meantime I want you to know that I always meet my payroll."

"Hey, I know that," Jesse protested. "Just wish the boys at Halstead felt the same way," he grumbled as he stalked back to his office.

I switched on the computer and began assessing the damage Halstead Industries had done us. Without their check we weren't so awfully far from Chapter 11 ourselves. We had enough in the bank to meet expenses for six weeks, but we weren't generating enough work to support four people. If something didn't change soon, I'd have to lay off at least one person, maybe two.

Chris was planning to leave in June when her husband finished graduate school and took a job somewhere. She was a good investigator and I'd miss her, but nothing like the way I'd miss Jesse. We'd worked together for over three years, and I'd watched him grow from an awkward, cocky kid to a self-assured, highly skilled professional. He was a tremendous asset to the agency, but more important, he was a friend. I enjoyed his company, and I'd miss him sorely.

I reflected that it was only a matter of time before he moved on. When he'd come to me, he'd told me that his ultimate goal was to become head of corporate security for a Fortune 500 company. Every client we worked for had ample opportunity to observe his competence. Any one of them would hire him when the right job opened up.

The Halstead bankruptcy definitely enhanced the appeal of the First Central case. Locating the missing man might not be so hard. He was an amateur and might make some fairly predictable moves. Finding him in fourteen days was another matter. You could do everything right and still not find a missing person in two weeks.

I was concentrating so deeply that I jumped a foot when Amy buzzed to announce that Peter was on the line.

"Hi, feel like celebrating?"

"Actually, no, I don't," I said.

"Trouble?"

"Some. Instead of celebrating, maybe you could come down and help me out."

"Sure. I'm through here for the day."

"Which means the porno king is snugly behind bars?"

"Yep."

"Fast work."

"Had to be. I was watching his studio when a woman brought two little kids, couldn't have been more than seven or eight. I didn't like the idea of what might be going on, so I went in as soon as she left. Caught the bastard with the kids and one adult actor, convinced him to give me the Carlisle film, tied the adults up in a pretty package, and called the vice squad.''

"And they pinned a well-deserved medal on you.''

"I'm afraid I left before they got there. They won't need my testimony, and I didn't want to explain the missing reel of film.''

"Of course. You were hired to protect the family honor, not play policeman,'' I said, remembering how Peter hated his employer's attitude.

"Well, I managed both and am now available to rescue a damsel in distress.''

"I will await you at the tower window.''

Peter's idea of an emergency was the threat of imminent bodily harm; I didn't expect him to rush over to deal with issues of cash flow. I was staring dully at the budget when Jesse appeared with the report on a case he'd just finished.

"Is this the three-stooges-try-securities-fraud?'' I asked.

"You got it. All our cases should be this easy.''

"I hope you didn't put that in the report. Makes the client cranky to feel they're paying for something they should have been able to figure out themselves.''

I hadn't intended to include Jesse in the discussion of whether or not to take the Mendoza case, but his future was tied up with the firm's finances just as mine was. "Stick around for a while," I said. "I'd like your opinion on something.''

Peter arrived radiating good humor and an obscene amount of enthusiasm. At six two he was only a couple of inches taller than Jesse and seven inches taller than me, but in his exuberance he always seemed to occupy much more space than either of us.

He'd obviously been home to change since his surveillance of the porno king. He was wearing clean jeans, a blue oxford cloth shirt, and his herringbone sport coat—a definite improvement over the ratty jeans and dirty shirt he'd been wearing for the last week to blend in with the south of Market and Tenderloin crowd. I couldn't tell whether he'd gotten a haircut, but his thick sandy hair waved instead of straggled, and his beard had been trimmed back to a reasonable length. He looked good enough to make me sorry I'd had to turn down his offer to celebrate.

Budgets are definitely one place where a picture is worth a thousand words, so I turned on the computer and pulled up the budget spreadsheet. Peter was used to operating on a shoestring, so the figures didn't faze him. Jesse didn't like shoestrings any better than I did, and he was long in the face by the time he'd gone over the numbers.

With that as background, I launched into a description of the First Central case. When I got to the part about the flaw in the computer system, Peter snorted, "Ain't technology wonderful?"

When I finished, they were both silent for a while. Finally, Peter said, "It's a hell of a gamble."

"Skip tracing isn't even our specialty," Jesse remarked.

"You could probably bring someone like Hank Lawes on board for that," Peter said. Hank was an old friend of his and an expert on locating people who didn't want to be found.

"We don't even really know that this Mendoza guy is a thief. In fact, we don't know that there is a theft," Jesse commented. "Might just be a case of an overanxious banker seeing monsters under his bed."

"If Mendoza is clean, finding him shouldn't be any problem, but if he is getting ready to enrich himself at the bank's expense, fourteen days isn't much time to track him down," I said.

"The ball game isn't exactly over after fourteen days," Jesse reminded me. "The bank still needs someone to find him and recover its money. The real time limit is how long they're willing to pay us to track him down."

Peter frowned. "Once he's got the money, they'll call in the cops and may not feel they need you anymore."

"I'd say they're very anxious to avoid public disclosure on this one," I said. "It might well be worth it to them to keep us on the case and wrap it up quietly."

We tossed the issues back and forth for a while and finally came up with terms that made me feel a bit less like a first-timer in Las Vegas. First, there'd have to be a hefty bonus if we did find Mendoza before the two-week deadline, and second, if we didn't, the bank would have to commit to giving us a minimum of one month beyond the deadline to locate him.

"You really think Hank Lawes'll agree to work with us?" I asked Peter.

"Depends some on his caseload. But Hank's a freelancer, babe. It's just a question of how much for how long. You get the bank to come up with enough incentive, Hank'll find the time."

"How about Hank's good friend Peter Harman?" I asked. "We can use all the help we can get on this one."

"I'm easy," Peter replied, "but we'll have to negotiate the fringes."

THE OBVIOUS STARTING point was Daniel Martin. I called. He cleared his throat and coughed when I mentioned the finder's fee and the six-week minimum contract.

"I'm not authorized to approve that amount," he said.

Unsure of whether I was sorry or relieved, I asked if he wanted me to suggest other firms that might handle the case. "Oh, no," he said. "I just need to discuss the matter with my superiors. I'll try to get back to you today."

I reported the conversation to Jesse and Peter. "They'll come around," Peter said, "but I'd read that contract closely and make sure there aren't any loopholes."

"I fully intend to," I replied. "That's what I pay Stephen Chin an arm and a leg to take care of."

Jesse nodded. He knew from experience that "Good morning" was the only thing you got from Stephen for less than $200 an hour.

An hour and a half later, Martin called with word that the terms I had outlined had been accepted on the condition that we begin work on the case immediately. Peter took off for Orinda to deliver the film he'd "found" that morning to his client; Jesse set out to see how much of our already-reduced caseload we could either finish up quickly or put off for a while; and I awaited Daniel Martin, who had promised to bring me all the information he had on James Mendoza.

The file on Mendoza wasn't nearly as thick as I'd expected. You'd think that before asking someone to find the flaws in your computer system, you'd run an extensive background check. Martin had spent a lot more time examining Mendoza's computer expertise than figuring out whether he was the kind of guy to offer the keys to the vault.

First Central wasn't the first company to get careless with background checks. I spent a fair amount of time tracking down people who would never have gotten their hand in the till if someone had checked on where those hands had been before.

I did learn that Mendoza had served in the army from 1968 to 1970 and been sent to Vietnam. He'd attended the University of California as an undergraduate, worked for the Bank of California, and earned his MBA at the University of California Business School. He'd worked for First Central for eight years. Letters of recommendation and evaluations were all laudatory.

I had Amy copy the papers in the file. They weren't much, but they'd give us a place to start.

The next question was how Mendoza would actually get the money. I didn't think it would come in the form of a gift certificate. But when I tried to get information on the imperfect computer system, Martin clammed up entirely. That was a subject he was not prepared to discuss with a lowly private investigator, not today, not ever. That also wasn't so unusual. My clients start out having a hard time believing that anyone would rob them, and by the time they get to me, they've forgotten that anyone is honest.

I did manage to get the names of the other three men who'd worked on the committee with Mendoza. Martin wasn't too happy about having me interview them, and he was even less happy when I told him that we'd be interviewing everyone at the bank who knew James Mendoza. He lectured me on the need for secrecy; I informed him that I wouldn't take the case unless I got some cooperation.

Martin no doubt assumed that I'd walk into the bank and announce that Mendoza was about to rob it. No one had ever explained to him that PIs are right up there with lawyers when it comes to mendacity. I explained to him that I would create a cover story to mask the real reason for my questions. He reduced his objections from strenuous to halfhearted, and I accepted that as agreement.

"I will require frequent reports on your progress, daily at least," he said.

I shook my head. "I don't make daily reports. Often information gathered one day is refuted the next, or new information forces me to reinterpret what I know. A daily report can be very misleading, and it takes up valuable time. I prefer to wait until I have something concrete to report. As soon as I do, I'll call you."

"Ms. Sayler, this is not an ordinary case," he said sharply. "Time is very short, and I am responsible for your actions. I must be able to report on the progress of the investigation whenever my superiors require it."

I was getting tired of Daniel Martin. "If you want me to work on this case," I said in my best take-it-or-leave-it tone, "you'll have to allow me to do it my way."

He looked shocked. He probably didn't hear that tone often, especially from women. He coughed and looked down. "I'm sorry," he said slowly. "I don't mean to be difficult. I know that I'm not particularly good at dealing with people, and my wife tells me that I don't handle stress well." His voice had the same tight, controlled quality that I'd noticed when he first came to see me, and I could see the tension in his jaw when he looked up at me.

"This whole thing is a nightmare. They're already looking for someone to blame, and I'm first in line." Desperation and anger crept into his voice. "I've done everything expected of me and more, but if we don't find Mendoza, my career is over. And even if we do catch him, they may still dump me. My only chance is to convince the directors that I've done everything humanly possible to stop the theft. When they ask questions about the investigation, I need to have answers. I need to be on top of things."

I nodded and for the first time felt some warmth for the man. There was a human being under that bluff exterior, after all.

"I understand that written reports are time consuming," he said, "and I won't ask that, but I would be very grateful if you'd call me every day or so and tell me what's happening, even if there isn't much to report. That way I can keep my superiors informed."

"I'll do my best," I promised. "But don't expect a lot during these first days. Our main activity will be gathering information."

"Of course. I understand. But right now even bad news is better than no news." What he meant was that he'd rather tell his boss that the stupid investigator hadn't made any progress than admit he didn't know what was going on. I couldn't blame him for that.

Peter called with the news that Hank Lawes couldn't work with us full-time but was willing to consult on the case. He'd go over what we had and suggest how to get started tracing Mendoza, then answer questions as they arose.

"When can we meet?" I asked.

"Dinner tonight," Peter said. "He's working a tight schedule, but he can take a couple of hours between six and nine."

I groaned. "I hate dinner meetings. Where do you want to meet?"

"I suggested your place. We'll get more done there than in a restaurant. I can cook, or we can order Chinese."

"Let's order Chinese. I'd rather have you start interviewing Mendoza's co-workers."

"What kind of cover story do you want me to use?"

I paused to think. We needed a story that would make Mendoza's friends want to help us and would give us an excuse to ask the right questions.

"How about the old inheritance story—he's come into money, and we need to notify him and get his signature on some papers?" Peter suggested.

"We don't really know enough about him. What if all his family is already dead? Or so poor that an inheritance doesn't make sense?"

We kicked it around for a few minutes and came up with the story that we'd been hired to locate Mendoza to testify in a personal-injury case. An elderly woman had been injured by the careless driver of a BMW, and Mr. Mendoza had witnessed the accident and offered to testify on her behalf. The trial date had been moved up, and the attorney had asked us to inform Mr. Mendoza that we would need him weeks earlier than expected.

"That won't give us a chance to ask about the computer system," Peter pointed out.

"No, but we're not going to ask about the computer. Jesse'll go in separately to do that. He understands that stuff much better than either of us do. I'm going to ask Martin to bring him in as a special consultant, and he can stay undercover at the bank."

"Sounds good," Peter said.

I didn't think it would sound good to Martin. He clearly did not want anyone anywhere near his precious, though faulty, computer system, but I figured that I could sell him on the idea that Jesse was just getting information on Mendoza. Being a woman or a black can sometimes be useful in this game. I had a hunch that Martin was the type of man who'd underestimate Jesse's abilities, and Jesse was clever enough to play right into his prejudices.

"How good's your shuffle?" I asked when he came in to report on our active cases.

"Oh, ah shuffles real good, Miz Sayler," he drawled.

"Not that good, we're not going for slow-witted, just not too bright, the equivalent of dumb blonde."

"Well, that's really more your style," he pointed out.

I grimaced and explained the plan to him. "Try not to let anyone know how much you know about computers."

"Catherine," he said in his most irritating, smoothly patronizing tone, "I realize that all computers look the same to you, but God did not create them all equal. I know about the little guys; the bank has a big guy, a mainframe, and I don't know a whole hell of a lot about mainframes."

"Jesse," I said, trying to mimic his tone, "you learned about the little guys, you can learn about the big ones. I have every faith in you."

He groaned, muttered something I tried not to hear, and slouched out of the office.

I T WAS THE kind of day that convinces easterners to move to California. The middle of January and the sun shone brightly, with only a thin film of white clouds to soften the bright blue of the sky. But those of us who've lived here for a while know that you pay for all this sun when summer comes.

Last winter had been beautiful, sunny and dry; and this one was looking like more of the same. Without substantial rains we'd be facing serious drought by April. So, like all my neighbors, I soaked up the sun and felt vaguely guilty for enjoying it so much.

The Mendozas lived in the Sunset, the section of San Francisco on the south side of Golden Gate Park that stretches to the Pacific Ocean. Some developer had no doubt selected the name to suggest rosy skies over an aquamarine sea. The only thing visible most of the time was fog.

The houses were mostly modest two-story affairs tucked so tightly together that they seemed to form a low wall. Their picture windows stared out at the street like so many cyclopes' eyes.

The Mendozas' house was flanked on each side by ones that looked enough alike to have been built by the same contractor. Over the years the inhabitants of the stucco triplets had asserted their individuality; the house on the left sported a long flower box under the window, the one on the right, an ornate metal grill and wrought-iron numbers. The Mendozas had set their house off by lining their steps and porch with a set of earthen pots with bright pink and purple flowers.

I don't know exactly how I'd pictured Mrs. Mendoza, but I certainly hadn't expected her to be Japanese or six months pregnant.

She hadn't expected to open the door to a woman with a black eye, so we were even.

She wasn't a large woman, about five four; she'd be thin when pregnancy no longer conferred its soft roundness on her slender frame. The smile wrinkles around her eyes suggested that she was in her mid-thirties, probably just a couple of years younger than me.

"I work with Mr. Martin at First Central," I explained. "He's concerned about your husband, and he asked me to stop by and check on him."

Mrs. Mendoza said that was kind of him and invited me in. She had no accent; her family had probably been in the country at least as long as parts of mine. She was trying valiantly to maintain eye contact without staring at the flamboyant display around my left eye. Like everyone else, she wasn't successful.

The living room was right off the entrance hall. The furniture was contemporary—an off-white couch and gray chairs and teak tables—but the accents were Japanese. The overall effect was lovely and serene, a nice room to come home to.

She offered me a seat on the couch, and I was immediately struck by an intriguing sculpture that sat on the low table in front of me. As I studied it, I realized it was not a sculpture at all but, rather, a rock, about twelve inches long and nine inches high, with the bottom cut flat and mounted on a carved wooden base.

"That's a suiseki," Mrs. Mendoza said. "We found that particular stone in the Humboldt River."

"It's lovely. It almost seems like a tiny version of a mountain."

"Thank you. That's just what it is. Suiseki are stones found in streams or rivers. Over the centuries they are shaped and sculpted by natural forces until they come to resemble the mountains from which they came."

"The macrocosm reflected in the microcosm," I suggested.

She nodded. "Exactly. The only alteration that is permitted is the cut made to create the base so that it can be mounted on the stand."

"How do you decide where to cut the stone?"

"You know, I never asked. Jim just seems to know where to make the cut. He spends time with the stone, and when he's ready, he cuts it."

"You mean the stone is his?" I asked in surprise.

"Oh, yes. Everyone assumes that the suiseki are mine, but it was Jim who introduced me to suiseki. I enjoy going along when he looks for stones, and I've even found a couple of decent ones myself; but the best ones are his."

"Has he been interested in suiseki for long?"

She nodded. "From before we met. My father jokes that my Hispanic husband has more appreciation for my heritage than I do." She laughed. "I don't quite understand why Mr.

Martin is concerned for Jim. He's just out of town for a week or so.''

"It's not like Jim to disappear without notifying the bank."

"But I'm sure he called Mr. Martin. He told me he'd arranged for a short leave of absence."

"Are you sure he called Mr. Martin?" I asked. "Could he have called someone else?" I wanted First Central's big crisis to be a mistake. I didn't much like the idea of tracking down Mrs. Mendoza's husband.

"I don't think so," she said. "I'm fairly sure he said he'd talked to Mr. Martin."

"Do you know where he went?"

"To the mountains."

"Where in the mountains?"

"I don't know exactly. This is the last time before the baby's born that he could get away, and he wanted to do some cross-country skiing and maybe collect stones. He never has a plan for exactly where he'll go. He just sort of follows his nose."

"January seems an odd time for such a trip."

"It's not ideal for the stones, but the skiing should be good. And with this one on the way"—she patted her stomach—"who knows when he'll have time again."

"Had he been planning the trip for long?"

She shook her head. "No, things were slow at work, and he figured he'd better grab the time while he could. You know how it is."

I nodded, but not in agreement. Early January is one of the busiest times of the year in a bank.

"I still don't understand why Mr. Martin is concerned."

"Well, you know your husband works in a fairly sensitive area, and Mr. Martin doesn't like the fact that he can't contact Jim if he needs him."

"Oh, I see." A smile came to her lips for a moment, and I suspected that Martin might be one reason Jim needed time alone and beyond the reach of a phone. "Well, Jim will probably call me in a day or so, and I can ask him to check in or leave a phone number where you can reach him."

"Oh, good," I said. "That'll make Mr. Martin feel much better." I could have left at that point, with Suzanne Mendoza comfortably assured that there was no problem, but I wanted her just a bit uneasy when she answered the phone. Her husband hadn't actually violated the law yet. If he heard worry, maybe even fear, in her voice, it might shock him into returning home and giving up his plan.

"Did anything strange happen before Jim left?"

She looked surprised and shook her head, but even as she denied it, her expression changed just enough to contradict her words.

"Something did happen," I said. "What was it?"

"It wasn't anything. A friend came to visit, that's all."

"Something about that visit troubled you. I can see it in your face."

"It wasn't anything," she said. "It was just that I didn't know the man and he acted kind of peculiar. Things affect you more when you're pregnant." She ran her hand over the gentle roundness of her belly and smiled apologetically.

"Tell me about the man who came to see your husband." I was waiting for her to tell me that her husband's affairs were none of my business, but she didn't. She either had no idea that her husband might be an aspiring embezzler, or she was putting on one hell of a show.

She paused. "I didn't see him very clearly. He didn't come in. But he was kind of creepy. He almost seemed deformed. He walked with a limp, and his right hand was all scarred. It seemed strange that Jim didn't invite him in, but I don't think he'd have come even if he was asked. He just stood out on the porch shifting from one foot to the other and mumbled."

"Mumbled, you mean to himself?"

"No, not to himself, but when he talked. I guess he didn't really mumble; he just wouldn't look me in the eye. He was always looking down when he talked, and his voice was so low I could hardly understand him. In fact, after I called Jim, I came in here, and I couldn't hear what he said. They never did come in. They went for a ride in the car instead."

"When did the stranger come?"

"Friday evening, around nine."

"And when did Jim leave?"

"Sunday afternoon. He took off around two o'clock."

"Driving?"

She nodded.

"And he didn't tell you where he was going?"

"He didn't know himself, just that he was heading up to the Trinity Alps. We haven't been there in January, so he wasn't sure where he'd end up." She paused and gave me a nervous smile. "It must sound strange to you, but Jim does that a couple of times a year. He needs to get away by himself, and he makes no plans beyond a general destination. He says it lets him stay completely in the moment."

It didn't sound strange at all to me; in fact, it had great appeal. A stretch of days free from the tyranny of schedules and responsibilities with no one to please but yourself. I hadn't taken that kind of time in much too long. Too bad Mendoza hadn't either. "Had Jim discussed going away before the friend came?"

She thought for a moment and frowned. "No, I don't think so. But we'd planned to go away for several days after Christmas and gave it up because I get tired so easily. I think he just decided to go himself while he could."

"And he won't be gone long, I suppose."

She shook her head. "It's never more than a week or two."

There were a lot more questions I'd have liked to ask, but I could see that she was becoming uneasy, and I didn't want to push her too far. "Well, I guess there really isn't any cause for concern. I know Mr. Martin will be relieved."

I thanked her for her hospitality and rose to go. "If you need anything while Jim is away, please feel free to give me a call." I handed her the card with my name and the office number that Amy answered without identifying our business.

Peter was already at my apartment when I arrived home. "Did you feed the cat?" I asked as Touchstone hurled himself against my legs, meowing pitifully to inform me that he was on the verge of starvation.

"Of course," he replied. "I fed the whole goddamn menagerie, and don't let any of them tell you otherwise."

Touchstone was the only beggar; and at the rate he was putting on weight, I was considering renaming him Falstaff. The rest of the menagerie included Snake, a recuperating one-eyed garter snake that Touchstone had captured and released under my bed, and Reepicheep, my thirteen-year-old niece's gray mouse that was living at my house until she could convince her mother to let her bring it home—sometime in the next century.

I walked into the kitchen; the cat food can, the bag of mouse chow, and Peter's breakfast dishes sat on the counter. It occurred to me that for a woman who enjoyed living alone, I'd let my life get pretty crowded.

Peter and I agreed that we weren't ready to live together, but you'd never guess that from the amount of time he'd been spending at my place. Not that I didn't enjoy his presence; I did, more than I liked to admit. But I still wasn't ready for the greater demands that living together puts on a relationship. I'd been through that with my ex-husband. First you're lovers and everything's wonderful; then you're living together and things change.

I tossed the cat food can in the trash, the dishes in the dishwasher, and the mouse chow back in the cupboard and headed for the living room. Peter was stretched out on the couch with a book.

"*Brighton Rock?*" I asked.

"I finished that last night. I'm on to *The Power and the Glory*." Peter had taken to picking an author and reading all of his or her works. This time it was Graham Greene.

He closed the book and sat up. "Hank'll be here at seven, which gives me time to fill you in on Mendoza's fellow wage slaves before I go pick up dinner."

I settled in beside him and took a drink of his beer. "Hey, this is warm. Is something wrong with the fridge?" I demanded.

''Not so far as I know. Read English, drink English. That's ale; you don't drink it cold.''

''You going to go all the way and eat English?'' I asked with some trepidation.

''Hell, no, there are some limits, even for an extremist like me. Now, do you want to hear about Mendoza?''

''Of course.''

''Well, he's the Alan Alda of First Central—Mr. Nice Guy, very sensitive, concerned, friendly. Sounds like just the kind of guy to help a Little Old Lady who was hit by a BMW, if anyone knew where he was.''

''Which they don't.''

''Nope, but get this, several of them said that it wasn't at all unusual for him to take off with no clear destination. Seems he likes to go to the mountains and just hang out for a week or so, no set plans, no itinerary.''

''That fits with what his wife said. What else did you get?''

''Everyone agrees that he's a great family man. His wife's pregnant after years of trying, and he can't wait to be a daddy.

''Secretaries love him—he's friendly without being flirty, takes time to listen, empathizes with their problems. If he fools around, it's sure as hell not at the office.

''I asked about vacation spots, relatives, places he might have gone. Didn't get much. One guy said that he likes to go up north to the mountains, but he didn't know where he stayed or even if he always goes to the same place. He's got a mother and an aunt in some town in the central valley. That's it.''

''So everybody loves him, and no one knows where he is,'' I summed up.

''You got it.''

6

ETER VOLUNTEERED TO go pick up the food, no doubt to guarantee that at least some of the dishes would be spicy enough to burn a hole in his tongue. I went upstairs and changed into jeans and a sweater while I tried to remember why I had thought we had a prayer of finding Mendoza.

Hank Lawes arrived a little after seven. He was even taller than Peter, a large man, but not heavy. He looked like the Marlboro man forty years after—with skin the color and texture of old leather, blue eyes bleached gray, and a terrific head of thick white hair.

The first time he laughed, I fell in love with him. It was a deep, full, booming laugh, the sort that makes you look around to see what's so funny and who's having such a good time. He peered at my black eye and commented, "It's tough to keep Harman in line, huh?"

"Naw, but there is a reason that certain positions are not included in the *Kama Sutra*," I replied.

Peter choked, and Hank favored me with one of his marvelous laughs. The two men caught up on the doings of mutual friends while I dished out the food; then, over the Hunan prawns, I explained our problem.

Hank Lawes listened thoughtfully, then turned to Peter. "You taken to dressing in phone booths and developed some of that X-ray vision?" he asked.

"No, and I don't leap tall buildings in a single bound, either."

"Then you're in trouble, son."

"Needle-in-the-haystack time," Peter suggested.

"This country is the easiest place in the world to disappear. Just pick some medium-to-large city, pay in cash or traveler's checks, and unless you smack into a police car, there's no way anyone's going to find you. Needle in a haystack, hell, more like a bacterium.

"Now, lots of these guys will eventually trip themselves up. They'll use their social security card when they get a job or when they apply for a driver's license. But they may not do that for months or even years. And anyone smart enough to steal five million bucks can probably figure out that he shouldn't use his own social security number."

"But if you'd decided to find this particular bacterium, how would you go about starting?" I asked.

"Well, first you try to narrow the field, and to do that you have to know about the guy. People can change location, but they can't change personality so easy. So a guy who's a bowler, chances are, he's going to keep bowling; if he loves to sail, he'll settle someplace he can do that.

"You've gotta find out as much as you can about the guy and hope that what you get points you in a useful direction. If the guy's a stamp collector, you find out where he buys his stamps, what magazines he subscribes to, what stamp he couldn't resist trying to buy.

"The next thing is to narrow down where he might have gone. Chances are he didn't just pick a town out of the atlas. He probably chose a place he knows something about—not someplace he lived when he was younger, but maybe someplace he visited on vacation or maybe someplace he's heard a close friend or relative describe. You want to know where he's been on vacation, where he wanted to go, places he knows but isn't known.

"Then you put the places and the habits together. If you go to town X and your man is a bowler, you visit the bowling alleys. If he's a bird-watcher, you call the bird people. Every area you think he might be, you check out the places he might go."

"Piece of cake," Peter commented dryly.

"It's hours of interviewing friends, relatives, neighbors,

people he works with, wife's relatives—everybody who knows him. And from that you get mountains of information, and maybe none of it is even useful."

"Gee, you're just a real fount of optimism, Hank," Peter said. "If it's as bad as all that, how come you're driving a new Buick?"

" 'Cause I don't take cases like this."

After Hank left, I read over a copy of the interview form he gave his assistants, and Peter finished what was left of the wine from dinner. When I looked over at him, he was chewing on his mustache, always a sign that something was bothering him. "Peter?" I asked. "Is there something you aren't telling me?"

He turned to face me. "Yeah, we need to talk. Now's as good as ever, I guess."

With an introduction like that, I'd have preferred ever.

"I'm not sure I can help you on this case, Catherine. It just doesn't feel right. This Mendoza is a basically nice guy. Your client is a company that forecloses on farmers and won't lend money to people of color. To protect this august institution, we are going to run this poor guy to the ground and tack his hide to a fence. I don't think I want to be part of that."

I stared at him in amazement. "It's your decision," I said coldly, trying not to let the rising anger seep into my voice. "But don't forget that this 'basically nice guy' may be stealing five million dollars. And the fact that you don't like the people he's stealing it from doesn't make it okay."

"I'm sorry," Peter interrupted. "I said it poorly. I'm not excusing stealing. But this isn't my kind of case. Somebody's got to stop Mendoza; I'm just not sure I want it to be me."

"Don't want to dirty your hands in the evil corporate world?" I snapped. "Or isn't a little embezzlement a serious enough crime?" I paused to catch my breath. "And as to tacking someone's hide to a fence, that's a cheap shot, and you know it.

"I'm James Mendoza's best chance of staying out of jail.

If I can get to him before he gets to the money, his hide doesn't have to end up on anyone's fence.''

''You think you can get the bank to agree?'' Peter asked.

''They'll want his head on a pike, but they'll settle for a quiet termination. The alternative is a trial in which the weaknesses of their computer system become public knowledge.

''But if I can't get to him before he gets the money and the press gets the story, the law may be the least of his problems. His photo will be in every major paper along with the news that he has five million dollars of ill-gotten gains.''

Peter winced. He got the picture. All it would take would be the wrong person to recognize Mendoza's face and our ''decent guy'' would be a dead man. Anyone could kill him, hide his body, and steal his money. The police would continue to hunt for Mendoza while the killer walked off a rich man.

''Maybe you should pull out,'' I said. ''I don't want anyone in unless they're in all the way, and I can't afford to have you pull out in the middle.''

''You know I can't pull out in the middle. I'm just as compulsive as you are. Once the hunt's on, I get just as caught up in it. That's why it's time to decide now.''

''So?'' I asked.

''So . . .'' He paused. ''I'm in. I'm not wild about working for First Central, but you're right that Mendoza's better off with us on his trail than someone else.''

I nodded, glad Peter had decided to help but not exactly thrilled by the prospect of having to deal with his formidable social conscience on the job. It was bad enough to have him scrutinize my groceries for political correctness. I'd already given up grapes and anything from Nestlé; who knows what was coming next.

I fumed quietly while Peter went to the television and began fooling with the VCR.

''What are you doing?''

''I taped the news. Want to see if my porno king's on.''

I'd been so obsessed with James Mendoza that I'd completely forgotten that Peter had closed a big case that morning and had been planning to celebrate when I roped him into helping me. My indignation felt a bit less righteous.

The porno king was the big local story. An attractive brunette stood in front of a nondescript warehouse south of Market and explained that at ten that morning police had broken up a major pornography operation. The camera shifted to a ruddy-faced man in a rumpled suit, and Peter and I howled in unison at the sight of San Francisco's sleaziest vice cop.

"Oh, no! Bryson," Peter groaned. "Good thing I didn't stick around. He'd have busted *me*." Bryson had the temperament and intelligence of a pit bull, and he had a badge, which made him dangerous. He and Peter had tangled a couple of times; they agreed on one thing only, how much they disliked each other.

We watched in amazement as Bryson told the reporter how months of investigation had led to today's arrests. Peter moaned, "Oh, shit, I've made a hero of the schmuck. They'll probably give him a commendation." He shook his head and gave a hollow laugh. "Another good deed gone awry."

Any anger left over from our confrontation faded as I realized that the same oversized conscience that could be so irritating was also a big part of why I loved him. I reached for the remote control and turned down the sound. "We should be celebrating your capture of the porn king. Would you like to go out somewhere?"

I rubbed his shoulders and felt him relax a bit. "There's a bottle of Domaine Chandon Reserve in the fridge, shall I open it?" He nodded, and I headed for the kitchen.

When I got back to the living room, he was busy building a fire. I started on the champagne. "I guess we're not going out," I observed.

He wiped his hands on his jeans and joined me on the couch. "There are so many more interesting things to do here. I thought maybe you could show me some of that *Kama Sutra* stuff."

"I could try standing on my head," I offered. What he had in mind was less exotic and much more satisfying.

* * *

The black eye was a little less flamboyant the next morning. It still hurt, though, and it was obviously going to be with me for a while.

Peter headed back to the bank for more interviews, and I trudged off to the office. At nine o'clock I called Martin and asked if there was a chance that someone else at the bank had granted Mendoza a leave of absence.

"No," he replied. "It would have to have been approved by me, and besides, we're much too busy right now for anyone to grant a leave except in case of emergency."

I explained that I wanted Jesse to work undercover inside the bank. He didn't think that was a good idea and as usual explained his reasons at great length. If he was this helpful to the people designing the computer system, no wonder it had bugs.

After as much politeness and cajoling as I could stand at that hour of the morning, I hardened my tone and declared that he'd hired me to run the investigation as I saw fit and that was what I proposed to do.

"I'm sorry," he said. "Of course, you do what you think best." His voice sounded strained. I understood the way he felt. In a situation where you feel like things are out of control, it's damn hard to let someone else call the shots.

I tried to reassure him and explained that I wanted Jesse working as close to Mendoza's job as possible. I made a few not-so-subtle suggestions that he shouldn't expect too much of my assistant and figured I could leave the rest to Jesse's acting ability.

Despite my firmness with Martin, I wasn't at all sure of my next move. I wasn't ready to begin interviewing friends and neighbors quite yet. I'd established some rapport with Mrs. Mendoza, and that would be gone the minute she learned that I was questioning everyone who knew her husband.

There wasn't much chance of figuring out where Mendoza had gone when he left home, especially since he had a car. Anyone with a little imagination could get out of San Francisco in a dozen different ways, all of them impossible to trace.

Amy resolved the question of what to do next by reminding me that I hadn't finished the report on my last case. When it came to reports, this particular client reminded me of my least favorite high school English teacher. I'd saved him several hundred thousand dollars, but I knew that the moment I put words on paper, he'd find a way to question my basic literacy.

I was still pounding away on the keyboard two hours later when Amy announced a call on our unofficial line. It was Suzanne Mendoza, and her voice was on the edge of panic.

"Ms. Sayler, I'm terribly sorry to bother you, but I need help, and I don't know anyone else to call."

"What's happened? Has Jim called?"

"No, no, he hasn't, and someone else, another man, called and said not to worry, but I am worried. It's not like Jim not to call himself. And now there's that man—"

"What man?"

"Well, I can't be sure, of course, but I think someone is watching the house, and he followed me when I went out shopping this morning. I don't know what's going on, but I'm frightened."

"Are you at home now?"

"Yes," she said, so softly I could barely hear.

"Do you think you're in immediate danger? Should I call the police?"

"No. No, I'm not even really sure there's someone out there. But there's been a blue van parked on the street since Sunday evening, and my neighbor up the block thinks someone is living in it. She thought it was just a homeless person, but she noticed that when I went out, the man left the van and went around the corner; then he came back shortly after I did. It happened at least three times."

"Stay where you are. I'm coming right out. Don't answer the door for anyone you don't know."

7

I STRUGGLED TO keep my foot light on the gas pedal as I drove to the Mendozas' and considered what Suzanne's call might mean. It could be a clever way to divert attention from our search for her husband. But if that were true, she was the best actress I'd ever run into.

If someone was watching her, they must know that James Mendoza was about to rob First Central. Given the difficulty Daniel Martin had discussing the matter with me, I didn't think he was the source of that information. That left Mendoza himself.

I couldn't see him announcing his intention to rob his employer, but I could imagine that after a couple of drinks he might have talked too freely about his assignment to check out the computer system. Maybe even expressed amazement at the bank's decision not to fix the bug. Not the sort of thing you tell a stranger or announce in a crowded bar, but something you might chuckle over with a friend, or a co-worker.

If someone else was involved, it would explain several things that had been bothering me. Like why Mendoza had disappeared two weeks before he could get the money and why he'd left his wife behind. Abandoning his wife didn't fit with what we'd been told about the man, but running off to draw danger away from her did.

Another player could mean another handle on the case, which was one more than we had at present. It could also mean a much more dangerous situation than I'd expected. Mendoza had set out to commit a nonviolent crime; a third party was at least capable of intimidation, quite probably worse.

The blue van was nowhere in evidence as I pulled up in front of the Mendoza house. Suzanne opened the door even before I rang the bell.

"Oh, thank you so much for coming. I didn't know what to do. If only Jim were here."

This time I led her to the living room. We sat facing each other on the couch. "What exactly happened?" I asked.

She took a deep breath. "Well, first Jim didn't call. I was sure he'd call; when the phone rang, I knew it was him. But it wasn't. It was a man who said he was a friend of Jim's and that Jim couldn't call right now but he was fine and I shouldn't worry. He asked if I needed anything."

"And?"

"I asked why Jim couldn't call, and he said he was staying in a cabin with no phone, but he wouldn't tell me where the cabin was. I asked, but he just said 'back in the mountains' and 'off the road.' He said he could get a message to Jim if there was any problem. It's not like Jim not to call himself. I'm so frightened."

She looked as if she was about to cry, but something in the way she held herself told me that she was not looking for a hug or a shoulder to lean on. I put my hand on her arm. "Did the man tell you how to get in touch with him? Do you have his phone number?"

"No, he just said he'd call in a few days. I don't even know who he is. I feel so helpless."

"Was his voice at all familiar?"

"I'm not sure, maybe."

"Could it have been the man who visited Jim?" I asked.

"Maybe, but I don't know. That man mumbled, and this one spoke quite clearly. Besides, telephone voices are different from real voices. I don't know."

"Tell me about the man who's been watching you."

"Mrs. Wascovitch from up the street called this morning. Her husband died about eight months ago, and she doesn't have much to keep her busy, so she looks out the window a lot. She noticed a van parked in front of her house on Sunday evening, and she thinks that a man was living in the van and that when I went out, he followed me.''

"Did she get the license number of the van?''

"I didn't think to ask.''

The van could have been pure coincidence. But if it wasn't, it meant real trouble. If someone had been watching Mrs. Mendoza, he'd known enough to get the van out of there before I arrived. He'd either tapped the phone or was using sophisticated surveillance equipment.

I don't go in for that sort of thing. Most of it is illegal, and all of it should be. I've got catalogs full of nifty little devices; and in many cases I can't think of a single use for them that wouldn't cost me my license and probably a couple of years of my freedom.

Some, like directional microphones that allow you to listen to what's happening in a house down the block, are outrageously expensive; others are cheaper but take some expertise to rig and use. Anyone who uses either is probably a pro.

I talked a bit more with Suzanne, but she'd given me what information she had. She assured me that no strangers, except me, had been in the house for over a week, so I could rule out the possibility of a bug inside the house.

I asked if I could have a look around the outside. I didn't tell her what I was looking for, since knowing that someone could be listening to her every word wasn't going to do much for her peace of mind.

I started on the side of the house where the van had been parked, and it didn't take long to find the transmitter. It was hidden behind a small bush that was trying hard to become a tree. A thin wire led back to the garage door, through the garage to a storage closet. He'd done a good job of making it nearly invisible, brushing dirt or leaves over it and slipping it into a crack along the foundation.

The lock on the storage closet was a snap; I got it open on the first try, and I'm not even very good at that sort of thing. Inside the closet, I followed the wire up a wall behind a bunch of boxes to a spot on the ceiling where I found the tiny piece of metal that had picked up every word spoken in the rooms above.

How long had it been there? Just since the van arrived or much longer? I hoped Suzanne could give me some idea of that. I cut the wire but left everything in place.

I walked up the street to interview Mrs. Wascovitch. She was a heavyset woman in her late sixties with straight, dull gray hair pulled back into a severe bun. She wore a floral cotton duster and fluffy pink slippers on her feet.

She invited me into a living room out of the forties. Not just the furniture, but the ashtrays, picture frames, knick-knacks, everything had a forties feel to it. "What a nice room," I commented. "It reminds me of my aunt's house when I was growing up."

Mrs. Wascovitch looked about her as if noticing it for the first time. "Never used this room much," she said. "My husband liked a neat house, so I never let the kids in here. Always liked the kitchen better, anyway. And after the girls left, their room became a den. Now I sit in here a lot and look out the window." There was a heaviness to her statement, a sense of time weighing her down with the slowness of its passing.

"I understand that you saw someone watching the Mendozas' house."

"Seemed like he might have been. I can't be sure, of course, but that's what it looked like to me."

"What made you think he was watching Suzanne?"

"I didn't think he was watching anybody at first. Just assumed he was one of those homeless folks, living out of his car. We had a whole family stayed on the next block over a month ago, parents and two kids living in an old Chevrolet. I don't understand it myself. Understood the depression, nobody had much and some folks had nothing at all, but these days the country's so well off. How can there be families with no homes?"

I'd wondered that myself plenty of times and was still waiting for an answer. Downtown San Francisco had become a bit surreal—store windows proudly displaying $200 pairs of shoes and $1,000 watches while in the foreground, men, women, and sometimes children begged for spare change.

I passed up the big question and refocused on less cosmic and more immediate concerns. "What made you decide he might be watching the Mendozas'?"

"The second time that I saw him come back just after she did. Didn't even know there was anyone in the van till the first time he went out. I got to watching him because I was curious to see if he was living in his van. Not that I was opposed, so long as he didn't cause problems, but I was curious. Things like how do you find a toilet or take a bath. So I kind of kept an eye on the van."

She gazed out the window and seemed to forget I was there. She was like a windup toy that suddenly stops dead.

"The first time you saw him, did he seem to follow Mrs. Mendoza?" I prompted.

She brought her attention back to me. "Well, he didn't really follow her. He went around the corner. Hopped out of the van and walked real quick around that corner." She pointed to the corner two houses away. "Couldn't see where he went after that; but later, just after Suzanne came home, he came back around the corner and hopped back in the van. Didn't see him get out again all day. He must have some sort of toilet in there."

"Where exactly was the van?"

"Right there." She pointed to the curb outside. "Right in front."

She answered all my questions, and there was no cause to doubt her mental acuity, but she had an unsettling way of drifting off into her own thoughts. I trusted the accuracy of her information, but the interpretation was another matter.

She described the man as medium height, maybe around five feet eight or nine, brown straight hair that fell to his collar, no beard or mustache, dressed in faded jeans and a denim jacket. He hadn't looked dirty, really, but he was a bit scruffy.

The van was a VW, grayish blue with lots of dents and rust spots, plaid curtains on the windows behind the front seat. I asked if she knew the license number. The surprised expression on her face gave me the answer before her words.

"No, I guess I should have, but you couldn't see the license from here, and I don't go out much. Stairs are hard on my knees."

The heaviness in the room was getting to me. I caught myself on the edge of a yawn and shook my head to clear it. I thanked Mrs. Wascovitch for her help and dragged myself up from the chair.

Outside, the cool damp air was delicious. I breathed in deeply and walked all the way around the block. I wanted to see if there was anyplace the man in the van might have been going. There were no stores or phone booths.

Back at the Mendozas' I broke the bad news. Mrs. Mendoza's eyes grew large when I told her what I'd found in her storage room.

"Then someone *was* watching the house. But why?"

"I was hoping you'd know that. Do you have any idea why anyone would want to spy on you or your husband?"

She shook her head. "There's been nothing out of the ordinary until that man came, the one with the limp that I told you about."

"Anything unusual in Jim's work with the bank?"

She shook her head again.

"Wasn't he on a team to study weaknesses in the computer system?"

"Yes, but that was over a year ago. What would that have to do with all this?"

"As I understand it, that team discovered several weaknesses, one of which the bank chose not to fix," I said. "Jim's knowledge of the computer system includes the means to rob First Central of a large sum of money."

Her look of general confusion solidified into alarm. "You mean that someone might try to force him to tell them how to rob the bank?"

"It's possible."

"Then he's in danger; we have to find him."

I should have been smug and delighted. After all, my quarry's wife was about to become my chief informant. Instead, I felt distinctly uncomfortable. Sometimes you have to follow your gut feelings, and I decided that this was one of them.

"Suzanne, have you ever considered that Jim might be involved in a scheme to rob the bank?"

The look on her face was answer enough. "You know him, you must know—" Then, for the first time, suspicion crept into her face. "When you came here yesterday, you weren't really worried about Jim, were you? Who are you?"

Truth-or-consequences time. "I'm a private investigator, and I work for the bank. I won't lie to you; Jim's superiors are very concerned that he might use his knowledge to steal funds from the bank."

She stared at me with disbelief, then said, "I think you'd better go."

I didn't move. "I don't expect you to like what I've told you, but I think you need my help as much as I need yours. Whoever that was in the blue van, he's not on Jim's side. And his presence suggests that we may have more to worry about than the bank's money. My guess is that he's after Jim; and if that's true, you'd better hope I find him first."

Her anger melted into confusion, then distress, and her eyes filled with tears. I felt genuinely sorry for her, and I hoped to hell that she'd let me help her.

It took some talking and numerous reassurances that I would keep the police out of the case, but eventually she accepted the need for my help. I took out a notebook and my tape recorder, and we started with family members and their addresses. His mother, aunt, and two brothers lived in Modesto, a town in the San Joaquin Valley. His sister lived in L.A., and there were aunts, uncles, and cousins in a dozen cities around the state. We covered places she thought Jim might go and, finally, the organizations he belonged to. She brought me a roster of people in their church and put a check by those who knew him.

When she'd told me everything she could remember, I clicked the tape recorder off and said, "This is entirely confidential, but I need to know. Did Jim use any kind of drugs?"

"You mean illegal drugs?"

I nodded.

"No, definitely not. He did drugs when he first got back from Vietnam, back in the early seventies, but he stopped that long ago."

I asked if I could look through her husband's things to see if I could find any hint of why or where he'd gone. She agreed, and together we sorted through his desk and his dresser. All I discovered was that he kept his drawers considerably neater than I did.

"Is anything missing?" I asked.

Suzanne thought for a while. She shook her head. "I don't think so."

I picked up an eight-by-ten photo of a man from her bureau. The man had thick dark hair, a mustache and closely trimmed beard, and eyes a bit large for his face. It was an appealing face, not classically handsome but sensitive and warm. "May I take this to have a copy made?" I asked.

"Sure, but please be careful, that's my favorite picture of Jim."

"Do you have any snapshots that show him in profile?" I asked.

She went back into the extra room they both used as a study and walked over to the bookcase. A cluster of pictures in silver frames sat on the far end.

"Something *is* missing," she announced. "There was another photo here. It was an old one of Jim and his friends in Vietnam. They're all standing around with no shirts on holding cans of beer."

"Do you think it's gone or just been moved?"

"I haven't seen it anywhere else; it's always been here with the other pictures."

"Are any other pictures missing? Any of you?"

She looked through the house and reported that only the

one picture was missing. "Any reason he'd take that one?"
I asked.

She couldn't think of any.

"Do you know any of the other men in the photo?"

"No. I don't even know their names, but Jim's mother
would know. They were all from Modesto. It was an exper-
imental program or something, and they kept men from the
same town together in Vietnam."

"Did Jim tell you much about his experience in Vietnam?" I asked.

"When we first met, he'd only been home a couple of
years, and he talked about it some. He hasn't said much in
the last few years."

I needed to get back to the office, but I wasn't about to
leave Suzanne alone with the man in the blue van around.
It's tough to convince someone they need a bodyguard without scaring them to death. I don't think I succeeded.

I knew the perfect person for the job if she was free. Annlyn Spears was a graduate student at San Francisco State
College. When she wasn't studying chemistry, she was working on the next level of her black belt in aikido. She was tall,
stately, and quite capable of dealing with mysterious
strangers.

I'd employed Annlyn and her roommate, Sara Guiness,
on one previous case. Like most students, they could always
use some extra money, and they enjoyed the role of protector.
The client had loved them so much that she still sent them
boxes of chocolate chip cookies. I was disappointed to find
that only the answering machine was home at their apartment. I told it to have them call me ASAP.

"Do you have someplace you could stay until I get
someone to stay with you?" I asked Suzanne.

"I could stay with my brother and his wife."

I poked around a bit more while she called her sister-in-
law; Suzanne's side of the conversation was reassuring. She
was an awful liar.

8

I GOT BACK for the one o'clock staff meeting at one-ten, only to discover that Jesse and Peter weren't there yet. My assistant Chris had flown in from Tucson the night before and was in her office pulling together her report. She ogled my black eye and commented, "You bugged Jesse once too often about his spelling."

"No, I stuck up for you when he found out who'd eaten his entire stash of junk food."

Chris laughed and patted her thigh. "It's hard to hide the evidence." The evidence in her case was not a problem. She was disgustingly slender and could put away prodigious amounts of food without gaining a pound.

I gave the tape to Amy to transcribe and asked her to start on it immediately and to get me five copies as fast as possible.

Peter breezed in with his assistant, Eileen. "I've brought the virgin for sacrifice," he announced.

Eileen looked appalled. "Ignore him," I advised. "He's just having trouble admitting that he's working on a corporate case."

Eileen was young and idealistic and had found her way to Peter while searching for a career that was "socially useful." Anything involving working for a bank was a sort of moral lapse in their radical scheme of things.

She'd replaced her usual outfit of jeans and a sweater with a skirt and blouse, a subtle sign that she was serious about joining us on the case. She was even wearing a little bit of makeup. With her dark hair and very fair skin, she looked very pretty.

Jesse arrived a few moments later, and we got down to business. I explained the case and reviewed the Hank Lawes approach to finding missing persons. No one looked overly enthusiastic about the endless rounds of interviews.

"A Reebok case," Chris commented dryly. Her taste for expensive shoes with high heels and pointed toes, known around the office as Inquisition slippers, made her cranky about cases that involved legwork.

"Peter'll take the co-workers, Eileen and Chris can interview relatives, friends, and neighbors, Jesse'll be undercover at the bank, and I'll take the family."

"You got an organization chart on this bank?" Peter asked.

"Not a chart, but a general picture. Mendoza is in the Systems Division. Martin is a senior vice-president in the same division." Eileen looked impressed.

"That isn't quite as awe inspiring as it sounds," I cautioned her. "A senior vice-president is really a middle-management position. This bank has a chairman, a couple of vice-chairmen, probably six to eight executive vice-presidents, and maybe twenty senior vice-presidents."

"There are seven vice-presidents just in Systems," Jesse put in. "I can't tell exactly where Martin is in the pack, but I don't get the sense that everyone is in awe of him."

"Systems Division means computers, I assume," Eileen said.

"Right. And Systems is divided into a number of areas to service different departments in the bank."

"Where's Mendoza in the scheme of things?" Chris asked.

"He's a manager," Peter explained. "Started out as a programmer, moved over into management. He's sort of an interface between the programmers and the people who don't understand the first thing about computers. When someone has a problem with the system or needs to have it do something, they tell him the problem, and he figures out how to get the system to solve it."

"Or he explains the constraints and gets them to redefine

the problem so it's easier to work with,'' Jesse added. ''People who don't understand computers tend to believe they can do anything while at the same time not really trusting them at all.'' He turned and looked directly at me as he spoke, making clear that ''people'' included his technologically deficient employer.

''And the other guys on the team?'' Chris asked.

''One's a programmer on Mendoza's team; that's Nick Shultz,'' Jesse said, consulting his notes. ''The others are programmers on other teams.''

''I interviewed Shultz yesterday,'' Peter said. ''He seemed to be particularly close to Mendoza. You might want to hang out with him, Jesse.''

Jesse nodded. ''That'll be easy. Getting to know the other guys may be harder.''

''If necessary, we'll put Chris into the bank, too,'' I said. ''Give it a couple of days, then let me know if you need her.''

''Chris is better at hearing confessions than most priests,'' Jesse confided to Eileen.

Chris smiled. ''And when Jesse starts in with the compliments, it's a sure sign he's about to dump extra work on you.''

''We may not need you at the bank,'' I said. ''You can start by interviewing relatives. There's a sister and several cousins in L.A., an aunt and uncle in Bakersfield. The family is pretty spread around, but they're all in California.'' I slid some papers with names and addresses down the table. Chris grimaced as she read it.

I passed another set of papers to Eileen. ''I'd like you to interview friends from church and several other groups he belongs to. There's a list of guys he plays basketball with on Monday nights. I'm particularly interested in anything they have to say.

''When you finish with them, I'd like you to canvass the neighbors. The ones on the list are the most likely to know something useful, but you should talk to everyone. I want to know if anyone has seen anything strange on the street during the past two weeks.

"I also want you to spend time with Suzanne Mendoza. Get as complete a biography as possible on her husband. You can start with what she told me today; go over it and ask her to fill in any missing pieces. Try to get every place he's gone or talked about going since they met. It'll take time for her to remember it all, so stop by and see her every day or so. She's fairly fragile emotionally, so she can use all the support and comfort you can give her."

I gave the group a quick summary of what Suzanne had told me about her husband and described the missing photograph. "The men in the photo all came from Modesto, which is also where Mendoza's mother and aunt live, so I'll head up there tomorrow, probably spend Friday there as well."

With the basic stuff behind us, I moved on to the interesting part and told them about the bug at the Mendoza house and the man in the blue van.

Peter gave a low whistle. "All of a sudden this doesn't look like a classic embezzlement," he said.

"I figure that someone knows about Mendoza's plans, either a confederate or someone who wants to move in on him," I said.

"Could even be that our boy is an unwilling partner in this scheme," Jesse suggested.

"An outside player," Peter said.

Eileen looked confused, and he explained, "The guy who was watching Mendoza's house. We don't know who he is, where he came from, why he's involved. He's outside the game as we understand it."

"Never a good situation," I said.

"No," Peter agreed. "An outside player always makes things more dangerous. Now we not only have to find Mendoza, we have to figure out who else is looking for him and make sure our outside player doesn't get to him first."

Jesse shook his head. "I got a bad feeling about this case."

* * *

When the crew had filed out of my office, Amy stuck her head in. "Two calls," she said. "Annlyn Spears and your mother. Your parents are arriving on the fourteenth instead of the twelfth."

"Does my mother want me to call back?"

"She said you needn't bother, which means you should."

I groaned. My parents were coming next month for their yearly visit to the Bay Area. I could look forward to at least one painful talk about biological clocks, numerous dissertations on the virtues of marriage, and one dinner to which they would insist on inviting my ex-husband.

My parents could not accept the fact that I had divorced Dan, and they made no secret of their drive to reunite us. My dad is a cop. When I married another cop, Lt. Dan Walker of the SFPD, he had the perfect son-in-law. Unfortunately, sexual attraction cannot overcome basic incompatibility. Dan wanted to protect me; I wanted to run my own life, so after we'd fought about it enough times to figure out that neither of us was going to change, we'd separated.

I hadn't met Peter until the divorce was almost final, but that didn't prevent my parents from blaming him for the breakup. Everything about him—his profession, his politics, and his irreverent attitude toward authority—offended my father and worried my mother. During their last visit we had spent one of the longest evenings of my life trying to find something safe to talk about. I was not looking forward to a repeat performance.

I made the easy call first. Annlyn and Sara, being long on time and short on cash, were delighted by my offer of a job. They were ready to move in that evening, so I called Suzanne and arranged for her to meet them at her house at seven.

By the time I finished that call, it was almost five-thirty. I was due at the dojo in thirty-five minutes to teach the six o'clock aikido class. I'd have to call my mother later.

A dojo is the martial arts equivalent of a gymnasium. Ours isn't in one of San Francisco's finer neighborhoods, but the rent's good, and the upstairs room is nice and large. In stepping through the door, you move from late-twentieth-century urban blight to a stark white world of silence. The stairway is adorned with several large Japanese prints, but upstairs white walls surround mat-covered floors, and the only decoration is a photograph of Morihei Uyeshiba, the founder of aikido. Tonight a single red rose in a small vase sat on the low table before the photograph.

I arrived at five-forty and was immediately the center of attention. It was enough to make me wish I'd bought an eye patch. I escaped into the office, only to find Frank Gowan sitting behind the desk.

"Ouch," he said, looking at my eye. "That looks like it hurt." Frank was my first teacher. I respect him more than any man alive. He's a true sensei, not just a master of the physical moves but a teacher in the spiritual sense. He is the quietest person I know. To be with him in a room is to feel your mind clear and all the senseless chatter in your head die away.

"Yeah," I said, "but the bruise on my eye is nothing compared to the wounds on my ego."

He smiled. "I had a similar injury a few years ago. A beginner struck me in the face with a move that no one with any experience would have tried. It was so foolish a strike that I was completely unprepared for it. It taught me a valuable lesson about the dangers of expectations."

"It's not the punch you expect that knocks you down," I said, repeating a line I'd learned from him.

"And," he said, "knowing that is not the same as knowing how." I must have looked perplexed, because he laughed and said, "Knowing what you are supposed to do is not at all the same thing as doing it."

I nodded. "Too true," I said, then headed out to get dressed.

I looked around the class as I led them in warm-up exercises. Almost half the group had the aggressive good grooming and Nautilus-tuned bodies of true Yuppies. I'd finally gotten the Bruce Lee fans to settle down. Now I had the overachievers to contend with.

I demonstrated *morote-tori kokyuho* several times while the class knelt at the edge of the mat. My partner grabbed my wrist with both hands, and I pivoted to bring myself next to him and brought my arm up and back, forcing him to stretch backward. We held that position for a few seconds; then I brought my arm down to drop him on the mat.

"Practice just to the stretch a couple of times, then do the throw," I instructed them.

When I clapped my hands and bowed, they turned to each other and silently paired off. The overachievers were a real challenge. They'd been taught that success depended on assertion and confrontation, taking the initiative and dominating the opposition. Yet in aikido one deals with hostile energy by simply moving out of the way and directing the attacker's energy against him.

These corporate whiz kids had a lot of trouble getting out of the way; they were so anxious to begin their throw that they left themselves vulnerable. I moved among the partners, demonstrating how the attacker could punch or kick them if they got sloppy about moving out of the way.

They had another problem. Successful defense requires using an opponent's energy against him or her; to do that you have to sense and respond to that energy, be receptive before becoming active. Receptivity isn't something that's taught much in the Western world.

I clapped to end the practice, and the class knelt at the edge of the mat.

"As soon as you're out of the way, you blend with the attacker's energy," I reminded them. "You don't confront that energy; this isn't arm wrestling."

I signaled my partner to strike with a punch to my stomach, and as he did, I pivoted to the side and turned to face the same direction. As I moved, I raised my arm and rested my hand on his. He froze in place.

"Now," I said, "we're facing the same direction. I'm seeing the world just as he does. That's blending. Once you've done that, you can guide his energy." With that I grasped my partner's hand and finished the throw.

* * *

As I drove home later, I thought about the call to my mother. I tried to see the upcoming trip from her point of view. My parents' hopes of reuniting Dan and me were fed by the chemistry between us. I still found Dan extremely attractive, even if I couldn't live with him. Mom and Dad picked up on the first without understanding the second.

Since I knew that Dad genuinely enjoyed Dan's company and wanted to see him, I decided to set up a golf game for them. I could take Mother shopping, and all four of us need never be in the same room at the same time.

Later, Peter and I could take them to the beach or to the wine country. My dad and Peter both loved the outdoors; conversation there was bound to be easier than over the dinner table.

That settled, I went back to the First Central case. I wondered how the world looked through James Mendoza's eyes. Discovering that would be the first step to understanding where he'd gone and why. I hoped that some of the answers could be found in Modesto.

I T TAKES ABOUT two hours to get to Modesto unless you leave during rush hour, so I fixed myself some scrambled eggs and enjoyed a leisurely breakfast. Peter, never one to go to work any earlier than necessary, joined me; and Touchstone made his presence known by rubbing against our legs and trying to climb into our laps.

At nine o'clock I could no longer use the excuse of missing the traffic, but I had one last task before I left town. I didn't think Daniel Martin was going to be thrilled to hear that someone was watching the Mendozas, but I'd promised to keep him informed, so I called and gave him the bad news. There was a long silence.

"I don't understand," he said at last. "What does this mean?"

"Right now, anything I told you would be a guess," I said. "But it suggests that there is someone besides Mendoza involved in this, someone else anxious to know where he's gone."

"Oh, dear," he said. Then, after a pause, "Does Mrs. Mendoza know?"

"Yes, and I've hired someone to stay with her in case she needs protection."

"Good, that's good," he said.

"I'm going to Modesto today to interview Mendoza's mother. I plan to see several people, so I may have to stay the night. If you don't hear from me, you can assume that I haven't anything to report."

He thanked me and even attempted a joke about my calls being the best medicine for his ulcer. Mr. Martin wasn't a funny man, but it was nice that he tried.

I gave Peter a last kiss and headed out, looking forward to a ride in the country. The country, unfortunately, is getting farther from San Francisco all the time.

I'm used to the unrelenting urban ugliness of Nimitz Freeway, but I wasn't prepared for the subdivisions spilling out into the Livermore Valley east along 580. I remembered glass-gold hills with their twisted dark oaks and white-faced cattle; in their place I found gouged earth planted with rows of identical houses.

Beyond the suburbs, however, steep gray-green hills, terraced by generations of cattle, continued to defy the developers. In January of a normal year the wild grass that sprouts with the first rains would have covered them with a rich emerald carpet. But this year had been dry; and the short, stunted new grass was still overshadowed by the dry skeletons of last year.

I remembered Modesto as a town on the way to the Sierras. Located in the middle of the rich San Joaquin Valley, it was a welcome stopping point for an ice cream soda on the long, hot drive to Yosemite. I realized that I hadn't stopped there for a long time when I found that the number of Modesto off ramps had tripled.

Tracts of large houses had sprung up in place of orchards and fields. The town was in the middle of a building boom. I was pondering why a hot valley town was suddenly so popular when I remembered a newspaper article about supercommuters, people who worked in San Francisco but lived hours away in communities where housing prices were still low enough to afford.

The senior Mendozas' house was in the middle of an expensive subdivision that was at least ten years old. Suzanne had said that Jim's father owned a neighborhood grocery store; the large ranch-style house seemed a bit rich for a grocer.

A woman I assumed to be Mrs. Mendoza senior opened the door. She was dressed in a plum pantsuit with a pink blouse. Thick black hair tied back in a bun showed no sign of gray, but her face was richly etched with tiny lines. Suzanne had obviously warned her about my appearance. She was the first person I'd met who didn't react to the fact that I seemed to have grape jelly under my eye.

The living room had been done by a decorator whose ideas on design came from the Sunday supplement. Nice, probably expensive furniture, but large and heavy and a bit too much of it. I'd bet that most of the things in the room had been bought at the same time, right down to the glass ashtrays, silk flower arrangements, and reproductions in gilt frames. In a corner on a low table I spotted the remnants of the Mendozas' previous life—a forest of family photographs that spanned several generations, an old crucifix, and several small religious statues. The largest of the statues was a Virgin of Guadalupe that was probably older than Mrs. Mendoza. For the first time I realized that her son's home, with its lovely Japanese accents, contained no reflection of his Hispanic background. Why had he, I wondered, turned his back so thoroughly on his own culture?

"Suzanne tells me you're concerned about finding Jim," Mrs. Mendoza said. "I told her that I don't know where he's gone. I'm afraid I can't help you."

"He didn't tell you he was leaving?"

"No."

"When was the last time you spoke with him?"

"About a week ago." She paused. "Look," she said, "Jim's been going off on these little trips since he was old enough to drive. And we've never known where he'd get to. He doesn't know himself. He'll head for Yosemite and end up in Sonora."

"I'm afraid this isn't just one of those trips," I said. "Jim didn't tell his employer or anyone else at work that he was going. The bank is very worried."

"Worried? Why?"

I explained about Jim's study of the computer system and its potentially expensive bug.

"They think Jim's trying to rob the bank?"

"No accusations have been made, but they're very worried that he's disappeared with no explanation. He could probably clear it up very quickly if they knew where to find him."

"Anyone who knows Jim knows he wouldn't do a thing like that. It's because he's Hispanic, that's why they're going after him." Her mouth was set in a tight, angry line.

"It's because he's missing," I said. "God knows, there's plenty of prejudice in this society, probably even at the bank, but the bottom line is that no one would be worried if he hadn't disappeared so mysteriously."

The lines in her face softened from anger to worry.

"There's more," I said. "Someone installed a listening device and started watching the house shortly after he left. Suzanne called me when she realized she was being watched, and the man disappeared, but his presence means that some-one besides me is looking for Jim."

We sat in silence as Mrs. Mendoza came to grips with what I'd told her. Worry aged her face, but she held her body erect. There was no sign of weakness in her carriage. "If Jim had wanted people to know where he was going, he'd have told them," she said.

"He obviously felt he could handle the situation himself," I admitted. "But he may be up against something much bigger and more dangerous than he realizes. The man who watched his house is probably a professional crook. Jim may need help."

She considered again, struggling to decide how best to protect her son. Finally, she said, "What do you need from me?"

I told her, and she agreed to compile the lists—places he'd been or might go, people he knew and might contact, interests that might draw him to one place over another. Then I asked her about Jim himself, what kind of kid he'd been, what had happened while he was growing up.

Once she'd decided to help, she was unqualified in her efforts. There were no more questions about why I wanted to know or how something was relevant to Jim's disappearance. She spun out the story of her son's life as if I were a member of the family or a good friend rediscovered after many years.

Jim had been the eldest of four, two brothers and a sister. His father had owned a neighborhood grocery store where Jim worked from the time he was old enough to help out. When Jim was fourteen, his father bought the land for this house. It was outside the city at that time, since Hispanics couldn't buy in the better areas of town. Jim helped his father and uncle build the house. Mrs. Mendoza took pride in describing the special things they'd done that made their house superior to the newer ones that had sprung up around it.

Jim had always been a good student. He'd gotten excellent grades despite the demands of helping out at the store. He was working the cash register when lots of other kids were still struggling with math sheets.

Living in north Modesto, the Mendoza kids had been among very few Hispanics in their high school, and while Jim had experienced some prejudice, he was so outstanding that it didn't hold him back. He'd lettered in track and basketball and been one of the top ten students in the class. He'd planned to go to the University of California but changed his mind when several of his friends were drafted.

"He was that kind of boy," his mother said. "He wouldn't take advantage of the college deferment. He believed that if the country was calling men to war, he shouldn't duck out of the responsibility."

"I understand he was in a special unit with other men from Modesto."

"Yes, it was some sort of experiment." She paused, and her face took on a sadness. "It was a bad war, not at all like World War Two. He wasn't the same when he came home, not just older and wiser but real sad and confused. I remember he said something about wounds that don't show and don't heal.

"It took him over a year to get his life together. He just worked in the store and hung out with the other vets, drinking too much and staying out all night."

"Are any of those men still in town?" I asked.

"Yes, several of them at least. Let's see, there's Sam Connors and Terry Wheeler. They have a garage down on Scenic near the county hospital, and I think Craig Worth works there, too. There's another young man, a black man, teaches over at the high school, Modesto High School. I don't remember his name, but Sam or Terry would know."

"Were any of those men particularly close to Jim?"

"They were none of them close before they went to war, but when they came home, they were together all the time. Jim was especially close to Sam, I think. They spent a lot of time together. Sam's father had a stroke about six months after they came back, and Jim and Terry helped Sam with the garage. It was the best thing for all of them. Once they had to figure out how to run that garage, they started to settle down. Sam and Terry are still there, but Jim's dad convinced him to go back to school."

"He went to Cal in Berkeley," I prompted.

"That's where he met Suzanne," Mrs. Mendoza offered.

"He did real well there, majored in history but took all kinds of computer courses. I'm sorry his father didn't live to see him graduate. He'd have been so proud."

The rest of the story fit with what Suzanne had told me—a management training program at Bank of California, night courses on computer programming so that he could move into the Systems Division, and his move to First Central in 1981. I got Mrs. Mendoza to promise to call her sister and her other two sons to tell them I was coming to see them and to urge them to cooperate.

I was hungry, but a trip down the main drag made me feel like Alice in Franchise Land. Every fast-food emporium known to man found a spot on the strip. Even the places I didn't recognize looked like franchises. McHenry Avenue was probably the saturated-fat capital of the world.

I drove into the center of town to find a real restaurant and discovered that the strip had bled it dry. The only buildings that appeared to be in use were city and county offices and a couple of miniature malls. I finally found a small restaurant that may not have been any better than those on the strip but at least didn't look like it had been designed at Disneyland.

10

SAM CONNORS'S GARAGE was actually a body shop near the county hospital, which was conveniently located across the street from the cemetery. The body shop was only a little less run down than the hospital. Cars with battered fenders and ugly metallic scars waited outside with the same hopeless patience as the sick and indigent down the street.

In a dingy office at the front of the shop, a man in gray

coveralls poked away at a calculator with a hand that looked as if it'd had an unfortunate encounter with a meat grinder. A cane leaned against the wall next to the desk. I'd found James Mendoza's visitor.

He looked up at me and asked, "Can I help you?"

His voice was soft and deeper than I'd expected. He was a small man, shorter than I, but with a compact, muscular body. His closely trimmed dark hair was graying at the temples, and he wore silver-rimmed glasses and coveralls that looked like they'd been pressed.

"Mr. Connors?"

"Yes."

"I understand you're a friend of Jim Mendoza?"

Surprise and something else, maybe fear, crossed his face. "Yes," he said cautiously.

"I was wondering when you last saw him?"

His body tensed, and his eyes narrowed ever so slightly. He studied me very carefully. "Why do you ask?"

"I'm trying to find him, and I was hoping that you could help me."

"I would suggest you try his home in San Francisco."

"Did you visit him there recently?"

"I don't believe you told me why you wanted to know."

I'd hoped to put him in a position where he'd have to admit his visit or lie about it. He was avoiding doing either. I'm not fond of cat and mouse, so I said, "Jim left home shortly after you visited him. I was hoping you could tell me where he went."

Connors shook his head slowly. "No, I'm afraid I can't. I just stopped by to see him when I was in town. I don't get to the City often, and he doesn't come here much, so I hadn't seen him for quite a while. We just sort of caught up on old times. He didn't say anything about going anywhere."

"Well, he's gone, and his boss and his wife are worried. What exactly did you talk about?"

Connors tossed out enough generalities to earn him a Ph.D. in vagueness. I asked questions; he slid around them. We did that dance for long enough to convince me that he had more patience for it than I did. I asked to see Wheeler.

"Terry hasn't seen Jim for years," he said.

"I'd like to talk to him, anyway."

"He's working."

"So am I."

"Not for me, you're not. You want to talk to Terry or to me, for that matter, you do it after hours."

I backed down. "That's fair," I said. "Can I buy you a beer after work?"

He didn't look like he wanted a beer bad enough to put up with me, but he gave a resigned sigh and said, "Sure. We quit at six."

I took the chance and pushed just a little bit further. "Is Craig Worth here? I'd like to talk with him, too."

Connors shook his head, "Naw, he hasn't been around all week. He wouldn't be much help, anyway. He's not too clear in the head most of the time."

I thanked him for agreeing to give me his time, arranged a place to meet, and left him to his calculator.

I spent the rest of the afternoon with Mendoza's aunt and his two brothers. They were all cooperative and concerned but of very little help. The youngest brother, Mark, told me about several places he and Jim had wanted to visit as kids. He was the most open of the group, so I asked a few questions I wouldn't have asked the others, questions about why Jim seemed so different from the rest of the family and why they knew so little about what he'd been doing since college.

"Jim was the oldest, and I think Dad really pushed him. He wanted him to get out of Modesto, go to college, and be a real success."

"Seems to me that your dad was a real success," I said, thinking of the house I'd visited earlier in the day.

"He made plenty of money, especially for a Hispanic in this town, but I think he wanted more for Jim."

"And not for the rest of you?"

"He sort of mellowed over time. Things got easier, and

Mother really wanted us close to home. He encouraged us, but he didn't push us the way he did Jim."

I wondered how being the one who was supposed to succeed had affected Jim Mendoza. Had a good job at the bank suddenly not been success enough?

There was no way to see everyone on my list in one day, and I sure wasn't making that two-hour drive twice, so it looked like I'd be spending the night. I pulled out the AAA guide, found a motel that was centrally located, and made a reservation before I headed for my meeting at the bar.

The Angler was your basic smoky, noisy bar; it was not at all the place for a woman alone, which was probably why Connors had chosen it. Even in a bar a black eye gets a reaction. Men looked my way uneasily; then one boomed out, "Hey, darlin', you ought to get a guy who doesn't beat you." I ignored him and squinted through the thick haze. "Sam Connors?" I asked the bartender.

"There." He made a vague motion that was next to useless. I continued squinting and finally spotted Connors and another man at a table in the back. If they saw me, they sure weren't making any effort to get my attention.

I talk to a lot of people who clearly wish I'd go away, so their lack of hospitality didn't crush me.

Connors and Wheeler looked like an entry in the opposites-attract sweepstakes. Wheeler was the kind of guy people think it's funny to call "Tiny," at least six feet four, with large shoulders and chest and an even larger gut. Where Connors was tidy, almost fastidious, Wheeler was downright grubby. His dark hair was long and stringy, and his flannel checked shirt had more than a few miles on it.

I sat down at the table and introduced myself to Wheeler. He nodded. I asked about Mendoza. He hadn't seen him. I asked when he had last seen him. He didn't remember. I asked every question I could think of twice, then settled back and stared at them. Most people can stand only so much silence and will eventually start talking to fill the void. These two looked like silence suited them just fine.

I tried another tack. "You three were in Vietnam together," I said. Connors was staring at the table, so I couldn't see his face, but his body stiffened. Wheeler had a sudden coughing attack. "It must have been pretty rough."

"We got through it," Connors said.

"Who else was in your unit from Modesto?"

Connors hesitated. "Craig Worth, the guy you asked about this morning, George Davis, John Langer, and Luis Ramirez."

"Do you know where those men are now?"

"Some. Why do you want to know?" Connors asked.

"I'm talking to anyone I can find who knows Jim Mendoza. They may have some idea of where he might have gone."

"I doubt it. We don't stay in touch much anymore. But Davis is teaching school somewhere in Modesto, Modesto High, I think. Langer isn't around here. He comes through maybe once or twice a year, but we never know when that'll be. Ramirez died in 'Nam. And Craig's been off somewhere for several days. He couldn't help you, anyway. He gets real confused."

"When Craig's around, where does he live?" I asked.

"Different places; he sort of drifts."

I'd have to find Craig Worth, but I knew these two weren't going to be any help. I had one final question. "Did you call Suzanne Mendoza Tuesday night?" I asked Connors.

"No, I don't even know Jim's wife. Why would I call her?" Between the lack of light and the smoky haze, I couldn't see his face clearly. I couldn't tell whether he was lying, but I certainly didn't trust him. I was tired, and the smoke made my throat tickle, so I thanked the men for their time and retreated from the bar.

Outside I gulped in the cool fresh air. Just breathing the air in that place was probably equivalent to smoking a pack of cigarettes, and I hadn't even gotten any pleasure for my pain. But my time hadn't been completely wasted. Connors and Wheeler had reacted strongly to my question about Vietnam. Too strongly. I wondered why.

I checked into the motel and called my mother. She wasn't fooled by my let's-go-shopping-while-Dan-and-Dad-play-golf ploy, but knowing that I hate shopping almost as much as she loves it, she accepted my suggestion graciously.

Next I called Jesse to see how he was doing at the bank.

"You don't pay me enough for this kind of hassle," he complained.

"Which is?"

"Which is putting up with Daniel Martin. The guy is driving me nuts. He has to know everything I'm doing and everything you're doing and why we're doing it that way. I can't turn around without bumping into him."

"He's terrified of losing his job," I explained. "After all, he's the obvious scapegoat if we don't deliver. Hang in there, and I'll try to get him to give you some peace. Have you got anything?"

"In one day? No. The place is a madhouse. It isn't just the Carleton acquisition; the whole damn bank is trying to catch up with year-end transactions. There's so much volume that it'll take at least another week for them to get everything recorded and checked."

"Of course. I should have remembered that. They're supposed to get everything straightened out by the sixth business day after the end of the quarter, but with all the transactions at the end of the year, it usually takes a couple of weeks."

"You can imagine what it's like in the Trust Division; they're not set up to handle the end-of-year volume coupled with a major acquisition."

"All in all, an ideal time to take advantage of the flaw in the computer system."

"You got it. I have an idea worth exploring if I can get Martin off my back. As far as I can tell, Mendoza's team only investigated potential problems and solutions. They didn't work on how to catch someone if they actually tried to rob the bank. I don't know enough about the system to figure out whether there's a way to discover how and where the money's being paid out, but that's what I'm working on now.''

"Sounds good. Do you need anything?''

"If it looks promising, I'd recommend we turn it over to an outfit that specializes in computer crime. There's a guy on the peninsula who's supposed to be very good at this sort of thing. I'll have Amy do some checking to find out who's the best.''

"Martin won't like bringing in someone else," I predicted.

"Yeah, but it beats losing five million dollars.''

"It does that.''

It took some doing to find a restaurant that wasn't a franchise, but I finally found a little Mexican place that looked family owned. It was early, and I had the place to myself except for an Anglo family with two young boys across the room.

While I was waiting for my fajitas, a Hispanic man and his son came in. From across the room one of the Anglo boys called, "Hey, Carlos.'' The boy went immediately to the family, and it became apparent from his conversation that he and one of the boys at the table were classmates. I looked closer and guessed that they must be about fourth grade.

The Hispanic boy's father joined the conversation for a few minutes, then excused himself to go work in the kitchen. The topic turned to school, and the mother complained jokingly about her son's C's. She asked Carlos if he was having trouble, too, and he responded that he was doing okay.

"He got straight A's," the other boy reported.

Both mother and father expressed surprise and complimented the boy, but there was something patronizing, even a hint of distaste, in their tone. Carlos changed the subject quickly.

Laws have changed since Jim Mendoza was a kid, but attitudes take longer. I could imagine that he got a lot of mixed messages about his achievements. And very little real acceptance.

I was up early Friday, eager to get through my interviews and back to San Francisco. I had breakfast in the motel restaurant and skimmed the *Chronicle*. The front page proclaimed that crack-cocaine had turned the housing projects into a war zone; public officials expressed dismay, and the cops begged for more resources. On the same page administration officials denied that drug money had been used to fund the Contras. I turned to the comics.

George Davis was next on my list, and a phone call confirmed that he did indeed work at Modesto High School. The school secretary informed me that he was free period two, which started at 8:50. I grabbed my map and headed for my car.

I knew that something was wrong before I got to it. The window on the driver's side had been smashed. The prospect of replacing the radio for the second time this year infuriated me until I looked into the car and realized that there are much worse things than having your radio stolen.

11

I LEANED AGAINST the car and waited for my heart to slow down. The seats had been slashed, and an ugly red-brown substance that looked a bit too thick for blood was smeared everywhere.

On the driver's seat was a naked Barbie doll and a note. The doll had been mutilated. One arm had been wrenched off, and deep cuts covered the torso, legs, and remaining arm. The face had been hacked till the features were completely obliterated. The doll was smeared with the same reddish substance as the seats.

There was a piece of paper under the doll. I forced myself to pick it up. The words were scrawled in large letters with a red pen. It read, "If you don't want to end up like this, get out of town."

The violence of the scene sickened me. The seats weren't just cut; they'd been attacked and slashed again and again. My first reaction was revulsion and fear, but that quickly turned into anger. I'm very fond of my car. We've been through a lot together. I felt like an old friend had been attacked.

I walked back to the motel restaurant and ordered a cup of tea to take the edge off the adrenaline rush. The car presented a problem. I couldn't just leave it in the parking lot. Someone was bound to report its sorry condition before too long, and that could result in a call to the police. First Central was paying for discretion as well as skip tracing. Discretion meant no police.

I went back to the car and checked the trunk. The old blanket I keep for picnics was there, and I found a rain poncho tucked away near the spare. I covered the front seats with the blanket and as much as possible of the back with the tarp. I also pulled out a flashlight and checked to make sure that everything looked okay in the engine and under the car.

Back at the room, I called the office. Eileen was there, so she got the job. I asked her to call Connors's body shop from the Mendoza home, with Suzanne on the extension.

"Ask for Connors and get him talking," I said. "Tell him you were in an accident and banged up the front of the car and ask some questions about getting it fixed. I want Suzanne to listen to his voice and see if he was the man who called her about Jim. If he isn't the one, wait till the afternoon and try the same scam with Terry Wheeler.''

Eileen agreed to make the call, then passed the phone to Peter.

''Hi, babe, how goes the chase?''

''I've flushed something, and it sure as hell isn't a rabbit,'' I said, and told him about my car.

''Ouch,'' he said. ''You okay?''

''Of course I'm okay. It's my car that has the slashed seats. I may not be okay when I talk to my insurance man, and I will definitely not be okay after Alfonse, the high priest of Volvos, sees it. I may have to take it somewhere else to get it fixed.''

Peter laughed. He'd been along when I'd gone to Alfonse with my car, covered with spray-painted slogans from some nut who hated foreign cars. He'd reacted with shock and indignation, not only against the nut but against me as well for letting such a thing happen. I left feeling like a negligent parent.

''Any sign of our mystery man watching Suzanne Mendoza?'' I asked.

''All gone, as far as I can tell. I've checked the house for bugs, and it's clean; but there was one in the box on the telephone pole. You think the mystery man could be on your trail?''

''I sure haven't seen him, though my car may have. He's doing a hell of a job of being inconspicuous if he's around here.''

''It sounds like you could use someone else on your team. I'm not getting anywhere down here. I'd like to join you there.''

''Great. It looks like I might be spending some time here, and it will definitely pass more pleasantly with your marvelous body and scintillating personality.''

''You want me to bring anything?''

''How about an old blanket or sheet.''

''And a loaf of bread and a jug of wine?'' he suggested.

"The blanket is to cover the backseat of my car. You can buy bread and wine here, just bring thou."

"It'll take me a half hour to tie things up here; I should be there in three hours or so."

"Be sure to tell Amy to feed the menagerie. And ask her to call the dojo and get someone to take my Saturday morning class."

"Done," he said. "See you soon." He paused. "And don't crack the case before I get there; it'd spoil all the fun."

I promised to wait for his arrival. I wasn't anywhere near cracking the case, but I appreciated Peter's gentle efforts to protect me from myself. I thought about the delicate dance we did—he carefully guarding my autonomy and I struggling not to shut him out. A case like this was tough. I knew how much he wanted to protect me, to impose himself between me and any danger, and I also knew that I couldn't allow that.

I spent the rest of the morning going over everything we knew about Jim Mendoza and listing people to see and places to check. But I was just going through the motions. I couldn't shake the strong feeling that the answer was here in Modesto with Mendoza's army buddies.

Peter looked into the car, with its slashed seats and ugly dark stains, then at the doll. He shook his head and backed away.

"Not a pretty sight," I said.

"No, and there's no way to know whether you've got a psycho on your tail or just someone who wants to look like a psycho."

"I'm betting on the latter. None of the people I saw yesterday looked nuts, and they're the prime candidates for this job."

"Could be someone you haven't seen yet who knows you're here and doesn't want to see you."

"I suppose. What would you do if you were in my shoes?"

Peter considered the question as we walked back to my room. "You know me, long on muscle, short on brains. I'd probably go hassle all the people I'd talked to here just to see if I'd get a rise. See what they'd do next.''

That was about what I'd come up with. In aikido, the first thing you learn is to get out of the way of an attack, then use the opponent's energy to take him down. I needed to get that energy flowing before I could use it.

''It's probably time to bring in some heavy artillery,'' Peter suggested. ''Why don't you let me take care of this round of hassles.''

''You make a charming sacrificial lamb, but I'd rather keep them focused on one target. I'll hassle; you handle backup.''

Peter sighed. ''It isn't supposed to be this way, you know.''

''Welcome to life in the nineties. Don't mope just because I won't play the fainting maiden. If there's any real danger, I'll be only too happy to let you handle the rough stuff.''

''I can hardly wait. In the meantime, why don't I come along and stand menacingly in the background. It might make the guilty party just that much more nervous.''

I considered the idea. I certainly wasn't looking forward to confronting a person who slashed up dolls and maybe people, but I knew that my chances of getting a reaction would be destroyed by Peter's presence.

''No, I think I'd rather have you watching from a distance. Whoever slashed up my car must have been following me yesterday, and he was good enough to do it without my noticing. How'd you feel about tagging along to watch my back?''

''Will you wear your tight jeans?''

''You do have a one-track mind.''

''And you love it.''

''I do.''

The most likely candidates for car vandals were Connors and Wheeler. I couldn't see Mrs. Mendoza slashing seats, and all the members of the family seemed honestly surprised and distressed by Jim's disappearance. Wheeler and Connors, on the other hand, had been nervous and evasive from the minute I mentioned Mendoza's name.

"I think a trip to the body shop is in order," I said. "We'll see what Connors thinks about my slashed seats."

"You going to drive your car?" Peter asked.

"Sure, there's nothing wrong with the engine."

"You mind if I check it for you, just in case?"

When it comes to what's under the hood of a car, I'm barely literate. I accepted his offer with enthusiasm.

It only took a few minutes to confirm that my assessment was correct. "She ain't pretty, but she runs," Peter announced.

"Poor car," I said. "It hurts just to look at it."

"Cheer up. It matches your eye."

I threw the blanket over the front seat again and drove to Connors's body shop. I didn't like the idea of entrusting my car to the men who were its most likely attackers, but I needed to see their reactions and to let them know I wasn't impressed.

I pulled into the entrance to the garage and beeped the horn. Connors came out of his office in response. He looked surprised to see me. He also looked genuinely surprised to see my broken window. "You got a broken window," he said, stating the obvious.

"Yes, and that's not all." I climbed out of the car and pulled the blanket off the seat. His eyes widened as he looked at the slashed seats. His astonishment certainly appeared real, but there was something else, a guardedness that might have come from his general wariness of me or might have meant something more.

"Have you any ideas on how such a thing might have happened?" I asked.

Connors shook his head. "Lot of vandalism these days," he said.

"Somehow I don't think this was done by a stranger," I

said. "Especially since there was a note warning me to get out of town."

Connors looked very sober. He shook his head and said, "I don't know why anybody'd do a thing like that. Seems plain crazy to me. I can fix the window and seats for you, but it'd take time. I'd have to order them. Volvo dealer would be faster."

"I figure it must have been someone I talked with yesterday," I said. "That would be you, Terry Wheeler, or Jim Mendoza's family."

"Wasn't me," Connors said. "And I don't think it was Terry, either. You want to talk to him?"

I said yes, and Connors walked back into the garage to get Wheeler. I followed to prevent any private conversation.

Wheeler was banging out the fender of a new Honda Accord. Connors informed him that I'd like to speak to him for a few minutes and led the way back to my car. Wheeler was as surprised as Connors had been, and his nervousness was even more apparent.

"Someone wants me to leave town," I said.

"I told her it wasn't us," Connors interjected before Wheeler could say anything.

"Jesus, no," Wheeler said. "I fix cars, not mess 'em up."

"Did you tell anyone else about my visit?" I asked.

Both men shook their heads, but Wheeler's expression contradicted him. I looked straight at him. "Who did you tell?"

"No one. I didn't tell no one. There wasn't anything to tell," he protested a bit too vigorously.

"Well, you can tell whoever it was you didn't tell that I'm not leaving town until I get some answers. If you don't know where Jim Mendoza is, I think you know who does. And since I'll be here for a while you can order me a window for this car. It's an '84."

Connors headed back to the office to get the necessary forms, and Wheeler stood around looking uncomfortable.

He frowned as he looked at the car. "It's too bad," he said. "It's a good car." He sounded sad, as if the sight of such wanton destruction hurt him.

"You care about cars, don't you?" I said.

He looked surprised. "Yeah, I do. Not like animals or anything like that, but every car, it has a special feel to it. They're more than just a bunch of steel and a motor."

"I know. That car's an old friend," I said. "You must enjoy your work, taking a car that's all bent up and making it beautiful again."

He smiled. "It's kinda neat. I never done seats. We just work with bodies. I think someone who does upholstery could recover those seats for you."

"Might need new pads, though," Connors said as he emerged from the office. He leaned into the car and examined the seat. "Yeah, those cuts are deep. You'll need new pads. You'll probably have to order them from a dealer, but Terry's right, I'd go to an upholsterer. You want a recommendation?"

"Thanks, but that can wait till I get back to San Francisco. The window's more pressing."

"Shouldn't take more than a couple of days," Connors said. I noticed that both he and Terry relaxed when the conversation turned to cars. They clearly did not want to talk about Jim Mendoza, and I had a hunch that they generally found it easier to deal with cars than with people.

12

CONNORS AND WHEELER were lying. I was sure of it. They'd told someone else about my visit; and if they hadn't actually vandalized my car, they knew who did. I felt that surge of adrenaline that comes when a case starts to fall together.

I drove back to a coffee shop on the strip. Peter pulled in behind me, and we went inside. He ordered coffee. My stomach was still accepting only tea.

I told him what had happened. "So you'd put your money on his army buddies?" he said.

"They're hiding something. I'm fairly sure of that."

"You think they're in on the robbery?"

I shrugged. "They could be, or they could just be covering for him."

Peter nodded. "Yeah, he could have given them a story that had nothing to do with the bank."

"It's odd that after almost fifteen years of little contact he'd come to them, though."

"Not really. They were in Vietnam together. You go through something like that, you get real close to the people you're with. You've got a special kind of history together. I feel that way about guys I knew in Alabama. They asked for help, I'd give it."

"The fact that they fought together might make him more inclined to turn to them if there was physical danger," I said.

"Might," Peter agreed. "Whatever he told them, they're not going to talk to outsiders about it. I'd bet on that."

I nodded, reluctantly admitting he was right. The waitress came to take our order. After she left, I told Peter, "There's a third vet I haven't seen, Craig Worth. Connors claims that he drifts from one place to another and isn't around right now, but I'd like to know more about him."

"Like whether he fits the description of the guy watching Suzanne?"

"Yes, and like where he was this morning."

"I'll see if I can track him down."

Lunch arrived, and by the time we'd finished our cardboard club sandwiches, Peter had accepted my judgment on Modesto food.

* * *

When we got back to the motel, there was a message to call the office. Amy transferred me to Eileen, who reported that Suzanne was reasonably sure that Sam Connors was the man who'd called her.

"All right," I said. "We're finally getting someplace, though I have no idea where. I want you to do something for me; it'll probably take some time."

She volunteered for the extra time, and I asked her to try to find someone, preferably the commanding officer, connected with Jim Mendoza's unit in Vietnam. "You'll have to get specific information from Suzanne Mendoza—the exact name of his unit, where it was stationed, and when.

"See if she has anything with a commanding officer's name on it. She didn't know Jim while he was in the army, but he may have kept old papers, maybe even letters. I'll try to get the same information from someone in the family here.

"It's going to be a whole lot easier if we have a name. Once you've got that, Jesse can tell you where to go from there. If you don't get a name, he can tell you how to do it the hard way."

"I've got something else for you," she said. "It may not mean anything, but it could be a clue to the man who was watching Suzanne. When I canvassed the neighborhood, I found a woman around the corner from Mrs. Wascovitch who remembered seeing a tan Ford parked in front of her house for a couple of days. She does flower arrangements, and she had a wedding on Monday. She came home to pick up the flowers and found the Ford so close to the driveway that she couldn't pull in.

"It was gone when she got back from delivering the flowers, and an hour or so later it was back. She left a note on the window, and the driver moved it up the street."

"Did she see the driver?"

"No, and she didn't get a license, but she did notice that the front end on the driver's side was dented."

"Anything else?"

"Nothing. Just that it wasn't really an old car but didn't look new, either, and she thinks it was a compact, probably only two doors. But I have to tell you that this lady does not know much about cars, so I wouldn't trust the description too far. She wasn't even really sure it was a Ford when I questioned her. Ford could mean American made."

"Something's always better than nothing. Tell Annlyn, Sara, and Suzanne to keep an eye out for a smallish tan American car with a dented left front end."

"Already done."

"Good work," I said. I reminded her that we needed the information on Mendoza's commanding officer as soon as possible and promised to check in with her around five.

"You going to confront Connors about the telephone call?" Peter asked when I told him Eileen's news.

"He's already denied it," I said. "Right now I think I've poked at this thing enough. It's time to sit back and see what happens."

"As in spending the next several days sitting in a parked car?" Peter asked with a noticeable lack of enthusiasm.

" 'Fraid so."

"I got a better idea. Why don't we hire a couple of friends of mine to sit in the car so we can spent some of that time in bed."

How could I refuse? I leaned over, unbuttoned his shirt and kissed his chest, moved my lips up to his neck, then his ear. I guess he took that for agreement, because he immediately slid his hands under my sweater and began to unsnap my bra.

Before I lost all ability to concentrate, I pulled away and reminded Peter that until his friends arrived, Connors and Wheeler were still our responsibility.

"You are such a tease," he complained.

"Look who's talking," I replied. "Come on, we've miles to go before we sleep."

"Frost may have had sleep in mind," Peter commented. "I was planning on something else."

He called and arranged with his friends to handle the surveillance on Connors and Wheeler. They promised to get to Modesto as soon as possible, but it didn't sound like they'd be there till late evening. Peter headed off to watch the boys at the garage, and I went back to Mrs. Mendoza to see if she could help me find the name of her son's commanding officer.

Mrs. Mendoza was friendly but reserved. I don't suppose I'd have been too crazy about someone who brought the kind of news I'd brought her. I explained that I needed to find the name of Jim's commanding officer in Vietnam and wondered if she had any way of knowing. If she'd ever heard it, she had forgotten, but she suggested that it might be in one of Jim's letters from Vietnam. She wasn't exactly sure where they were, but she thought they might be in a box in the basement. "I tried to give them to Jim," she said, "but he didn't want them. He didn't want anything to remind him of the war. Someday he'll want those things, maybe when he has a son, so I'm keeping them for him."

It took about ten minutes for her to locate the box with the letters, which is a lot less time than it would take me to find anything in my basement.

She sat down across from me and held a shoe box filled with letters on her lap. She didn't offer to give them to me.

"I'm not asking to read the letters, Mrs. Mendoza. I don't want to invade your privacy or Jim's. I would appreciate it very much if you or someone else in the family would read the letters to see if they have the name of the commanding officer in them."

She nodded. "I'll do that for you. I don't see how it's going to help find my son or stop the people who are after him, but I'll do what I can."

"It might also help if you could keep a list of all the names that appear in the letters,'' I suggested. ''It's just possible that someone he knew in Vietnam is involved in this.''

She looked skeptical, but she agreed.

At four-fifteen, the phone in my room rang. Eileen announced gleefully, ''I haven't got the name, but I've got something almost as good. He's still in the military, and he's probably stationed someplace in the Bay Area.''

She explained that Suzanne remembered Jim meeting a man in uniform at San Francisco International Airport about a year ago. She was coming back from making a phone call when she saw the man walk up to Jim and speak to him. They only spoke for a moment, and Suzanne said she could feel the chill clear across the room.

''He told her the man was his commanding officer in 'Nam and that he was a real bastard. Suzanne says it's unusual for Jim to have a strong dislike for someone; he's generally pretty tolerant, but he really disliked this guy.''

''How do you know he's in the Bay Area?'' I asked.

''Suzanne heard him say something about how maybe he'd be seeing more of Jim now that they were in the same neighborhood. He said it in a real nasty way, almost like a threat.''

''Very interesting,'' I commented. ''But she doesn't have a name.''

''Unfortunately not. Looks like the ball's in your court.''

''I hope so. I hate to think how long it might take to dig that name out of the military.''

Eileen also told me that Jesse was still complaining about Martin, and I remembered guiltily that I hadn't called him as I'd intended. I promised again to call, and Eileen told me that Jesse was making progress on his quest to find a way to catch Mendoza when he claimed his money. I hoped it wouldn't come to that, but it made me feel better to think we had a fallback position.

I called Daniel Martin. He asked six questions before he stopped for breath. I began to wonder if he'd make it through the fourteen days.

I answered the six questions, mostly with "Nothing to report," and told him about my car. Before he could fall apart on me, I explained that the threat was probably a sign of progress. "I've made somebody nervous," I said, "which suggests that someone here has something to hide."

"Like Mendoza's whereabouts?"

"We can only hope."

That seemed to cheer him substantially, but not enough to prevent him from complaining about Jesse. He found Mr. Price's presence at the bank disruptive and saw no reason why he should continue to be there, especially now that we had a good lead in Modesto.

"Not a *good* lead," I cautioned, "a possible lead. And I'm afraid you'll have to accept my judgment that it is essential to have someone undercover at the bank. Some of Mendoza's colleagues may know something that would be useful to us, and they won't confide it to a total stranger."

He groused a bit more. I cut that off by reminding him how important it was that we take every precaution. "You don't want any questions about our thoroughness," I pointed out.

No, that was one thing he definitely did not want. I suspected that having Jesse looking into the computer system was another thing he wouldn't want, so I tactfully didn't mention it.

The first of Peter's "surveillance experts" arrived around ten; his buddy was fifteen minutes behind him. They introduced themselves as Bert and Ernie. Bert was tall, lean, and wore a serious, almost-mournful expression; Ernie was short and round and laughed a lot. Thirty years ago, they'd probably have called themselves Abbott and Costello.

I'd had them stop by my office to pick up the portable phones we use for surveillance. I took one for my car and gave them the other two, then sent Bert to Connors's and Ernie to Wheeler's, told them to check in after the two men got to the garage, and settled back to wait for Peter.

He was still half-frozen when he returned to the room, complaining that the fog made it nearly impossible to see the houses. "Poor baby," I said. "Surveillance is the pits."

"True, but tonight was not a complete waste," he announced as he took off his shirt. "I have now memorized all of 'Fern Hill' and the first half of 'Do not go gentle into that good night.' "

"Fern Hill" is hardly a love poem, but I think I fell in love with Peter, or at least had the notion that I might love him, the night we discovered our shared passion for Dylan Thomas. After an evening of Greek food, half-drunk on retsina and ouzo, we began quoting lines from "Fern Hill" to each other, argued vigorously over phrases we couldn't quite remember, and ended up making love on a blanket in his backyard.

" 'Now as I was young and easy under the apple boughs,' " I began, and he joined in and continued when my memory failed. I fell silent and watched him. The hair on his chest had traces of gray, but it was still thick and curly, and his body was defined by muscle rather than fat.

I applauded when he finished and reached up to pull him down onto the bed. "Come here and I'll show you something almost as good as the 'lamb white days,' " I offered.

He accepted with his usual enthusiasm.

I woke up before Peter the next morning, and my stomach informed me that it was in no mood to wait till he got around to thinking about breakfast. I put on jeans and a sweater, grabbed the room key, and headed for the restaurant.

The world outside my door drove all thoughts of food from my mind. Thick tule fog had descended like a curtain, erasing the main building and its restaurant and replacing them with only a few ghostly shapes that hinted at familiar structures. I could see the sidewalk at my feet and dimly make out the fence around the swimming pool several yards away, but that was all. Everything else—the trees, the buildings, even the cars in the parking lot—had disappeared into a silver-white void.

I rushed back into the room to tell Peter, only to discover that this was not his first tule fog and that he did not share my enthusiasm for a morning walk. I didn't argue; the idea of walking alone in the silence appealed to me. Had I been less anxious to explore or Peter been more awake, one of us might have realized what a foolish idea it was for me to wander into the dense fog by myself.

13

I HEADED DOWN the residential street behind the motel. Normally, elm trees formed a green canopy high above the street, but today a curtain of white stretched just above my head, swallowing all but the dark trunks that stood sentinel between the walk and the curb. Cement paths wandered away from the sidewalk and disappeared before reaching their houses.

Somewhere an engine idled, but sound was muffled by the fog, and I couldn't tell whether it was ahead or behind me. The noise became louder until two points of red light glowed dully through the fog. I was glad not to be in a car in this stuff. Walking was fun; driving would be Russian roulette.

I walked toward the park at the end of the block. The car drove past me as I reached the corner, and only after it had passed did I become aware of a second sound. It was a soft regular sound. I stopped to listen. The sound stopped. I walked again; the sound resumed. I was being followed.

I turned to look behind me but saw only fog. If my follower was unarmed, I could probably take him. My training in aikido gave me the advantage, even with a large, athletic man. But if he was armed, I could end up dead. It didn't seem worth the risk.

I was at the edge of the park now. If I couldn't see my follower, he couldn't see me either. Once I was on the grass, my footsteps would be silenced. There'd be no way he could be sure which direction I had taken.

I took a few steps into the park and waited. I stood in the middle of a white void and forced the image of the mutilated Barbie doll from my mind. This was not a time to think about anything; thoughts would distract me from what was happening and slow down my response. I centered myself with my breathing and waited.

The footsteps had stopped. My follower was also waiting. I figured I could outwait him. But as the minutes dragged by, with only the sound of water dripping from the trees and the gray formless mass around me, waiting got harder. The damp air was cold on my face, but inside my leather jacket it felt as if someone had turned up the heat. My mouth was so dry that it was hard to swallow.

I didn't like the fact that he could come from any direction. What if he'd passed me unseen in the fog and doubled back? I pushed the thought from my mind. In the dojo I sometimes practiced with a blindfold so I didn't know where an attack would come from or what form it would take. But in the dojo I knew that the attackers weren't armed. Again I pushed the thought from my mind. I wasn't doing such a great job of staying focused.

When I thought I couldn't stand it much longer, I heard a muffled crack, as if someone had stepped on a small branch or twig. He was moving again, but where was he?

He almost walked right by me. If he'd been a foot farther away, we'd never have seen each other. He was stalking; his body slightly crouched, and I knew as soon as I saw him that he was trouble. He spotted me and turned. He held an open switchblade in his right hand.

He was a big guy, tall but not heavy. I waited and hoped he hadn't been trained in the martial arts. He took a couple of cautious steps toward me, holding the knife in front of him. Then he lunged, aiming the knife for the middle of my body.

I pivoted out of the way and grabbed his hand at the wrist. Stepping back, I brought my other hand up and bent his arm back toward his body, pressing my thumb into the tendons of the back of his hand and torquing the wrist until the knife pointed at the ground.

He yelped and dropped the knife. Before he could recover, I let go with one hand, straightened and raised his arm, and stepped under it. I ended up with him in a *sankyo* grip, his shoulder rotated forward, with his elbow in the air, and his hand palm out, held against my chest.

Sankyo doesn't look like much, but when you put that kind of pressure on the shoulder joint, even a small movement is intensely painful. My assailant lashed out at me with his free hand; I turned toward him, putting more pressure on the hand held against my chest. He howled, pulled back, and began swearing vigorously.

I didn't want to leave a switchblade in the middle of a park, so I said, "We're going to bend down now, just bend your knees and go with me." I took him down, grabbed the knife, and straightened up before he could get into any more trouble. Closing the knife while keeping my prisoner under control was a real trick, and I thought as I stuffed it in my pocket that it undoubtedly qualified as a concealed weapon.

I needed to get my assailant back to the motel, where Peter and I could question him, but in my efforts to evade him, I'd lost track of where I was. We stood in the midst of a space without definition. Not even a tree trunk marked one direction from another.

Deciding that hesitation was the worst response, I moved forward, maintaining the pressure of my prisoner's elbow to encourage him to walk ahead of me into the fog. When we reached the swings, I knew I'd gone in the wrong direction, but I also knew that we'd reached the middle of the park and that if I turned around I'd probably end up somewhere near the point at which I had stepped off the sidewalk.

We reached the sidewalk, but I couldn't be sure it was the right sidewalk. I paused and uncertainty loosened my grip. Unable to strike at me, my attacker pulled away in the opposite direction. I grabbed his collar and pulled, and he fell backward. Had I been more centered, I'd have simply let go and allowed him to fall, but in the fog I was disoriented and a bit slow, so he knocked me off balance, and I went down with him.

It was worse for him than for me. I landed hard on the best padded part of my body, but I held on to his hand, and that wrenched his arm painfully. He fell onto his shoulder, and his head got a good bang on the cement.

"You've broke my arm," he screamed.

"I'll do worse than that if you try anything again," I said, trying to sound tough. "Now we're going to get up, and if you want to use that arm again, you'll be very careful to do exactly what I tell you."

I got us on our feet without losing control of him. He moaned every time his arm moved. My tailbone hurt like hell, so I wasn't too sorry for him.

It was slow going. Between the fog and the problem of steering my prisoner, it was a long way back to the motel. The worst part was that until we reached the fence around the parking lot, I wasn't sure I was going in the right direction.

I banged on the room door, hoping Peter wasn't at breakfast. There was a muffled "Just a minute," and a couple of minutes later, the door opened. Peter stood there, half-awake, dressed only in jeans. He woke up fast when he saw us.

I pushed my attacker into the room and let go of his hand as I shoved him into a chair. He grabbed his shoulder and whined again, "You broke my arm."

"I doubt it, but that's what you get for playing with knives," I said. I pulled the switchblade from my pocket and handed it to Peter.

He winced as he examined it. "He came after you with this?"

I nodded. "And now I want to know why."

The man in the chair didn't look very fierce now. He was about six two and skinny. His dirty blond hair hung limply to his shoulders, and a scraggly reddish beard covered the lower half of his face. He looked up at me, but the pupils of his eyes couldn't seem to stay in one place. They flicked rapidly, almost bouncing from side to side. I wondered what he was on.

"Who are you?" I asked.

"I don't have to talk to you."

"No, you can talk to the police, about assault with a deadly weapon. How much time do you do for that, Peter?"

"Depends on your record. You got a record, pal?"

His voice said no, but his face contradicted it.

Peter smiled. "Hope you're right, because if you got any kind of record, you'll be doing hard time for going after a woman with a knife." He walked over to the phone and picked it up.

The man watched Peter cross the room; his pupils were jumping even more wildly. As Peter lifted the receiver, he cried out, "Hey, man, no. I was just trying to scare her."

"A knife in the midsection is definitely scary," I said. "Who are you, and why were you following me?"

The man hesitated. Peter dialed a number.

"Okay, okay, don't call the police."

Peter held the phone. "Answer the lady's question," he ordered.

The man's body slumped in the chair. He spoke to the floor. "My name's Worth, Craig Worth." Peter and I exchanged glances, but Worth was studying the floor and didn't notice. "I just wanted to scare you, to get you to leave town."

"Why?"

"You're making some people unhappy."

"So they asked you to scare me off."

"No, no, they didn't ask me nothing. But I don't like to see my friends upset, so I thought I'd do them a little favor."

I thought of my disfigured Volvo. A little favor indeed. I was sorry I hadn't broken his arm.

"Who are the friends?" I asked.

He was silent. Peter picked up the phone again and dialed one number. Worth sat and massaged his arm. Peter dialed a second number. Worth showed no sign of stopping him. "So you're going to take the fall for your buddies. Very noble. Except it won't be too hard for the cops to figure out who they are. They probably won't appreciate police attention." He dialed a third number.

"Wait. It don't have nothing to do with them. They don't even know what I did."

"You think the police will believe that?" I asked. "I'll bet Connors and Wheeler'll be furious."

His head snapped up when I said their names. There wasn't much question who the friends were.

It got easier after that. Worth bitched and moaned a lot and retreated into silence a couple of times, but we got the story from him. He'd noticed the light in the body shop on Thursday night and had stopped by. Connors and Wheeler were discussing my visit and our meeting in the bar, and they were clearly upset. Worth didn't understand exactly what was going on, but he knew that they were afraid of me. He'd decided to solve the problem for them.

"So you slashed my seats and carved up a Barbie doll as a warning," I said.

"I didn't mean any real harm. I just wanted to scare you. I wanted you to go away. That's all."

Worth didn't fit the description of the man who'd watched the Mendoza house, but I wanted to see his reaction, so I asked, "Why were you watching Jim Mendoza's wife last week?"

He looked genuinely confused. "I didn't," he stuttered. "I didn't even know she was here."

"Where's Jim?" I asked.

Worth didn't know. He thought maybe Jim was in San Francisco, but he wasn't sure, because Connors talked like he was someplace else.

"Where else?"

"He didn't say. Maybe I misunderstood. I get confused real easy. I done a lot of drugs, and the war really messed up my head. Sam and Terry kind of look after me. That's why I didn't want to let anyone hassle them."

We tried different questions and some of the same ones, but we'd gotten all we could from Worth. He didn't have a blue van, and he didn't know anyone who did. He didn't know that Connors had gone to the Bay Area to see Mendoza. He didn't know much.

I wasn't sure he was telling us all there was, but I didn't expect to get any more out of him.

"I think I'll go see what Sam Connors thinks of this," I announced.

Worth jumped out of his chair. "Don't do that, please. Sam'll be real mad at me. He hates it when I do crazy stuff. Please don't tell him." He looked like a frightened ten-year-old. It was hard to believe that this was the same man who'd tried to stick a knife in me less than an hour ago.

I didn't really know what to do with Worth, but I wasn't about to let him go, so Peter agreed to stay with him while I went to Connors's. As I headed for the door, Worth collapsed into the chair with his head in his hands and began mumbling to himself.

Once outside I discovered that the tule fog had only improved a bit and that it was much too foggy to drive around unfamiliar streets.

"How long will this last?" I asked the desk clerk.

"Sometimes fog lasts most of the day, but this one seems to be lifting. Another hour or so, it should be pretty well burned off."

An hour or so. My stomach announced loud and clear its ideas on what to do with the time.

Peter had already made coffee for himself and Worth with my little portable coffee maker, so he was happy to let me have first shift at the restaurant.

Once inside the warmth and comfort of the restaurant, I got hit with a screaming case of delayed shock. My mind replayed the scene in the park, with special emphasis on the size and length of the knife blade.

We work with wooden knives in the dojo, and I was well prepared to deal with the real thing physically, but nothing prepares you emotionally for a confrontation with death. In the park, my body had reacted as it was trained to do. Now my mind and emotions were catching up, and they weren't doing too well. I ordered a pot of tea, hoping it would stop my stomach from flipping around, and discovered that my hand shook when I picked up the cup.

I took several deep breaths and just sat quietly until the shakes passed. Nothing on the menu looked compatible with my adrenaline-drenched stomach, so I ordered toast. Outside, the fog wasn't lifting much that I could see, so I picked up a newspaper and took my time with breakfast.

I tried to talk to Worth a couple of times while Peter was having breakfast, but he seemed to have shrunk into himself, and he wouldn't respond to me. Occasionally he'd talk to himself in a crooning tone, telling himself it was all right and repeating that he didn't mean any harm.

Just before Peter got back from breakfast, Bert called to say that Connors was at the garage. Wheeler hadn't arrived yet. "Isn't this fog something," he commented. "He could have walked right past me last night and I'd never have known."

I couldn't say much with Worth sitting across from me, though I don't think he would have noticed. He was too absorbed in his own misery to pay much attention to anything else. We waited for the fog to burn off.

14

SAM CONNORS WAS alone in his office at the garage. "I don't have that window yet," he said when I walked in.

"Craig Worth tried to kill me this morning," I said.

Connors practically bounced out of his chair. "Oh, no. No. He was calming down, and he's been clean for weeks." He seemed to remember me belatedly. "It's your fault," he said. "You coming around here with all those questions and getting everyone upset. That's why he flipped out. He was doing fine."

"People who are doing fine don't vandalize cars, threaten other people, and attack them with knives."

Connors sat down heavily. "He came after you with a knife?"

"This morning, in the fog. And if I hadn't known how to defend myself, I could be dead now."

"Oh, shit," he said, and followed it with several other colorful expletives. "Where is he?"

"He's in my motel room, with my partner. What happens to him depends on you."

"You haven't called the police?"

"Not yet. Maybe I won't need to, if I can get some information from you and if you can get him into some kind of treatment program."

"He's got a counselor over at the VA; I can call him."

"First let's talk about Jim Mendoza."

"I've already told you that I don't know anything about him."

"You also told me that you hadn't spoken to his wife, but I know that you called her Tuesday night and told her you knew where Jim was."

"I didn't."

I gave him my best give-me-a-break look and turned to leave. "Maybe the police can straighten this out."

"No," he cried. "No, okay, I did call her."

"And . . ."

"And I asked if she needed help and told her I could contact Jim if she needed anything."

"So where is he?"

"I promised him I wouldn't tell, and I won't. A guy needs time to himself sometimes. Women don't understand that. He's not fooling around on her. He just wanted some time to himself."

"Sit down," I said. "It's time we talked."

He sat down at his desk, and I took the straight chair he kept next to his desk for customers.

"I'm not here because Jim Mendoza's wife thinks he's fooling around. I'm here because there's a good chance that he's involved in illegal activity and that someone else is after him."

His eyes, already magnified slightly by the glasses, grew larger. "That's the craziest thing I ever heard. Jim's not involved in anything illegal. The guy works for a bank, for chrissake; they don't hire people who break the law."

Such touching innocence! And he seemed to mean it. "What exactly did he tell you before he left?" I asked.

"He said he needed time to himself before he got bogged down in being a father. He asked me to keep an eye on his wife in case she needed anything."

"Why'd he come to you instead of someone in San Francisco or a member of the family?"

"I supposed he figured I'd understand. We were real close in 'Nam. He knew he could count on me."

"Sam, you seem like a good friend, maybe too good a friend. If Jim is involved in something illegal and you cover for him, you'll be an accessory. He'll get away scot-free, and you'll go to jail."

"What crime is he supposed to have committed?" he asked uneasily.

"Embezzlement."

I could have sworn that his face registered relief. "I'm not worried about that," he said. "Jim isn't involved in anything illegal."

"Do you know anything about the man who watched his house and followed his wife for two days after he left? Or the tap on their phone?"

"What're you talking about?" He was visibly shaken, and I didn't think it was because he was concerned for Suzanne. He had reason to fear someone following Jim Mendoza. Sam Connors was not as innocent as he pretended.

We sparred back and forth for a while, and finally Connors asked, "What are you going to do with Craig?"

Worth was my bargaining chip, the best chance I'd gotten so far at forcing Connors to tell me where Mendoza had gone. I could force him to choose between the two men, offering him Worth's freedom for Mendoza's whereabouts, but I wasn't ready to gamble on it. If he chose to protect Mendoza, I'd have to send Worth to jail, and there wasn't much chance any of the vets would speak to me after that.

"What do you think I should do?" I asked.

"If you turn him in, they'll send him away; and I don't think he could take that. He was never that together, even as a kid. His old man signed him up for Vietnam when he was seventeen because he caught him smoking dope. What a joke!" Connors laughed harshly. "Sent the kid to dope central just because he was smoking weed."

He paused and wiped his glasses on his shirt. "Craig was too young; he couldn't handle it. I don't know that any of us handled it, but we got through. He just sort of dug himself a hole and climbed in with every kind of drug he could find.

"And when he got home and no one seemed to think the war was such a great idea anymore, so we were just an embarrassment, you know what his superpatriot old man did?

He threw Craig out of the house because he caught him smoking dope. Threw him out and told him he wished he'd died an 'honorable' death in Vietnam.''

Connors shook his head and sat quietly for a minute. ''He never had much of a chance with that crazy family,'' he said bitterly. ''We took better care of him than his parents ever did.

''People who didn't go don't know what it was like. Watching your friends die and never knowing who might be Charlie. Going over to defend your country and ending up killing little kids. Our first night out on patrol, we blew away a whole family by mistake. They weren't supposed to be there; only Charlie was supposed to be out at night. So when we heard someone on the trail, we opened fire, killed a woman and three kids. The only one left alive was a baby.

''And you know what? No one back at camp gave a damn. The commanding officer just said they shouldn't have been there and not to worry about it. Guys made jokes about 'our big kill.'

''None of us ever really got over that night, but Craig took it hardest. His older sister had a baby about the age of the one that was left. It drove him nuts that no one cared what happened to the baby. They said we should just have left it.''

Connors's voice was strained, and tension tightened his lips and pursed his mouth. He took his glasses off and went to work polishing them, ducking his head so I couldn't see his face. It had cost him to tell that story. He was pitching for my sympathy, and he'd gotten it.

''I don't want to cause Craig any more trouble,'' I said. ''But how do you know that he won't try something like this again and maybe kill someone or get killed himself?''

''He's not really dangerous,'' Connors said. ''He went after you because he was worried about us, almost like a dog goes after someone who threatens its master. Now we know that can happen, we can have his counselor work with him on it, and we'll be more careful so it doesn't happen again.''

I didn't believe that Worth wasn't dangerous, but I knew that a stint in jail wouldn't make him any less violent. The only chance to turn his life around lay in therapy, and he sure wouldn't get that in jail.

"All right," I said, hoping desperately that I wouldn't regret it. "What do we do now? He's in pretty bad shape, rocking and mumbling to himself. I don't want to put him out on the street like that."

"I'll come with you and take him home. Terry can stay with him today, and one of us will be with him until we're sure he's okay. He won't cause you any more trouble, I promise you that."

I accepted his promise. I wasn't nearly as worried about what Worth might do to me as I was about what he might do to someone else. I knew that letting him go was a risk. If I'd known the price of that risk, I'd never have taken it.

Connors drove behind me to the motel to pick up Worth. The disturbed man jumped up and began apologizing the minute his friend entered the room. Connors went to him, put his arm around him, and began speaking quietly. Beneath his tightly controlled exterior, there was a gentleness that surprised me.

"This lady's being real nice to you," he told Worth. "She could call the cops on you, but she's not going to. Will you promise not to bother her again?"

"I promise," Worth mumbled, still not looking at me.

"Remember, you made that promise to me," Connors said, and Worth nodded. A promise to his friend obviously meant a lot more than any he would have offered me.

Peter put his arm around me. "You okay?" he asked.

"I'm fine," I said. "Why should I let a little thing like a man with a knife bother me?"

He hugged me and held me against his chest. It felt good and safe, and we stayed that way for a long time. Finally, I pulled away and kissed him lightly.

"Back to work?" he said.

I nodded.

"Then I should tell you that Mrs. Mendoza called. She asked to have you call her back."

"I think I've found what you want," she told me. "There were several officers he mentioned, but two of them were killed. I don't know what happened to the other two, but their names were Westin and Cochrain. Jim didn't think much of either one of them."

I thanked her for the information and had her spell the names. She said that she hoped it would help and asked why I was so concerned with people Jim knew so long ago. The truth was that I had no idea what Jim's disappearance had to do with his experience in Vietnam, but I had a strong hunch that there was a connection.

In this business, you poke around until something doesn't feel quite right. Then you poke at that something until you begin to understand what's going on. It's not very scientific, and my clients would be appalled to learn that's what I do, but it usually works. Mrs. Mendoza probably didn't want to hear it, either, so I gave her my one-size-fits-all excuse—that it helped to know as much about his past as possible.

I CALLED EILEEN with the two names Mrs. Mendoza had given me. She had the names of all the military installations in a hundred-mile radius but didn't know if she could get anything on the weekend.

I had a list of Mendoza's high school friends and even an address for his best friend, Joseph Avila. The phone book yielded an address for George Davis, the high school teacher who'd served with Mendoza in Vietnam. Peter took Davis; I called Avila.

Joseph Avila's wife informed me that he was at their restaurant in West Modesto. She gave me the address.

Avila was about five seven, stocky, with powerful arms and shoulders. His thick black hair had just a touch of gray. I found him in the kitchen chopping onions and issuing orders in Spanish to two gangly teenagers, who responded with the sullen compliance of the truly put upon. Avila ignored their nonverbal messages and tossed out orders a mile a minute. I couldn't understand much of what he said, but the tone was unmistakable.

He lit up with a smile that filled a good part of his face when I mentioned Jim Mendoza. He hadn't seen his old friend for years, but he told me that when they were in high school they were "like this." He held up two fingers pressed tightly together.

He turned the knife and onions over to one of the boys, poured two cups of coffee, and led the way out into the restaurant.

"Tell me about Jim," he said, forgetting to ask why I was there.

I told him about Mendoza's job at the bank, his marriage to Suzanne, and the baby that was on the way. "He'll be a good father," Avila announced. "So he ended up working with computers? It figures. He was one smart guy, smartest guy in our class, really, though the Anglos didn't like to admit it."

"What was he like as a kid?"

"Smart, funny, had a great sense of humor. A good person, good friend. Seemed like he was good at everything he did."

"A model student."

"Well, he wasn't quite the model kid teachers thought he was," Avila confided with a smile. "I mean, we did things they wouldn't have believed."

"Anything dishonest?"

"Hell, no, just screwing around. Jim set real high standards for himself. I suppose he got that from his father. As long as I could remember, his dad had him working at the store; and he was always telling Jim that he had to get A's so he could go to college."

"So he followed all the rules," I prompted.

"All the important ones," Avila said. "But I'll tell you one thing about Jim, and not many people know this, he loved to beat the system. He got free Cokes for the senior class by ordering them on the cafeteria account number. And once, we rewired the PA system so that everything said in the principal's office was broadcast into all the classrooms." He laughed at the memory of it.

"What was so great was that the principal was this very proper guy who'd chew you out if you said 'damn,' and the whole school heard him tell the football coach that he wanted the 'fucking team to stop screwing around.' "

We both laughed at that. "We had some good times," he said. Then his smile faded, and he added, "But it wasn't all just fooling around. I mean, you could rely on Jim, no matter what. My dad died when I was in the tenth grade, and I had a bad year. My grades went down the tubes. I did a lot better the next year, but my grade point wasn't good enough for state college. Jim knew all about it, so one day he stole my transcript from the counselor's office and changed the grades."

"That's real friendship," I said.

"They'd have thrown him out of school if they found out," Avila said. "Not many people take a risk like that for a friend."

He took a drink of the thick black coffee he'd poured for us and smiled. I took a very small sip, in deference to my stomach. "Hey, I been talking your ear off, and I don't even know what it is you want. What can I do for you?"

"Jim left home last Sunday without telling his wife where he was going. She's very worried, and she needs to get in touch with him. I told her I'd help her find out where he'd gone. I thought maybe you'd have some idea."

He laughed. "That's just like him. He was the most organized kid in school, but give him a week off and a back-pack, you never knew where he'd end up. Tell her not to worry. He's just up to his old tricks.''

"But this wasn't vacation time; and he didn't tell anyone at work that he was leaving,'' I said.

He looked skeptical. "That doesn't sound like Jim. He's not the kind to cause anyone to worry. Maybe there's trouble in the marriage and he just needs some time away.''

I told him that someone had tapped the Mendozas' phone and that a man had been watching their house just after he'd left, but Avila had decided that the woman was the problem, and he wasn't about to help another woman track down his friend. He just shook his head and said, "He just needs some time to himself.''

I didn't push things. I wasn't going to change Avila's mind, so I thanked him for talking to me and left.

The visit wasn't a complete waste. I'd learned a couple of useful things, the first being to let Peter handle interviews with Mendoza's friends. Maybe they'd be more open with another man.

The Jim Mendoza that Avila described was both a good friend and a man who'd bend the rules to help a buddy. He was also someone who enjoyed risk. The pranks Avila described might not have been very risky for an Anglo, but for a bright Hispanic kid in the early sixties, they could have meant serious trouble.

Peter was already at the motel when I arrived. George Davis was out of town for the weekend and wouldn't be back till late Sunday evening. I described my meeting with Avila.

"Interesting," Peter said. "We don't have any of the usual reasons why Mendoza should rob a bank. The financial report shows him with plenty of savings and no real debt. He's a guy who lives carefully within his means, has no expensive tastes, no sign of drugs or gambling. There's enough in the family that he doesn't need to bail out any relatives.''

"I didn't go over the report on his family. What's in there?''

"Typical hardworking immigrant tale," he said. He dug through the papers he'd brought with him from San Francisco and tossed me the report on James Mendoza's parents. "Grandparents immigrated from Mexico in 1917 during the revolution. The father had a mom-and-pop grocery store in West Modesto, not a gold mine, but it generated enough extra so that he could buy several houses in the neighborhood. He rented them out, used the rent to buy the next house, till he had a nice real estate portfolio."

I got the picture. The houses weren't worth a lot in the forties and fifties, but like Andy Warhol's soup cans, they'd grown in value well beyond anyone's expectations. I scanned the figures on the report. Money was not likely to be a problem for anyone in the Mendoza family.

"So he's got enough to live comfortably," I said. "But everyone has his own idea of 'enough.' Maybe he wants more than comfortably, especially now with a child on the way."

"Or maybe he wants to help a friend," Peter suggested. "That would fit better with the picture I have of him."

"And the risk would appeal to him," I added. "But not if it endangered his family. If he'd just stayed put and hidden the money in a Swiss account, they probably couldn't have pinned it on him. After all, there were at least five people who knew about the hole in the system and many more who could have stumbled on it."

"That's the way I see it. So his disappearance means that something went wrong."

"I sure hope we can find him before that something catches up with him," I said.

We spent the next couple of hours going over the reports Peter had brought. Amy had put together a list of thirty-seven places that had come up in interviews. Most were in northern California and Oregon, though there were several foreign countries and a sprinkling of places across the United States. I couldn't see how we could check all of them in the nine days remaining. And that was only the preliminary list.

Connors was our one solid lead. He'd admitted knowing

where Mendoza was even as he refused to give me the information, and his reaction to the news that someone was watching the Mendoza house suggested that he knew his friend's absence was more than an innocent desire for time to himself.

"Connors must have some means of getting in touch with Mendoza," I reasoned. "Do you know how to tap a phone?"

"Yeah, it's not hard."

"Can you tap Connors's phones?"

"Sure. I just put on my lineman belt, shinny up the pole outside his house, and attach the bug. I can give Bert the receiver and have him tape the calls as they come in. But that won't tell us where he's calling."

"No. What we really need is his phone records."

"If you don't want to ask Dan, I can get Matt to get them."

"No," I said. "Not this time. Any cop who helped us would be in a very dicey position if Mendoza succeeded in robbing the bank. We need another way."

"There's always a way, my love."

"Meaning?"

"The phone company doesn't give out the records, but they employ lots of people at minimum salaries who have access to the records. One of those people may be willing to help a struggling private investigator if he or she is properly compensated."

"Whoa, wait a minute, one of those people might also decide to turn us in, and that little caper could cost us our licenses."

"It could cost you or me dearly, but it wouldn't cost Bert much. One of his talents is the ability to look borderline retarded when he wants to. I've seen him do it to sucker people at a card game. In fact, that's how we met. I saved him from being creamed by a guy who didn't like the idea of losing to someone he thought was dumber than he was."

"So we give Bert some money and a phony story, and he tries to find us an employee with not too many scruples."

Peter nodded, and his crooked smile reminded me that he

just loved to run a good scam. There was a reason I didn't ask him to help me very often.

"I'll need to go back to the City to get the stuff for the tap," he announced.

"Why don't we go back down tonight. There's really nothing to do here except keep an eye on Connors and Wheeler, and your guys are doing that."

"Sounds great. I could use a home-cooked meal and a night in my own bed, or yours."

Driving back to the City felt like being on vacation. Peter had a new tape of the Seldom Scene that we listened to several times. Then we ambled back in time with the Grateful Dead and Credence Clearwater.

"Tell me about the two characters we're leaving in charge of things in Modesto," I asked. "Bert and Ernie aren't their real names, so who are they?"

"They're a couple of independent filmmakers. They wouldn't be any good if things got rough, but they're good at following people. I've used them before."

"Filmmakers?"

"Aspiring. Actually, they're cameramen, and so far their only credits are porno films, but they're saving up to go to the Art Institute."

I groaned. That was one point we would definitely omit from my report to Daniel Martin.

16

PETER PICKED UP the supplies he needed to bug Connors's phones and headed back to Modesto Sunday morning. I spent most of the day talking with Eileen and Chris and going over the information they'd amassed. Chris had traveled all over the state to interview relatives and gotten nothing more than a long list of places Mendoza had been or might have wanted to go. Eleven towns, all in northern California and Oregon, had been mentioned by more than one person, so we got out the atlas and planned Chris's next few days.

We went back over the full list of places, looking for ones that seemed particularly likely. But it was James Mendoza, rather than the towns, that interested us. Each of us seemed to feel that if we could just understand the man well enough, we could break the case. Our task was to figure out where he'd gone, but the question that gripped us was why. Why had this man who didn't seem to care much about material wealth decided to risk everything by embezzling money?

People don't alter the patterns of a lifetime easily. Most of the guys I catch have been cutting corners for years. Their appetites grow to the point that someone notices them, and they get caught. They always pretend, and frequently believe, that this was the first time, but that's rarely the case.

There was no evidence of Mendoza cutting corners, just the opposite. If money and status had been of great importance to him, he'd have made a different set of career choices. His wife told us that he'd consciously rejected chances to compete in the fast-track executive derby because it meant too little time for family and friends.

When someone who's basically honest sets out to break the law, there's always a reason. It could be overwhelming financial need—a medical crisis in the family or a son's gambling debts—or retaliation against poor treatment by an employer. But there's a reason. I wanted to know James Mendoza's reason.

By four o'clock my head was beginning to ache, and my body was stiff from sitting still for too long. I sent Eileen and Chris home and went out for a long walk.

The weather was cool, but the sun shone brightly, and there wasn't anything vaguely approaching a rain cloud in the sky. I thought of the strange weather of last year and wondered if the greenhouse was already heating up. The politicians maintained that last summer's scorching weather was just a fluke. They'd probably still be saying that when the Midwest dried up and blew away.

I hiked up to Alta Plaza Park and sat on a bench and watched various combinations of dogs and people pass by. Two jays tried to outshriek each other, and a gopher worked diligently pushing dirt up out of his hole. I waited for him to make an appearance, but he was too busy with housecleaning chores.

When I got home, a delicious aroma met me at the door and informed me that Peter was back from Modesto. He was at the stove, doing something with Italian sausage, tomatoes, and red onion. I came up behind him and gave him a big hug.

"Hey, don't feel up the help," he objected, not too strenuously.

I ignored him and ran my hands up over his chest, then down to his thighs.

"Not hungry, huh?"

"I didn't say *that*." I moved my hands to scratch his back. "I just can't resist your body."

"That's one of the things I like best about you," he said.

Dinner tasted as good as it had smelled, and a Ridge Zinfandel made it even better. After a couple of glasses, the problems of First Central seemed a bit less pressing.

"I should do the dishes," I said without much conviction.

"But you're not going to."

"Make me a better offer."

He did, and several hours later, when the doorbell rang, the dishes were still on the table. I pulled on jeans and a sweater as Peter struggled to disentangle his clothes from mine and got to the front door breathless and disheveled.

It was Jesse. "Sorry to disturb you," he said with a knowing smile as Peter arrived behind me.

"All work and no play," Peter said.

"You're letting this hippie corrupt you, boss lady," Jesse

warned with a laugh as we walked into the living room. "Hey, you're fading," he observed as he conducted an elaborate examination of my eye. "You know, green just isn't your color."

I'd had the same thought when I looked in the mirror that morning, but I didn't appreciate Jesse reminding me. "Did you come all this way just to torment me, or do you have something useful to offer?"

"I think we have a good chance of catching Mendoza when he grabs the money," he announced. "I can't be sure because Martin is guarding the system like an old mother bear, but if things work the way I think they do, it's possible."

"What do you need?"

"I need you to convince Martin to let an independent computer security firm analyze the problem. I've talked to Computer Security of Sunnyvale in very general terms. They're the people to handle it."

I'd managed to dodge Daniel Martin for two days. I'd have to see him Monday, before I returned to Modesto, so though I wasn't optimistic about our chances, I agreed to give it a try. "Don't expect too much," I said.

"This is our best shot if we can't find him first," Jesse argued. "It'd be crazy not to try it."

"Where did you get this charming idea that rationality affects human behavior?" I asked.

"Not rationality," Jesse said, "self-interest. I have great faith in self-interest."

I called Martin first thing in the morning. He wanted a report, but he still didn't want me to be seen at First Central. I wondered if he'd feel differently if I didn't have a black eye. Probably not.

Daniel Martin arrived at my office forty-five minutes later. He was still immaculately groomed, but his eyes had a haunted look, and the bluish crescents under them suggested that he wasn't sleeping too well these days.

"There are only seven days left," he said. "Do you have

anything at all for me?'' The imperiousness was gone from his tone, replaced by desperation.

I gave him a report on what we'd learned. He looked like it was all he could do not to reach for a Maalox.

''There must be some way to get Connors to tell you where Mendoza is.''

''I've asked him. He's refused to tell me,'' I said. ''There isn't much more I can do legally.''

''There must be something. Offer him money.''

Ah, the thirty-pieces-of-silver gambit. ''They're close friends,'' I said. ''I don't think money will do it.''

''Don't be so sure,'' he said. There was an unpleasant eagerness in his voice. ''How much would a man like Connors take?''

More than a man like you, I thought. ''I really don't think it's a good idea,'' I said. ''It might well make matters worse.''

''Shouldn't you bug his phone?''

''That's illegal,'' I explained. ''If I were to do it, it's not the sort of thing that you'd want to know.''

It took him a minute to figure it out, but finally he nodded his head and said, ''Oh.''

Before he could come up with another brilliant idea, I said, ''I will do everything in my power to find Jim Mendoza in the next seven days, but even if I don't find him in time, we may still be able to save the bank's money. I've done some research on this, and I think there's a good chance that a computer security firm could devise a way to—''

He shook his head. ''No, no, we can't,'' he said, and this time he did reach for some kind of medicine. He peeled a couple of tablets off a roll and began chewing them. The action was so automatic that I wasn't sure he was even aware of doing it. ''That's been studied at length, and there is no way.''

''It's my understanding that the study covered how to correct the error that would allow someone to steal the money; it did not cover how to catch the thief at the time when he or she pulled the money out of the system. That's what I want to look at now.''

He studied his hands. "I just can't authorize that," he said. "We can't afford to have even a suggestion that our deposits are not fully protected, especially now." His tone put the "now" in italics and underlined it.

"As you may know, Japanese banks have been extremely active in acquiring banking institutions in this country. There are really only a few left that don't have American subsidiaries. We understand that one of those has expressed interest in First Central."

"And you're afraid that First Central would be considerably less attractive if it were hemorrhaging money through a hole in its computer system."

Martin winced and nodded. "Let's just say that we are very anxious to prevent any discussion of this problem before it is resolved." He rubbed the bridge of his nose as if he had a headache. "My superiors are already under a good deal of pressure, and not everyone agrees with my handling of the situation. If I were to suggest bringing in another organization—"he paused and shook his head "—well, it would not be well received."

I nodded. Better to take a strong position and lose millions than to reveal that you weren't entirely on top of things and have someone else save the money for you. With a possible takeover in the air, everyone was protecting their posteriors. Hiring me to locate Mendoza was good procedure. Hiring a computer security firm to do something your own team should have done could be embarrassing.

I was getting ready to take off for Modesto when Eileen breezed in. "I've got our man," she announced. "He's Lieutenant Colonel Clarence Westin, stationed at the Presidio, and he has something to do with readiness for National Guard and Reserve units."

"You're sure he's the guy?"

"He's the only Westin or Cochrain in the Bay Area. That's all I can promise."

"Did you get me an appointment?"

"He was supposed to be getting back from Camp Roberts

this morning. His secretary is a Sergeant MacKenzie. He says Westin's calendar is clear this afternoon, but he couldn't promise that he'd be able to see you.''

Come-wait-around-and-maybe-someone-will-talk-to-you is not one of my favorite investigative techniques. I groaned.

"I could call at one and try to get you an appointment," Eileen offered.

"No, they can't say no if we don't ask. Better I should go and sit until he feels inclined to see me. Where am I going?"

She gave me the address, and I dug through my desk for a map.

17

THE PRESIDIO SITS at the northern tip of San Francisco, overlooking both the Bay and the Pacific. It is just about the only large, undeveloped piece of land in San Francisco except for Golden Gate Park. The military has done far better by the land than the developers would have, and there are still wonderful groves of trees and large areas of open space. For a military base, it's pretty neat.

Colonel Westin's office was in a large three-story building that looked like a blockhouse. It probably dated from the early 1900s, but the builder had made some effort to recall the Presidio's Spanish origins, so the building was covered with stucco and roofed with red tile.

Inside, it was standard military, a stark entrance hall with plaques and flags on the walls and a young man in uniform behind a heavy wooden desk with nothing but a phone and a logbook on it. I signed in and got directions to Westin's office.

The office was on the second floor. A well-polished young sergeant sat at a metal desk in a small outer office.

"Sergeant MacKenzie?" I asked.

"Yes, ma'am."

"I'm Catherine Sayler. Eileen Watson from my office called you earlier to arrange an appointment with Colonel Westin."

"I told her I couldn't promise anything. The colonel is just back from an inspection trip, and he has a lot of paperwork this afternoon."

"I understand fully," I said. "But I was hoping he could give me just a few moments of his time. I promise not to take long." I was lying, of course. I wanted to take as much of his afternoon as I could get away with, but nobody'd ever let me in if I told them that.

"What shall I tell him is the subject of your visit?"

"I'm doing a background check on a man who was under his command," I replied.

Sergeant MacKenzie went into the colonel's office and returned almost immediately. "He's on the phone right now, but he'll see you in a few minutes."

The few minutes stretched to twenty before Colonel Westin buzzed the sergeant and told him to send me in.

Westin stood as I entered and offered me a chair beside his desk. He was tall, about six two, and muscular. He had nice shoulders and a broad chest, but also the suggestion of a paunch that he probably worked real hard to keep down.

The colonel sat down behind a metal desk that was tidy to the point of austerity. An in-out box with neatly stacked papers sat at the right front corner and a telephone at the left. A computer with the screen glowing green was positioned just to Westin's left, and a pad and pencil were centered before him. The walls were decorated with brass plaques, photos of groups of men in military uniform, and a couple of pictures of a woman and two blond-haired children. The best feature of the room was its window, which looked out on a stand of eucalyptus trees.

"Sergeant MacKenzie tells me you're doing a background check on someone under my command," he said.

"Not someone under your command currently, someone from your unit in Vietnam," I corrected.

He frowned. "I don't know how much help I can be to you, Ms. Sayler. There were a great many men under my command in Vietnam, and it's been almost twenty years."

"I understand that it's a long shot, sir. I don't really expect you to remember individuals, but I was hoping you might have some form of documentation that would help me."

Westin frowned. "The documentation you're seeking is a personnel record. We can't release such files to a civilian."

I nodded, groaning inwardly about the amount of time and finagling it was going to take to get those files. "Of course, I understand that. But I was hoping to convince you to review the record and tell me anything that might be germane to the case I'm pursuing. The men I'm interested in served together in a special unit made up initially of men from a single town, Modesto. Their names were Jim Mendoza, Terry Wheeler, and Sam Connors."

The change in Westin's expression was extremely subtle, but it was enough to tell me that he'd recognized at least one of the names.

"And why are you interested in these men?" he asked with studied casualness.

"I'm not at liberty to discuss that," I replied, enjoying the sudden reversal of our positions. "But it has to do with a case that may involve criminal activity."

Westin nodded. "I see, well, I do remember them, Mendoza in particular, and if he's involved in your case, I'd advise you to be very careful."

I tried not to look startled. "Oh? What makes you say that?"

"The man is most certainly a crook and quite possibly a killer as well," he announced.

I stared at Westin in shock. My first thought was that maybe he meant Worth or Connors. But it was clearly Jim Mendoza's name he'd responded to. I was grateful when his intercom buzzed and he answered the phone, giving me a few moments to digest the bombshell he'd just dropped.

When he put the phone down, I asked, "Can you tell me more about him?"

Westin cleared his throat. "I can't prove any of this. If I could, Mendoza and the others would be in the stockade; but it's true."

I nodded. "I certainly appreciate your willingness to tell me about it."

"The unit you're interested in was my first stint in 'Nam. I hadn't been there a month when one of them fired on the CO. It was in the middle of a firefight, so I assumed it was the VC shooting at his chopper, but a few weeks later he was fragged, that is, killed by one of our own men, and I subsequently learned that some of the enlisted men had put a bounty on him. They collected money as a reward for the man who killed him."

"And you think Jim Mendoza killed him."

"If Mendoza didn't pull the trigger, he sure as hell knew who did. He was clearly the leader in that group, and he was already involved in black-market activity."

"Can you tell me about the black-market activity?"

"Look, Vietnam was no church picnic, and the draftees weren't all choirboys, so there was a certain amount of pilferage. And there were wheeler-dealers who would've sold the bullets out of their buddies' guns for a buck. We caught the ones we could, but you don't have a lot of time for playing policeman when you're fighting a war.

"The guy I replaced knew that Mendoza was up to something. All the Mexicans stuck together and covered for each other, and Mendoza got real chummy with the bunch in Supply."

Westin said "Mexicans" in a tone that suggested the word left a bad taste in his mouth. I wondered how much his obvious prejudice might color his judgment. "Was there any other proof that they were stealing supplies?"

"Supplies disappeared whenever that bunch was around—

blankets, medical supplies, C rations. And it wasn't the sort of stuff that guys stole for their own use. You expected pilferage of certain drugs, but not of others; and the Mexican Mafia, as we called them, had strange tastes. I figure they were selling things into the civilian black market, maybe even to Charlie.

"The lieutenant before me caught Mendoza and a buddy red-handed with a generator one day. They claimed they were just delivering it for a friend in Supply, but they didn't have any paperwork, and the guys they claimed to be delivering it to hadn't ordered it. The Mexicans in Supply backed them up and claimed it was just a snafu, and the war heated up about that time, so no one followed up on it. After that, they were a lot more careful."

"You say that Mendoza was the leader. Can you tell me anything about the other men—Terry Wheeler, Sam Connors, Craig Worth, Jim Davis, John Langer, or Luis Ramirez?"

Westin shook his head. "They blend together for me—except for Ramirez, and I'll tell you about him in a minute. Wheeler and Connors were dopers, I think; Worth, too. Don't really remember Davis or Langer." He leaned back in his chair and shut his eyes for a moment. "No, wait, I think Langer was the guy who had some sort of training in unarmed combat, some martial art. He was a doper, too."

"And Ramirez?"

"Ramirez was Mendoza's buddy. Killed in action, supposedly, but if you want my opinion, I think Mendoza may have killed him. You see, Ramirez knew who fired those bullets at the CO; and he was getting ready to tell me. I think Mendoza realized that and killed him before he could talk."

"Do you have any solid evidence?"

"If I did, I'd have had Mendoza in front of a court-martial. It's the easiest thing in the world to kill a guy during wartime. Some guys get separated from the platoon, by the time you find them, one's dead. The others say it's a sniper or a booby trap. Who's to know?

"As I remember, there were four or five of them—Mendoza and Ramirez, maybe a couple more of their bunch, and a new guy. They got separated from the main platoon just about the time Charlie hit us in an ambush attack. When we found them, Ramirez was dead, and the new guy had disappeared. Very convenient, wouldn't you say, since if they had killed Ramirez, the new guy would have been a witness."

"Did you ever find him?"

"Not as far as I know. I think he's still listed as missing in action."

"And Ramirez was shot."

"No. You can always run ballistics tests on weapons and bullets. Mendoza was too smart for that. He used a grenade; there wasn't even much left of the body."

I was so busy thinking about what Colonel Westin had told me that I turned in the wrong direction when I left his building. I'd walked about half a block before I figured out why the parking lot that I expected to find wasn't there. Feeling foolish, I turned around and headed back in the right direction.

A shrill scream shocked me out of my thoughts. Across the street a little girl pulled at her mother's arm and howled in fury. The mother seemed unconcerned by the piercing shrieks that sent chills up my spine. As I watched the battle of wills, I noticed for the first time a tan Ford at the curb. There was a dent in the front fender.

There are probably thousands of tan Fords in the Bay area, and some of them are bound to have dents in the front end, but I'm not big on coincidence. The car at the curb fit the description of the one the man who'd watched Suzanne Mendoza had used to follow her, so I looked carefully at the Ford, noted the license number, and decided to keep my eye out for it in the future.

* * *

I found Eileen and Peter at the office. They were both as shocked by Westin's revelations as I was. None of us wanted to believe that Jim Mendoza was a killer. Eileen, who had spent many hours with Suzanne Mendoza learning everything she could about the man, resisted the idea most vigorously.

"You said yourself that Westin doesn't like Hispanics," she pointed out. "Maybe his suspicions are just an extension of his prejudice."

I wanted to agree with her. I'd spent the last week learning about Mendoza. I felt as though I knew the man, and what I knew I liked. I didn't like the idea that he might be a murderer.

"It puts his relationship with Connors in a new perspective," Peter pointed out. "They were both there when Ramirez died. At the least, they've shared a very powerful experience; at the worst, they've conspired to kill a man."

When I told them about the tan Ford, Peter let out a whistle. "Our outside player?" he asked.

"Seems like a real possibility," I said.

"Could it be Westin?" Eileen asked.

I shook my head. "I don't think so. The Ford was at the curb; his car should have been in the parking lot. But we'll know soon enough." I took out the scrap of paper with the license number on it and walked over to the computer. "This is where an on-line data base comes in very handy," I said to Peter, who has never been overly impressed with the virtues of technology.

"But I didn't think Motor Vehicles gave out that information anymore," Eileen said.

"Not to investigators," I replied, "but it's still available to representatives of insurance companies. As of January first, I am a representative of Continental Casualty."

"And Joe Preston owns a piece of your time," Peter said. "A fine example of the age-old principle that restricting access to information doesn't protect it, it just makes the information more expensive."

I nodded ruefully. "You should have a name and address by tomorrow morning," I told Eileen. "Check it out and call me in Modesto."

18

P ETER AND I managed to get off for Modesto just after three, which meant that the traffic was already beginning to thicken. It was Peter's third trip in two days, and the drive was losing its appeal. First he complained about the traffic; then he raged over every new development that had converted green rolling hills into scarred earth and ticky-tacky houses.

I agreed with him about both, but I couldn't stand the heavy dose of negative energy he was putting out, so I turned the radio on loud. Unfortunately, it came on with the news segment of "All Things Considered," and we spent the next fifteen minutes listening to accounts of environmental disasters and carnage in Central America. Finally, I put in a tape of chamber music, and we both relaxed a bit.

Bert and Ernie reported that the phone taps were working, but there'd been no calls concerning Mendoza. Wheeler hadn't come into the shop all day, so both men had been needed for surveillance; consequently, Bert had been unable to try to get Wheeler's phone records.

I'd had Eileen start background checks on Connors and Wheeler. Peter and I planned to do the same thing in Modesto. There was no way to do it without the men finding out, but that was just fine. I wanted to step up the pressure on them.

* * *

I slept poorly and woke early. My teeth were fuzzy, and my hair stuck out at six angles. All I needed to do was spray it purple and I could pass for punk. Instead, I doused it with water and pushed it around with a brush. My black eye was now somewhere between green and yellow; it was not an improvement.

As usual, Peter was blissfully asleep.

Outside, the weather was slightly foggy and cool. It was a quarter to seven, and the coffee shop wasn't open yet. Yesterday's adventure had left me a bit chary of early-morning walks, which was exactly why I decided to take one today. As I walked through the parking lot, I kept an eye out for tan cars. There weren't any, and the only tan car on the street next to the motel was a Datsun. I walked for several blocks and saw a couple of cars that were about the right color, but neither was a Ford, and neither one had a dented front fender.

Then, as I turned back to the motel, I noticed the Garden Motor Inn across the street. There wasn't any garden that I could see, just a two-story stucco building with a couple of anemic palm trees in front; but there was a tan Ford—the same one I'd seen at the Presidio.

Having just discussed electronic eavesdropping at some length with Peter, I understood at once the significance of the fact that the rooms of the Garden Motor Inn were on a direct sight line with the back side of the section of motel where we were staying. I hurried to the room to get Peter.

It took a while to get him to wake up, and my attempts to lure him out of the room met with good-natured but firm resistance. Finally, I whispered in his ear, "This room is full of bugs, the electronic kind. Just get up and get out of here so we can talk."

That did it. He was up and dressed and out of the room faster than I'd have thought possible. He walked me away from the room, then asked, "What's going on?"

"I've found the tan Ford, the one that was outside the Mendoza house last week. It was parked outside Westin's office at the Presidio, and now it's across the street. It's in front of a motel room almost directly across from ours; the reception should be excellent.''

Peter swore. "I should have been looking for this. I knew we had an outside player.''

"Before you beat yourself up, remember that there are two of us in this. I didn't see it coming any more than you did.''

"Well, it's not all bad. We know where he is, we don't have to go looking for him. Early morning's my favorite time for heart-to-heart chats.''

"You're just going to burst in on him?''

"No, I'm going to wait till he comes out, and the place I'm going to wait is the backseat of his car. But first, I think I'll get my gun, just to make sure he understands I'm serious.''

Peter leaned into his MG and lifted the platform back of the seats to get to the gun he kept hidden behind the battery. I didn't think this was such a great idea, but I didn't have anything better to suggest.

"You ever smash that car up, and the mechanic is going to get a big surprise,'' I observed.

He pulled the gun from its plastic bag and, folding his jacket over it, extracted himself from the car. Somehow Peter and his MG always reminded me of the circus act in which a clown on stilts gets out of a car that seems about half his size.

I was still trying to figure out why this was a bad idea when we walked around the building and discovered that the tan Ford was no longer at the Garden Motor Inn.

Peter swore again, this time even more colorfully.

"He must have seen me,'' I said.

"Or he was listening and realized something was up.''

"Where do we go from here?'' I asked.

"First thing is to make sure there really are bugs,'' Peter said as we headed back to the room. He stopped. "If he's bugged the room, he's sure to have bugged the phone, too. It might be useful to let him think we hadn't found that one.''

"Won't he assume we would?''

Peter thought for a minute. "If he's using RF transmitters

and we use a Hound Dog to sweep the place, it won't pick up the phone bug unless the phone is actually in use. We could stage our own little radio drama, let him listen to us sweep the room. You can ask about the phone; I can tell you the Hound Dog says it's clean.''

I smiled. ''It'd probably work. Most crooks underestimate the intelligence of honest people.''

''Okay, let's go take a look.''

We found the first one where we expected to, up behind the curtain. It was an innocuous little thing, a flat, circular piece of metal about the size of a dime. It was small enough that I knew if there were others, we'd never find them all without some help.

''How long will it take you to get a Hound Dog so we can sweep this place?'' I asked.

''I'll call and have Eileen bring it up,'' Peter said.

''I've got a Faraday cage at the office,'' I told him. ''Have her bring it up so we can keep the little monsters for future use.'' Faraday cage is a fancy name for a metal box that blocks the bug's ability to transmit; it's a sort of electronic Roach Motel.

''I've got a Faraday cage, too,'' Peter smirked. ''It's called tinfoil.''

''Cheaper, I'll admit,'' I said, ''but I don't have to worry about throwing *my* bugs out with the trash.''

We called Eileen on the room phone just to reassure our listening friend that the idea of a phone tap hadn't occurred to us.

I looked at my watch and realized that if I skipped breakfast I could still catch George Davis at the school during his free period. I took Peter outside and told him where I was headed.

I found George Davis in the teachers' lounge with a cup of coffee, half a sweet roll, and a stack of papers in front of him. He was tall and slender, with broad shoulders and a gymnast's build. His skin was a deep brown, and though there were a few gray flecks in his hair, his face was smooth and almost unlined.

I introduced myself, and he looked disappointed. "I'm sorry," he apologized, "I was expecting someone from the county office. What can I help you with?"

I explained that I was looking for James Mendoza and I understood that they had served together in Vietnam. He hadn't seen Jim for a number of years but recommended that I look up his parents, who he thought might still live in Modesto. I pretended to be surprised and thanked him.

"Were you and Jim together in Vietnam?" I asked.

"Yes, there were a bunch of us from Modesto there together. In fact, if you can't find Jim's family, you could ask Sam Connors or Terry Wheeler. They have a body shop out on Scenic, I think, and one of them might know. They were closer to Jim than I was."

"And Luis Ramirez was part of that group?"

"Yeah, but he didn't make it back," he said quietly.

"Were you with him when he was killed?" I asked.

He shook his head. "No, I'd been wounded about two weeks before, and I was still in the hospital."

"One of the reasons I'm looking for Jim is to find out more about what happened to Luis Ramirez. Perhaps you could help me."

"I can't tell you much. Terry or Sam could tell you a lot more."

"I'll definitely see them," I said. "As long as I'm here, do you mind if I ask a couple more questions?"

He shrugged. "Sure," he said. "I have another twenty minutes before class, and I've read as many fanciful explanations of the Civil War as I can take. It's hard to believe that any of these kids have been in my class for the last two weeks."

"Was Luis particularly close to anyone in Vietnam?"

"Yeah, he and Jim were real tight. Jim was like an older brother to him. They were always hanging out together. They spent a lot of time with a bunch of Hispanics over in Supply."

"What happened after Luis was killed?"

"I heard about it in the hospital. One of the other guys told me. When I got back about a week later, Jim was still pretty torn up about it."

"Was there anything different?" I asked.

"What do you mean?"

"I don't know," I said. "I was just wondering if you noticed that anything had changed."

"Of course, things change," he said almost angrily. "You see your best friend blown to hell so there aren't hardly enough pieces to bring back, things change."

I nodded. "How did it change Jim?"

He thought for a minute. "It's funny, he didn't get stinking drunk or stoned all the time the way I'd expected him to. He and Sam got real close, I think. Like he sort of adopted Sam to take Luis's place."

"They were closer than they'd been before?"

"Yeah, I think so." He looked up as if he were trying to remember something. "Seems to me that, before, he and Luis hung out mainly with the Hispanics. But after Luis was gone, Jim and Sam got real tight. I guess that's how they handled it."

We talked a bit more, and just as it occurred to him to ask why I wanted to know all this, the bell rang. He said a hasty good-bye, grabbed his stack of papers, stuffed the last of his sweet roll in his mouth, and headed for the door. I'd been saved by the bell.

I met Peter back at the motel at ten; we found a quiet corner of the coffee shop that was currently much more private than our room. It'd be at least an hour before Eileen arrived with the Hound Dog, and while getting the bugs out of the room would make me feel better, I realized that it wouldn't bring us any closer to Jim Mendoza or the mysterious "outside player" who was so interested in our progress on the case.

I told Peter what I'd learned from Davis. "It isn't much, but it tends to support Westin's story. If they did kill Ramirez, it would explain why they were so close afterward.''

"And if only one of them killed Ramirez, it would provide a great opportunity for blackmail.''

"Maybe right after it happened, but once the blackmailer stayed quiet for a while, he'd be an accomplice; and the army could just as well decide to try them both. There weren't any other witnesses. Mendoza could just as easily have accused Connors. I think it'd been a draw.''

"Except that their commanding officer hated Hispanics,'' Peter reminded me.

"A fact I'm sure he never hid from Mendoza,'' I added.

"Yeah,'' Peter said, "but I still have trouble buying Mendoza as a murderer.''

"Welcome to the club,'' I said ruefully. "Unfortunately, it's getting easier all the time.''

19

FOUR CUPS OF coffee and two trips to the rest room later, we had hashed the case over and speculated on the identity of the outside player till we were sick of it.

"So what it comes down to,'' I summarized, "is that he's either out to find Mendoza and hoping I'll lead the way, or he's working with Mendoza and is keeping an eye on me to make sure I don't get too close.''

"Or he's kidnapped Mendoza and wants to keep you away,'' Peter added.

"Possible, but not likely. If our man is working with Mendoza or has kidnapped him, why bug Mendoza's house?''

"To find out what's being done about his disappearance.''

"He'd get pretty limited information there. But if he's out to find out where Mendoza's gone, then it makes all kinds of sense to bug the phone and the house. If I had to bet, that's where I'd put my chips."

Peter nodded. "Me, too. Though I wouldn't bet the whole stack."

That settled, we moved on to the death of Luis Ramirez. I didn't know what his death had to do with First Central's money, but I had a hunch that if I knew more about it, I might have the key to cracking Sam Connors's code of silence.

A call to Mrs. Mendoza revealed that Luis Ramirez had a brother, Raoul, who lived in Modesto. Peter offered to take Raoul out for a beer and see what he could learn about Luis's death. I accepted with the galling realization that he'd get more out of Raoul than I would.

"Ask if anyone else has approached him about Luis in the last several months," I suggested.

"Our outside player?"

"It's possible. There's something going on we don't understand, and it seems to have to do with what happened in Vietnam."

Eileen arrived about fifteen minutes later, just in time to save me from a fifth cup of coffee. She had the information on the mysterious tan Ford. The license number was registered to James Phelan in Rohnert Park, California. Phelan had a silver Toyota that had been missing a license plate for a couple of weeks.

Peter shook his head. "The guy's a pro; I'd bet on it."

"Well, so are we," I said.

We explained our little phone charade, then headed for the room. The cleaning crew was just finishing up. I wondered what juicy tidbits they'd unknowingly provided our hidden listener, then realized that unless he spoke Spanish, he wouldn't have understood much of what they said.

We swept the room and found four more bugs. One was

behind the head of the bed, which I realized, with some chagrin, would have provided a nice, clear recording of activities in the immediate vicinity. Before we popped the bugs into the metal box, I asked about the phone, and Peter assured me that it was clean.

We really didn't have anything for Eileen to do in Modesto, and I wanted her working on the background reports on Wheeler and Connors. I also asked her to check out whether anyone on our list of Mendoza's friends or associates had been stationed at Long Binh while he was in Vietnam or shortly thereafter.

"I'm particularly interested in anyone who came into his life in the last nine months."

She agreed to start Chris on that as soon as she got back.

"I think you'd better get a second Hound Dog and sweep the office," I added. "And have Jesse check the phone box at the pole. If our outside player is bugging me, you'd better assume that someone could be bugging the office as well."

"No need to make Jesse check the pole. I can take care of it," she announced proudly.

Peter nodded. "Climbs a pole faster than me, and looks a lot better doing it," he added.

Eileen blushed, but she was clearly pleased. I gave her the box with the bugs, and she headed back onto the freeway.

"We'll have to sweep it every time we come back," Peter pointed out as we walked back into the room.

"I think we should assume that the cars are bugged, too," I said.

"Oh, yes. But cars are too damn hard to sweep. It's easier just not to say anything important."

"He'd be taking a considerable risk to come back here," I said.

"Yeah, and I don't think he will, but we'll sweep, anyway. Dodging this guy could get to be a real drag."

"I don't want to dodge him. I want to catch him. I want to know why he's after Jim Mendoza."

"Okay," Peter agreed. "I'll go along with that. You have a plan in mind?"

I didn't. "We'll need some sort of trap, I suppose. Without the bugs, he'll need to follow me much more carefully. If we could find the right place, we could set him up, have him follow me into a place with only one way out, and you could be behind him."

Peter considered the idea. He did not look enthusiastic. "I don't know," he said. "We're converting a nonviolent situation into one that could be very dangerous. Right now he just wants to know where you're going. If we try to trap him, he might well become violent."

"It's a risk," I agreed, "but we're running the same risk down the road, assuming we can manage to find Mendoza, and then we won't be calling the shots."

Peter frowned.

"We have to stop this guy now. If he is dangerous and he gets to Mendoza first, it's bad for the bank and worse for Mendoza. If he's still on our trail when we find Mendoza, he could go after all three of us."

"We need a dead end," Peter said. The frown I'd read for disagreement was merely concentration. "I might have the place. Let's take a drive."

It wasn't terribly far, but we got lost a couple of times before we figured out how to get there. After several wrong turns, we ended up at the Tuolumne River Regional Park.

The park was a long strip of land on the north bank of the Tuolumne River. The west end, nearest the entrance, sported lawns and play structures. Farther along, picnic tables and benches had been placed at several points, but the park was mostly open land with a broad path that ran beside the river.

A single road led into the park. The entrance was marked by a steel bar that could be swung across the road to close it at night. The road snaked along the north side of the park. A high fence on the other side marked the edge of the municipal airport.

* * *

We parked in the parking area at the end of the road and walked to the edge of a bank that sloped down to the park. The picnic area below us had enough tables to accommodate several church congregations, as long as they were compatible. Beyond the tables, the park reverted to natural habitat. Underbrush grew wild, and after a short distance the path disappeared into trees.

We followed the path to its end and checked out the maintenance road that ran from the parking lot along the edge of the park. The area was deserted except for a couple of men fishing in the muddy river and a woman walking her dog. Peter made a detailed map of the area from the picnic tables to the end of the park and a less detailed one of the road leading into the park. Finally, he announced, "I think it'll work."

"So tell me," I asked.

"If we can get him to follow you into the park, I think we can trap him. To do the job right, we need five people. One at the gate to let us know he's in, and also to close the bar to keep other people out, one down the path from you in case he tries to go that way, and one to back me up when I come up behind him."

"We could use Bert, Ernie, and Jesse," I suggested.

"No, Bert and Ernie are great for surveillance, but I wouldn't want to put either one of them in a situation like this. I've got some guys back in San Francisco I'll call."

"Why do I have the feeling I shouldn't ask too much about these guys?"

"Because you're smart enough not to ask what you don't want to know," he replied with a grin. "We'll need some little walkie-talkies. I can get them in San Francisco."

"You can have your men pick them up from my office. Are you planning to carry a gun?"

"Of course. I'm not fooling around with this guy."

"I don't want a gun," I said. "I don't have a permit."

"You wouldn't carry a gun even if you had a permit," Peter commented, knowing my dislike of guns. "You won't need one, but if there's trouble, drop to the ground, because the guy behind you will be armed."

"All this assumes that our man will follow me into the park. We have to give him a good reason; otherwise, he could just wait outside till I come out."

"We know there's no way out, but he won't know that unless he's from around here or he's studied a map. Still, it'd be best to give him a good reason to want to stay close to you."

"We can put the phone bug to use," I suggested. "I'll call Amy and tell her I'm fairly sure that Mendoza's here in Modesto and I've set up a meeting with a man who'll take me to him. He'll have to follow me."

"He could still wait outside the park."

"He could, but I don't think he'll risk it. If he thinks I'm getting close, he'll want to be right behind me."

Peter nodded. "I think you're right."

"How fast can we put this thing together?"

"With luck, by tomorrow. Let's find a phone and see if I can arrange for backup."

It took a couple of calls, but Peter found his men and arranged for them to drive up to Modesto early the next morning. I didn't see any point in confronting Connors with Westin's accusation, but I thought it might be interesting to hear what Worth had to say about his war experiences.

Peter had discovered that Worth didn't drift nearly as much as Connors had led us to believe. In fact, he lived in a little cottage about six blocks from the body shop. The cottage was owned by Sam Connors. We picked up a six-pack and a bottle of bourbon and headed off to see Craig Worth.

20

Worth's cottage was set back from the street in a section of town with older, smaller houses. It wasn't the high-rent district, but most of the houses were well maintained, with neatly tended yards. Even Worth's lawn was mowed.

We knocked on the door and waited, then pounded and waited. Music played faintly inside the house. Peter pounded again. Finally, the door opened.

Worth was wearing jeans and a red plaid flannel shirt. He looked considerably better than he had when Connors had led him from our room, but that was still a long way short of good. His hair was greasy, and his clothes were wrinkled and hadn't seen a washing machine for much too long.

He looked surprised and a bit confused, then wary and hostile. I suppressed the temptation to stick out my hand and announce, "Hi, I'm the lady you tried to skewer."

Peter held out the booze and said, "No hard feelings about Saturday. Mind if we come in for a drink?"

Worth considered; then a slow smile lit his face. "Sure," he said.

We followed him into a room that was not so much furnished as piled. There were piles of books and piles of records and piles of clothes. On closer inspection I could make out a mattress covered with a blanket and some pillows that probably served as a couch and a couple of plastic lawn chairs buried under piles of papers and clothes.

Worth scooped a pile of clothes off one chair and offered

it to me. Peter shoved some stuff on the mattress aside and settled in, and Worth joined him there. Our host passed around the beer; then, after taking a long drink from his can, he began rummaging around next to the couch. He came up with a stash box and extracted a hand-rolled cigarette.

"Want some dope?" he asked.

Peter smiled broadly and said something anachronistic like "Far out," and Worth lit the joint.

This was no time to get high, but refusing Worth's offer might well destroy the camaraderie that we were trying to build, so when he passed me the joint, I took a drag, held the smoke in my mouth, and didn't inhale. Worth was neither interested nor observant enough to tell the difference.

Peter took a deep drag, leaned back, and sighed contentedly. He picked up a Grateful Dead album that was next to the couch and started a conversation about the rock group. I stayed quiet and tried to fade into the background. It wasn't hard, for the conversation had turned to football, and the two were doing a male-bonding number and had completely forgotten my presence.

I reflected that women were never unaware of the presence of men in this way. From the time I'd been small, I'd been able to sit quietly just off to the side of a group of my father's friends and listen to them discuss police business. I'd discovered that if you didn't act interested or draw attention to yourself, you could be nearly invisible.

And it still works. Sit quietly and look uninterested, and you become invisible. We keep an eye on those more powerful than ourselves and ignore the powerless. Sometimes it can be very useful to be invisible.

Peter turned the discussion to the war.

"You in 'Nam?" Worth asked.

Peter shook his head. "No, man."

Worth looked at him suspiciously. "You one of them protesters?"

Peter nodded, his eyes half-closed. "Yeah, I lost a couple of good buddies over there. Pissed me off to see good men sent to die when the government didn't even know what the fuck it was doing.''

Worth nodded. He, too, had a sleepy, stoned look. His was real. "You were smart," he said. "Smarter 'n me. I believed all that patriotic bullshit my dad handed me.''

They sat in silence for a few minutes. Peter said lazily, "I bet you saw some shit over there.''

Worth nodded.

"You were with Jim, right? He said you guys had some deal going with Supply.''

Worth laughed. "Yeah, man, we could get anything, anything we wanted. He tell you about the generator?''

"Was that when they nearly caught you?''

"No, man, that was the air conditioner, or maybe it *was* the generator.'' He laughed.

"What'd you do with all that stuff?''

"Didn't he tell you?'' Worth was rosy now, well past suspicion. "It was for the orphanage, man. Didn't he tell you about Xuan and the kids?''

"God, I don't know, I was too stoned, you know, man.''

Worth laughed. "Man, that was the best outfitted orphanage in 'Nam. Xuan needed anything, we'd get it for her. We found this baby, see.'' He paused, and his face told me that he still wasn't ready to tell *that* story. "And the priest, he told Jim about Xuan. Boy, she was something. I'd have married her if she'd been willing to come to the States, but she wouldn't do it, wouldn't leave those babies.''

"Man, I'll bet the brass'd been pissed if they'd ever caught you.''

"Shit, the guy we got near the end of our tour was always after Jim. Hated Mexicans, especially Jim, 'cause he was smart. Everybody was stealing shit, but it was Jim he wanted to catch.''

"Jim said something about them thinking he shot some big-shot commander or something.''

"The CO,'' Worth said as he lit a second joint. He uttered a colorful string of obscenities to describe the commanding officer, then took a long drag of the joint and passed it to

Peter. "Somebody fragged him," he said with no sign of regret. "I put a week's poker winnings into the bounty. Man, it was worth it."

"And Jim did him?"

"Hell, no, at least I don't think so. I don't know who did him, but I don't think it was Jim."

"But somebody thought so," Peter prompted.

"Must have been the platoon commander, Western or Winston, some damn name like that. He's the guy hated Jim. I can see him thinking it was Jim. He rode us all real hard about it." He sucked on the joint again. "No, you know, it was Luis he was after, I bet. I mean he was always on Luis's case, calling him in, giving him extra duty, shit like that. He was after Luis."

"Wasn't Luis the one who got killed?"

"Lots of guys got killed," Worth announced heavily. "Lots of guys."

"Not Luis."

"Yeah, Luis, he ran into a booby trap on patrol." He went on to describe in distressing detail the effects of a booby trap on the human body.

"So you were with him?"

"No, not that time, but I had another buddy ran into one maybe twenty feet from me. He was in front of me, could have been me just as easy."

Worth was retreating into himself. His smile was gone, and he looked like he was remembering things that no seventeen-year-old should see.

"I guess Jim and Sam got real close after Luis died," Peter said.

"Yeah, they were with him on patrol that night. It really messed up their heads, man. They wouldn't even talk about it. For a couple of weeks, they were like always going away, just disappearing. Or they'd be together and wouldn't want anybody else around."

"You must have felt real left out," Peter suggested.

"Yeah, not by Jim, but you know, Sam was like a big brother to me, and all of a sudden, he didn't want me around.

He was real good to me, Sam was, still is. This house is his, you know.''

"He's a good man," Peter said.

"Damn right," Worth agreed emphatically. "Damn good.''

He finally remembered my presence. He peered at me through the smoky haze. "But you don't like Sam," he accused. "You're the one got him all upset.''

"I didn't mean to upset him," I said. "I'm just looking for Jim. I don't know why he got mad at me. Why'd he get mad at me?'' I mimicked Worth's whiny tone.

That stopped him. He frowned as he tried to concentrate. "I don't know.''

"Why won't he help me find Jim?'' I made it sound more like a complaint than a question. "I gotta find Jim; his wife's gonna have a baby.''

Worth shook his head. His eyes had a blank look, and he was just on the verge of falling asleep. "He's a good man," he repeated. "He's got his reasons.''

Peter mumbled something about moving on, thanked Worth for the weed, and we headed for the door. Once we were outside, I took several deep breaths. My tolerance for smoky rooms goes down every year, and marijuana smoke is just as hard on the eyes and throat as cigarette smoke.

When we reached the car, I congratulated Peter. "That was a remarkable performance. How did you manage to keep from getting stoned? Or have you developed the ability to concentrate while under the influence?''

"It wasn't particularly good stuff, and I only inhaled a couple of times.''

"Still, I can feel the effects just from being in the room.''

"Well, you are, after all, not quite so experienced in these things as I,'' he said.

As we drove back to the motel, he asked, "Do you buy the story that they were stealing for the orphanage?''

"I do," I replied. "Connors told me that on their first patrol they accidentally killed a woman and some kids, only the baby survived. He said that it upset them all but that Worth was particularly guilt racked."

"So they adopted an orphanage to assuage the guilt."

"Seems like a pretty good way to deal with it."

"Better than most," he said.

"It's still not over for him."

"It's not over for any of us," Peter said. "The superpatriots are killing Nicaraguan peasants to prove they're still number one, and the left is trying to pretend that Daniel Ortega is Ho Chi Minh."

"We're probably always fighting the last war. My dad kept talking about Hitler and the price of appeasement all during the Vietnam War. He just couldn't see that it was a colonial war."

"It's because no one in this country studies history," Peter declared.

"If that were a problem, the Europeans ought to be real pacifists, and I don't see any evidence of that."

Peter shook his head. "No, pacifism doesn't come easy to any of us, I guess."

"How did you stay out of Vietnam?" I asked.

"I dodged the draft, and because I was smart and white and knew who to ask for help, I succeeded."

"You don't sound happy about it."

"Well, I'm damn sure not apologizing. The war was wrong, and all the Rambo movies and patriotic bullshit from the White House doesn't make it right. But it's hard to feel morally superior about a position that so clearly serves your best interest."

"What would you have done if they'd caught up with you?"

"Gone to Canada, probably. That's not what I should have done. I should have gone to jail; that's what the really courageous guys did."

"You could have been a CO."

"A conscientious objector? Not hardly. COs don't get involved in the kind of work I do. I do it because I believe in it, but I also enjoy it. And the stuff I enjoy about it is what men like about war. You know what scared me most about

Vietnam, not that I'd have hated it—but that I'd have enjoyed
it."

He pulled into the parking lot at the motel, shut off the car
engine, and sat staring straight ahead. I realized how for all
of us who came of age in the late sixties and early seventies
the war was a defining experience. You went or you didn't,
but the fact of it and the decisions it forced us to make marked
us for the rest of our lives, just as the depression and World
War II had marked my parents.

Peter had done what he thought right but still had no sense
of peace from it. Craig Worth had done what he thought right
and was even more tormented. The thing was a wound that
still refused to heal.

Peter went off to see Raoul Ramirez around eight. It was a
good time to catch someone at home, and we hoped he'd
have finished dinner by then and be relaxed and sociable. I
couldn't stand to spend another evening going over the case,
and the prospect of trapping our "outside player" tomorrow
made me jumpy.

Finally, I found the address of a bookstore and went in
search of something to get me through the evening. I browsed
through a table of paperbacks and stopped before a cover
with a gritty black-and-white portrait of a soldier. *Paco's
Story*, last year's winner of the National Book Award, had
been touted by some as the great Vietnam war novel. As I
paid for it, I realized that I don't like to read about war. It
astonished me that Peter and other men could consider war
exciting or desirable. There surely was one of the major dif-
ferences between the sexes.

It was almost midnight before Peter got back. When
he came in, he brought the bar with him, or more accu-
rately, on him. The room was instantly filled with that
unique mixture of stale cigarette smoke, spilled beer,
and the mingled odors of too many human bodies sand-
wiched together for too long. He collapsed into a chair
and announced, "I'm getting too old for this. I just can't
drink like I used to."

Having made the same appalling discovery myself on numerous occasions, I was sympathetic. I dug through my bag for the bottle of 500 milligram tablets of vitamin C. "Take six of these," I suggested. "They won't make you feel any better right now, but they'll spare you the hangover tomorrow."

Peter nodded and counted them out. "Got any aspirin? My head already hurts."

I dug around and found some of that, too. Having done my good deed, I couldn't keep my curiosity on hold any longer. "So what did you find out?"

"I found out that Raoul Ramirez is one of the world's more suspicious men, that he can drink like a fish, and that he expects his companions to keep up with him."

"That's it?" I asked impatiently.

"Damn near. No one else has asked him anything about his brother's death or Jim Mendoza for years; no strangers have approached him in the last six months; and he doesn't know anything more than that his brother was killed by a booby trap while he was on patrol."

Peter yawned. "However, I did get one interesting thing. He's still nursing a grudge against Mendoza. Seems he feels that Mendoza manipulated his brother, that Luis would do anything for Mendoza, and he's always felt that Luis ran into the booby trap because Mendoza sent him on ahead."

"Anything to support that?"

"Not that I can tell. There's probably some jealousy and the desire to find someone to blame. But the part about Mendoza manipulating Ramirez fits with what Westin told you."

I nodded. "Funny that it's such a different picture from the one we get from the people at the bank. People change over time, and he was young in Vietnam, but they don't change that much. It's almost like we're talking about two different men."

"Maybe, maybe not. Maybe he just got a lot smoother over time, and the reason everyone loves him is that he's so good at psyching them out. That does happen. Con men and bigamists do it all the time.''

"But con men don't adopt orphanages.''

"Not usually,'' Peter agreed.

The bar smells were getting to me, and Peter was having trouble keeping his eyes open. "Why don't you take a shower and go to bed,'' I suggested.

"I'd rather shower tomorrow.''

"Not if you're planning on sleeping in my bed,'' I insisted. "Come on, I'll soap your back.''

I led him to the bathroom, and he let me take his clothes off as if he were a little kid, but once he was undressed, he was a lot less like a little kid and also less tired than he'd seemed.

"Now yours,'' he announced as he began unbuttoning my blouse.

The room filled up with steam as we stepped under the caress of the hot water. I rubbed the soap into a rich lather and began smoothing it over Peter's body, working across his broad shoulders, down his back to his narrow hips, and down his powerful thighs. By the time he turned around so I could start up the front, I was as turned on as he was.

He covered my body with soap, taking a lot longer on the breasts and thighs than was strictly necessary; then we stepped back under the hot water and rubbed the soap off each other. We played around under the water for a while, but making love to a half-sober man standing up under a shower is a tricky business, so we climbed out and toweled each other off, then headed for the bed.

21

PETER'S BACKUP MEN arrived early. He'd had them take a room at the edge of town, and we met them there. The room was small and the men were large. I found their aggressive masculine energy a bit overwhelming, sort of like wandering into the 49ers locker room just before a game.

Peter introduced them with single names only, which reinforced the sense that I might be dealing with candidates for the FBI's short list. If I'd been a casting director, I'd have snapped up Al and Roy for extras in a tough waterfront barroom scene. The third, Stubbs, couldn't have looked less the part. He was about five four, weighed no more than 120, and had a boyish grin. If you looked at his eyes, however, they were anything but boyish. I always assumed that the reference to "cold eyes" was a literary device; but this guy convinced me otherwise.

There was no small talk; Peter got right down to business. He handed each of the men an envelope with cash that they accepted without checking the amount. These guys didn't look like they needed to worry about being shortchanged. I was still trying to figure out how to account to the bank on my expense sheet for all the cash we were disbursing. There were no categories for "bribes" and "hired muscle."

Peter gave them copies of the map he'd drawn of the park and went over the plan. Al was to take cover in the bushes along the trail at the point where I would stop as if waiting for someone. Peter would hide in the rest room beside the path from the parking area so that he could come out behind the man following me. Stubbs would be fishing just upstream from the rest room, which put him behind Peter in case our man made a break for it. Roy would be in a parked car near the gate to the park. Peter gave him a walkie-talkie so that he could alert us when our quarry followed me in.

"We don't know what he's driving," Peter said. "He had a tan Ford, but he'll have ditched that, since we recognized it. Watch for a white male, thirties, medium height, brown, straight, longish hair. Let me know when he's in. Then close the gate and put your car where you can block the road if he gets away from us."

"When do we do it?" Stubbs asked.

Peter looked at his watch. "The best time is morning; the park'll be pretty empty till lunchtime. If we can set it up fast, we could do it before eleven."

Peter and his friends went off to check out the park. I went to find a pay phone and call Amy. I explained the setup to her and told her to expect my bogus call from the motel in a few minutes.

"None of it will be true, of course, but it should get our outside player's attention and head him in the right direction," I told her.

"I hope you'll be careful," she said. "It sounds dangerous."

"We'll have a small army out there," I pointed out. "I don't expect any trouble." As I said it, I was aware of a feeling in the pit of my stomach that contradicted my words. "There's one more thing I need from you. Our outside player will be a bit bolder if he believes that Peter's not around. Wait about an hour, then call the room at the motel and tell Peter that he's needed back in San Francisco this afternoon."

"I'll give him a court appearance," she suggested.

"Great."

Before I hung up, she added, "Those of us who get to sit this one out would appreciate a status report as soon as it's over."

"You got it."

* * *

Back at the motel there wasn't much to do after I'd called Amy with the phony-meeting story. Time passed slowly as I reviewed our plans and tried to reassure myself that there really was very little danger.

After what seemed like several hours, Peter returned and announced that we were ready. He was carrying his jacket, and when he tossed it on the bed, I saw the Colt Commander he had in his hand. I was jumpy enough without the gun. Its presence was an unwelcome reminder of the seriousness of the situation.

Peter stuck the gun into his pants just back of his right hip and pulled his jacket on to cover it.

"Better be careful or you'll shoot your ass off," I said.

"That'd be real unfortunate."

"A tragedy. It's one of your best features." I gave him an appreciative pat.

The phone rang, and I realized it had only been an hour since my first call to Amy. She asked for Peter and delivered our prearranged message that he was needed in court that afternoon. He grumbled but agreed to start back immediately.

Amy has a flair for the dramatic, and she played her role for all it was worth, making Peter repeat the time and location of his court appearance. "Yes, I understand. I'll leave right now," he said, giving me a wink as he hung up.

He gave me a quick kiss, but I grabbed him and held him against me for several moments. "Be careful," I whispered.

He kissed me again. "Always. You be careful, too."

I gave Peter a twenty-minute head start, then set out to my car. The morning fog had lifted and been replaced with a whitish haze. The air was cool, and the sun struggled to produce even modest shadows. At the zenith, the sky was only a milky blue.

I tried to spot someone following me as I drove down McHenry but couldn't pick anyone out. I kept my speed down and didn't push any of the lights. When I left the main street and headed into an industrial area where there was less traffic, a dark-colored car followed, but it was too far away for me to see anything of the driver or even be sure of the color.

The drive to the park seemed much longer than it had when I'd taken it with Peter. The speedometer said thirty-five, but it felt like I was crawling. Just before the entrance road, I spotted a dark red car that looked vaguely familiar. I figured it must be Roy's.

As I drove down the road to the parking lot, a small plane suddenly flew in front of me about a hundred feet above the road. It startled me, and I almost hit the brakes, then realized it must be coming in for a landing at the airfield on my left.

I parked in the lot and started into the park, forcing myself to walk slowly and trying to move naturally. Moving naturally becomes nearly impossible when you think about it. My mind flashed back to a high school fashion show in which the woman from the store kept urging us to "walk naturally," making us more and more self-conscious until we almost forgot how to walk at all.

I passed the rest room where I assumed Peter was hiding and headed toward the path. Off to my right, Stubbs was almost invisible, sitting against a tree near the river's edge with a fishing pole extending out over the muddy water.

I'd gotten the hang of moving "naturally," but walking down that path slowly, eyes forward, turned out to be a lot harder than I'd expected. It's creepy to know there's someone behind you. And I did know he was there. I could feel him.

The problem, I realized, was that I was a decoy, the passive player in the game. The confrontation was to be between Peter and the man behind me. In aikido, when an attacker approached from behind, I was trained to spin around or to respond to the first indication that a blow was coming. I concentrated on my breathing and centered myself, focusing my attention as I do in the dojo.

I was almost to the point where I was to stop when I heard Peter's voice.

"Hold it, pal," he yelled.

As I turned around, the sound of two quick gunshots exploded in my ears. I should have hit the ground, but I knew something had gone wrong. I couldn't see Peter or the other man, but I knew those gunshots weren't Peter's.

My heart was pounding, and my chest felt tight as I raced back down the path. Al was right behind me, and as we came around the turn, there was a splash and a couple more shots. Stubbs was firing into the river. Peter lay crumpled on the ground.

He was on his left side, and I could see the ragged hole where the bullet had torn through his jacket below the shoulder. I sank down beside him and turned him over as gently as I could. The front of his shirt was bright crimson. I caught my breath and forced back a wave of fear.

He was still conscious. His eyes squeezed shut, and he gasped and clenched his jaw against the pain as I held him. I blinked back tears and, without even consciously willing it, cut off all emotions and went numb inside.

Al leaned over us, and Stubbs ran back from the riverbank. "The bastard got away. I don't think I even wounded him." He knelt beside Peter. "Two shots," he said. "Did they both exit?"

"I don't know," I said. "I saw blood only on his shoulder before I turned him over."

Stubbs reached under Peter and with surprising gentleness moved his hand over Peter's back. There was no blood when he drew it out. "Clean," he said. "That means there's still one in there."

I looked from Peter's pain-racked face to his chest. There were clearly two wounds, both on the right side, one in the shoulder and the other in his chest. He was bleeding so heavily that I couldn't tell exactly where either wound was located.

"We've got to get him to a hospital," I said. "He could bleed to death."

Stubbs nodded grimly. "This stuff on the outside's not so bad; it's what's on the inside you gotta worry about."

I heard a loud cracking behind me and looked around to see Al dragging a couple of dead branches toward us. "Can't wait for an ambulance," he announced, "take too long."

He took off his jacket and folded it on top of the branches to make a litter, then slid them under Peter's back. "We gotta keep him as still as possible," he explained.

Peter was visibly paler and had lost consciousness, but he came around with a jerk and a loud groan when Al moved him onto the branches. Everything seemed to take too long, and I could see the bloodstains growing with each second. I tore off my leather jacket and spread it over Peter to try to keep him warm. "Hurry," I urged them.

Al and I lifted Peter's body from each side while Stubbs took his legs. Peter's body jerked rigidly with each movement. Each step on the long trip to the car sent spasms of pain through his body, and I felt every one of them.

The climb up the bank to the parking lot was the worst part. The ground was uneven, and at one point Al slipped. Peter let out a strangled cry as we struggled to keep our balance. His breath came in gasps.

"You drive," Al told Stubbs. "Me and Roy'll check out around here, then split. We'll meet you back at the motel."

"We don't know where the hospital is," I said.

I was close to losing it. I forced myself to calm down and found the map of Modesto on the front seat. I gave it to Stubbs, then I grabbed the portable phone from the trunk. Dialing 911, I explained that we had a serious accident with heavy bleeding and probable internal injuries and needed to get to a hospital immediately.

"Take him to Doctors," the voice commanded. "Where are you now?"

I told him.

"Do you know how to get to McHenry?"

"Yes."

"Take McHenry to Orangeburg, turn left on Orangeburg. Doctors is in the second block on your right."

We put Peter in the backseat, and I slid in the other side to cradle his head in my lap. He'd probably have been more comfortable without me, but I couldn't stand to be separated from him, even by the seat.

He was frighteningly pale, and he seemed to fade in and out of consciousness. He grunted occasionally from the pain, and I thought I could also hear a wheeze. I noticed for the first time the blood on my own hands. How long, I wondered, did it take to bleed to death? Stubbs's reference to "what's on the inside" came back to me, and I realized that the blood I could see might be only a fraction of what he'd lost. I swallowed hard and bit my lip.

Roy was at the gate. He seemed to move in slow motion as he got out of his car and swung back the iron bar. Stubbs yelled at him to go pick up Al and we sped out of the park and up Santa Cruz Avenue. It was an industrial area, and Stubbs picked up speed fast. When we reached the more populated streets, drivers hit the brakes and watched their lives pass before their eyes. The way he drove, Stubbs was either a race-car driver or a getaway man.

I tried to concentrate on making sure Stubbs took the best route, because I couldn't bear to think about what might be happening to Peter. I tore part of the sheet that was covering the backseat and held it against the shoulder wound to try to stanch the bleeding. "Hold on," I whispered. "Hold on."

WE PULLED INTO the emergency entrance of the hospital. They were expecting us, and a crew rushed out with a gurney. As they lifted Peter to the gurney, one of the orderlies asked, "What happened?"

"He's been shot," I told her. "Twice, and one's still in there."

I tried to stay with them as they rushed Peter into a treatment room, but a nurse who looked like she moonlighted as a wrestler stepped in front of me. "We'll need you to fill out some forms, dear," she said. "There's nothing you can do for him in there. They'll take care of him."

She led me to a window in a glassed-in cubicle and shoved some papers at me. "Does the patient have medical insurance?" she asked. Not "Is he seriously wounded?" or "What exactly happened?" or even "Is he allergic to any drugs?" Just "Can he pay?" I silently congratulated myself on getting Peter to agree to join my health plan six months ago. The months of hassling and cajoling were all justified when I answered, "Yes."

The tone of her questions was sharp and suspicious, and I couldn't figure out why until I realized what we must look like, a man with two bullet wounds brought in by a woman with a black eye. Not a hospital's idea of desirable clientele.

"Before we go on," I interrupted, "we have the same blood type. Can you use my blood for him?"

"We'll have to type and cross you both, but if you're compatible, you can donate for him. You have to understand that there may not be time to use your blood for surgery." She called for a technician, who appeared with the usual gigantic needle, mumbled, "Make a fist," and poked me with the needle. He wasn't very good, and it took a couple of tries, but for once I didn't really care.

"That's a stat," the nurse reminded him. "Type and cross for the gunshot patient." The technician nodded and disappeared.

She went back to the forms, and we covered allergies to drugs and finally the hard one, "What is your relationship to the patient?" That was a question Peter and I had spent a fair amount of time discussing, not always calmly. He wasn't even my roommate, since I'd opposed his moving into my apartment and refused to move into his. Realizing that I might not be allowed into his room if we weren't related, I mumbled, "Wife," and hoped Peter didn't have a heart attack when someone called me Mrs. Harman.

We finished the interminable list of questions, and I was about to ask about Peter when two uniformed officers appeared at my side.

"You with the man with the gunshot wounds?" one of them asked.

My first reaction was anger. Peter might be dying and these bozos wanted me to fill out a police report. I pushed back the anger and pleaded, "Please, not now, not till I know how he is."

Before they could respond, I dashed toward the door they'd taken him through. A nurse grabbed my arm. With all the blood on my clothes, I didn't need to tell her I was with Peter. "Please," I begged, "Is he going to be all right?"

She held my arm and motioned to another nurse. Something in her manner warned me that I must sound a bit hysterical. The last thing I needed was a tranquilizer, so I lowered my voice and said, "I'm sorry, can you please tell me about my husband's condition?"

She relaxed a bit and shook her head at the other nurse. "Your husband is in surgery now. They'll let us know as soon as they can, but that may be an hour or so."

"How serious was the blood loss?" I asked.

"I can't tell you; they'll have to assess that in surgery." Now that she knew I wasn't going to get hysterical, her manner softened. She put an arm around me and said, "Let me take you to the surgery waiting room. They'll bring you word there as soon as they know something."

I thanked her, and she led me down the hall. The boys in blue followed us. The next hour was going to be the longest in my life, and I figured that the only way to get through it would be to find something to occupy my mind, so I forced myself to deal with the problem at hand.

I hadn't thought about trying to explain this mess to the police. But I knew instantly that they would not appreciate our little setup. Daniel Martin had hired me to spare him any contact with the police; and our last conversation had made clear that he valued discretion above all else. But it wasn't really Martin I was worried about. It was Jim Mendoza. Once the police were on the case, I'd lose all chance of negotiating a quiet settlement and keeping him out of jail.

We took an elevator up one floor, and the nurse led me to a room with industrial-gray carpeting, a tweedy couch, and several slightly saggy armchairs. On one wall a hospital-green curtain covered the window of the nurses' station next door. In the corner a television advertised soft drinks to the empty room.

She left with assurances that she'd notify me as soon as they knew anything. The cops stood just inside the doorway, awkwardly waiting for me to sit down. I stared at them and became what they expected—a sobbing, incoherent female. It wasn't all that hard. I just let out all the emotions I'd carefully kept in check. The officers escorted me to a chair and sat by stoically as they waited for me to regain control of myself.

I wondered how much these guys knew. If they'd seen Stubbs, they should be able to figure out that there was no way he and I could carry anyone as big as Peter for any distance. If they'd seen the car, they ought to be suspicious as hell. And even if they'd missed both Stubbs and the car, there was my appearance—a woman with blood all over her and a black eye did not inspire confidence.

Finally, I asked for a glass of water, and while one of the officers got it for me, the other offered me a tissue. I'd decided to tell them the truth, as far as possible, omit the important things, and go vague when we hit the tricky parts. I told them that Peter and I had been up in Modesto on business and that we'd been walking in the park. I explained that I'd been ahead on the path and had heard but not seen the shots.

"What did you see when you came back down the path, Mrs. Harman?" asked the older officer, who'd introduced himself as Sergeant Larsen.

"I saw Peter on the ground with blood on his jacket, and I caught a glimpse of a man jumping into the river. I assumed that was the man who'd shot Peter."

"He jumped into the river?" the taller, younger cop repeated, making no effort to hide the incredulity in his voice. He looked as if he couldn't be more than eighteen.

"Yes. I guess that was the only place to go. I was on one side of Peter, and there was a man running toward us from the other side."

"Who was the second man?"

"I don't know. I'd never seen him before," I said. "He was in the park, and he came running up when Peter was shot. He helped me carry Peter to the car, and I guess he realized that I wasn't in any condition to drive, but I never asked his name."

"Do you know where he is now?"

I shook my head. "Downstairs, maybe."

They asked for a description, and I gave them one of Stubbs, knowing that he'd be nowhere near the hospital by now. Larsen sent the younger cop downstairs to look for him.

"Do you have any idea who shot your husband, Mrs. Harman?" Larsen asked.

I shook my head. "I have no idea who he was," I said quite honestly.

The nurse interrupted us to tell me that I could donate blood for Peter and led me to a room where they laid me down on a table and drew the blood. I'd done this a dozen times and never really comprehended what it meant. As I watched the bottle fill, I realized that the blood flowing from my vein would soon become part of Peter's body. That is, if he survived long enough to need it.

The nurse gave me some orange juice to drink and asked if I'd like to rest there for a while. I realized when I stood up that that might be a good idea, but I figured I'd better get through the police interview while I still had some cope left. The effort of keeping up the naive, bereaved wife bit was getting to me.

The younger cop was back when I returned. I probably wobbled a bit when I entered the room, because both officers jumped up to take my arm. Once we were settled, Larsen asked, "Is there any reason someone might have wanted to hurt your husband?"

It wouldn't take them long to find out that Peter was a PI, so I didn't try to dodge that one. I told them that he might well have enemies in San Francisco, but that he hadn't taken any cases in Modesto, so I didn't think he'd have any enemies here.

With the news that Peter was a PI, I could see their approach to the case change. They wanted to know all about the cases he was working on. I told them that I had no reason to think that there was any danger involved in any of his current cases, which had been true until about half an hour ago.

"What brought you here, ma'am?" the younger man asked.

"I was doing some research for a report I'm writing, and I didn't want to be alone, so Peter came along." To forestall any questions about the fictitious report, I burst into tears and demanded, "What kind of world is it where you can't go walking in a park? Why would a man just shoot someone he didn't even know?"

I'm sure they'd asked themselves that question before. They just shook their heads and said, "We're sorry, ma'am."

They asked more about what had happened in the park. Since I hadn't seen anything, I didn't have to lie much. I drew them a map of the area where we'd been and agreed to go back to the park with them later if they needed me to.

"But not today, please. I have to stay here until he's out of surgery."

"Of course," Larsen said, "it can wait until tomorrow, and we may not need to ask you to go back there at all. I do have one more thing I need to ask you to do for us." His tone was apologetic. "It's standard procedure in a case like this to do a simple test on the hands of those who were present to determine whether or not they've fired a gun."

It took a minute for that one to sink in. I'd been so busy keeping them from finding out what we'd been up to that I'd missed the fact that I was the obvious suspect. "Oh, of course," I said quickly. "Can we do it here?"

The younger cop went back downstairs to get the GSR kit. They took out a disk and peeled off the paper, then pressed it against my fingers and hands. It didn't take long and was less messy than getting thumbprinted for a driver's license. Given the way I looked, I wasn't surprised they were suspicious.

"I know I must look like a tough customer or a battered wife," I said, touching the bruise beneath my eye. "It's been so embarrassing. I got it when my two-year-old niece hit me with a truck." As I said it, I realized I should certainly have been able to make up a more believable excuse. But the older cop smiled and nodded.

"My wife's got a chipped tooth where our son tried to feed her with a spoon when he was a toddler," he said. "Kids."

"We don't have any," I said, and started to sniffle, hoping that would end the interview.

Sergeant Larsen patted my arm. He took my address in Modesto and told me that a detective would contact me in a day or so. "If there's anything you can think of that might help us catch this guy, please call this number," he said as he handed me his card.

I thanked them and they left. I still had at least half an hour to wait.

I noticed that the green curtain had been moved so that the nurse could keep an eye on me. I moved to get a clearer view of her. She looked up and smiled.

I felt light-headed, and my mind seemed to dart from one thing to another. At the center, popping up to confront me each time I turned away from it, was the terrifying reality that Peter might die.

The phone at the nurses' station rang. I studied her face for some sign. She made some notes, then hung up. When she looked up, she shook her head and mouthed, "Not yet." We went through that ritual several more times, and with each ring, my heart pounded, and I could hardly breathe.

With the fifth call there was a subtle change in her posture; then her face broke into a smile, and she gave me the okay sign. She made some notes, then hurried into the waiting room.

"Good news," she said. "Your husband is out of surgery. They've removed the bullet from his lung, and his condition is stable."

"Does that mean he's going to be all right?" I asked.

She nodded. "So far so good."

"Can I see him?"

"He's still under the anesthetic," she said. "And he'll be in the recovery room till he's stable and the anesthetic has worn off. That'll be at least an hour. Then we'll move him to the ICU. You can see him there, but he'll be woozy, and you shouldn't stay long."

"Can I talk to the doctor?" I asked.

"Certainly. I'll ask him to stop by; it'll be about fifteen minutes."

I sank into the chair with a sense of immense relief. The nurse eyed me with concern. "You donated blood, didn't you?" she asked. I nodded and found I could hardly keep my eyes open.

She left me but returned a few minutes later with a soda, a sandwich wrapped in clear plastic, and a candy bar. "You need to eat, she said, "especially after donating blood. You're getting faint."

I did feel pretty wretched, but I didn't think it had much to do with food. My system was so pumped with adrenaline that I felt vaguely nauseous and light-headed, and my stomach had been tying itself in knots for the last two hours. I forced myself to eat the food she'd brought and discovered that I did feel somewhat better.

The doctor arrived in his baggy green one-size-fits-all surgical clothes. A funny muffinlike hat perched on his dark curly hair, and his hands were covered with talc, making them a ghostly white. He had a full dark beard that hid his mouth, but even though I couldn't see a smile, there was something reassuring in his expression.

He introduced himself as Dr. Berger and informed me that the wounds looked worse than they were. One bullet had gone straight through the flesh below the shoulder bone, causing a lot of bleeding but not doing any serious damage. The second bullet had struck a rib and glanced off into the lung. It had lodged near the edge and done some damage, but the lung hadn't collapsed, and the actual area affected was relatively small.

He explained that the blood loss had been significant but that they'd avoided giving Peter blood during surgery by using saline and lactated Ringer's to keep his blood pressure up. They'd give him the blood drawn from me after he stabilized.

"We've put in a chest tube to drain the wound. I don't know how long he'll need that. Once it's out, he'll still be very weak for quite a while. He's a very lucky man."

The ICU is a scary place; when you need all that high-tech equipment, you know you're in trouble. Peter's skin had a grayish cast, and all the vitality seemed to have drained from his body. There was an IV tube in his arm, an oxygen tube attached to his nose, and a drainage tube stuck in his chest that dripped pink fluid into a jar on the floor.

I pulled a chair near his bed and put my hand on his arm. His eyes opened, and he croaked, "Hi babe." The effort of speaking seemed to exhaust what little energy he had. His eyes blinked shut, and I couldn't tell if he was still conscious. I gripped his hand. "Don't try to talk," I said, "just rest.

"I love you," I whispered as I raised his hand to my lips.

He nodded and pursed his lips into a kiss, then drifted off again.

I sat beside him for a long time, just grateful to be able to hold his hand.

Finally, the nurses chased me out. I didn't want to leave the hospital, but I realized I'd better find my car before it got dark, so I wandered back to the parking lot. I figured it wouldn't be near the door, so I walked all the way around the lot. The walk felt good but didn't produce my car. I could have called Stubbs, but somehow I preferred walking to talking, so I headed out to the street to see if he'd left it parked there.

I found it on a side street just beyond the parking lot. Stubbs had rearranged the blanket on the front seat and had replaced the bloody sheet on the back with a blue blanket that looked like it had probably come from his motel room. The door was open, and I'd slid in and sat down before I realized I didn't have keys. After a quick search I found them under the passenger's seat.

I knew I should eat something for dinner, but I wasn't hungry. I was still numb. The nurse had said Peter was stable, but he looked terrible, and I didn't want to be away from him. There wasn't anything I could do, but I didn't want him to be alone. Truthfully, *I* didn't want to be alone.

Finally, I drove back to McHenry and found a restaurant that looked like it might serve soup. Soup and tea always seem like comfort foods, maybe because that's what my mother used to feed me when I was sick.

I was hungrier than I'd realized, and after a second bowl of soup I realized that Jim Mendoza wasn't going to come home by himself just because Peter'd been shot. I found a phone and called the office. Amy was still there. I realized with some guilt that she was waiting for my call.

I told her what had happened and asked her to tell Eileen. "She's very attached to Peter, so she'll really need some support," I said.

"Of course," Amy replied in a tone that informed me that I needn't have mentioned it. "Now, how are you doing?"

"As well as can be expected," I answered, feeling the sting of tears and swallowing hard. "Eileen will probably want to come right out, but I'd rather she wait a day until Peter's a bit stronger."

There was a click on the line, and Jesse came on. "What happened? Are you okay?"

I ran through the story again, and when I finished, Jesse murmured, "Oh, shit, Catherine, I'm sorry." It was all I could do not to break down and bawl, but when he asked if I'd like him to come to Modesto, I said no.

"I do a lot better in situations like this without too much sympathy," I said. "Besides, I need you at the bank."

I didn't feel much like calling Daniel Martin, but I had promised to keep him informed, and there was no way to gloss over the fiasco in the park. He was shocked and shaken; and true to form, it did not bring out the best in him. He was far more concerned with the risk of police involvement than he was with Peter's injuries.

"I haven't told them a thing about Mendoza or the bank," I said to reassure him. "If they do investigate, they'll be looking into the cases Peter was handling."

"You *must* keep them away from the bank," he said. "Any publicity and they'll fire me on the spot. It's awful here. People won't look me in the eye; they avoid me in the hall. It's as if they all know that I'm on my way out. I feel like a leper."

Social ostracism didn't seem like such a big thing alongside a chest wound, so I wasn't in the mood to hold Martin's hand. Still, I felt more pity than anger for the man. Peter's wounds would heal; the holes in Daniel Martin's soul would not.

When I got back to the hospital, the nurse in the ICU looked at me as if maybe she should find me a room. "You need to go home to bed," she announced.

"I don't think I'd sleep," I said. "Can I just sit in his room? I won't wake him."

She smiled and nodded. "He's doing fine. I know it looks scary, but he's coming along fine."

I thanked her and settled down in the chair.

23

PETER LOOKED A little better the next morning. His skin was still grayish, but his eyes had some life in them. The tube was still in his chest.

"Some people will do anything to get out of work," I said.

He made an attempt at a smile and said, "And you're always telling me how safe your work is."

I bit my lip, and he said quickly, "Hey, just kidding, I set the thing up, remember."

"It was my idea," I said guiltily.

"Hey, things happen, you know that. No guilt trips. I won't be able to complain if you look stricken every time I gripe, and in a situation like this, griping is one of the few pleasures left."

The nurse came in to take his temperature. "Oh, I didn't realize you were here, Mrs. Harman," she said.

Peter had a coughing fit that must have been painful. He submitted to having his temperature taken, and when she'd left, he turned to me and said, "Did I miss something while I was out?"

"I figured they'd be more comfortable with 'wife' than 'squeeze,' " I explained.

Peter smiled devilishly. "And here I thought that on my deathbed you'd finally decided to make an honest man of me."

"Well, I certainly hope it's not your deathbed," I said. "I'd like to think you have a few more miles left." I didn't tell him that I'd spent much of the last eighteen hours thinking about how very much I wanted Peter to remain a part of my life.

My marriage had taught me that just because you love someone does not mean that you can live with him and that when a lover becomes a husband, it can ruin a perfectly good relationship. I didn't want that to happen with Peter. But sitting in the surgery waiting room, I'd realized that he was already a much bigger part of my life than I'd admitted to myself.

"The police will probably be in to interview you," I said.

"I don't know nothin'."

"Right. As you might guess, we were simply walking in the park when by some freak accident you were shot by an unknown assailant."

"Sure. Of course. You think they bought that bullshit?"

"Probably not, especially since they know you're a PI. They do not know that I am a PI. I told them I was here to write a report and you'd come along to keep me company."

"And what is the nature of this report, should they ask?"

"I managed to stay vague on that. How about Vietnam veterans?"

Peter nodded. "Covers the ground."

"They'll want to know what you're working on."

"I've got a couple of things on the back burner that should satisfy them. I might even tell them about the porno king."

"That should contribute nicely to your relationship with Bryson."

Peter laughed, then winced. "I'd like to say it only hurts when I laugh. Unfortunately, it just hurts more." He looked down at the tube sticking out of his chest. "How do you like my new look? Think I can pass it off for a tie?"

"Only in L.A. Pink was never one of your best colors."

I could see that even our short conversation exhausted Peter, so I told him it was time for me to go so he could rest.

"One thing, Catherine," he said seriously. "This guy is a pro. When I yelled at him, he dropped, rolled, and squeezed off two shots before I could fire. No one but a pro could have pulled that off."

"Was he expecting you?" I asked. "Did we miss a bug someplace?"

Peter shook his head. "No, he wasn't expecting me, but he has incredible reflexes, and he's a damn good shot."

"That's what Stubbs said. I sent them back to San Francisco, but they wanted me to tell you they're available if you need anything. Al says to let him know if you get a line on the shooter and he'll take care of him for you."

Peter shook his head. "He'd do it, too."

"Did you get a good look at him?"

"Not really. He was moving too fast. But he fits the description you got from Suzanne's neighbor—about five eight, maybe a little taller, medium build, with longish brown hair."

"Could he be a vet who was specially trained?"

"Could be. He could be anybody. The point is he's dangerous, very dangerous. And he's still out there. I want you to be careful."

I nodded. "I'll be careful. Pink isn't my color, either."

Outside, the sun was still trying to shine. If you looked up, the sky was a milky blue, but at the horizon it was buttermilk haze. My leather jacket had blood all over it, which left me with just a heavy sweater, but it was enough for the mild Modesto winter.

I went straight from the hospital to Connors's body shop. Wheeler was working on a car by the door and greeted me with "We got your window."

"I need to talk with both of you," I said grimly.

Wheeler called to Connors, who appeared from the rear of the shop. "I told you we don't have time to talk during work," Connors said. "Besides, we don't have anything more to say to you."

"Well, I have something for you. Someone shot my partner yesterday and damn near killed him. I'm tired of playing games."

Both men looked genuinely shocked.

"It wasn't Craig Worth," I said.

They made no effort to hide their relief. "Then I got no idea who it might have been," Connors said.

"Maybe, maybe not, but there're things you're not telling me that might help me figure out what's going on. Indirectly, you're just as guilty as the guy who pulled the trigger."

"The hell we are!" Wheeler exploded. "You come in here making threats and causing trouble, and then you go blame it on us. We got nothing to do with anybody getting shot."

Connors was calmer. "What exactly happened?"

I told them about the outside player, the bugs, and the setup. "He's the same guy that was watching Suzanne Mendoza, and you're the ones who know where Jim is, so you're part of this."

Connors shook his head. He looked worried. "But I don't know why anyone would be following Jim."

"I explained that last time we talked. In only a few days Jim will withdraw five million dollars from First Central Bank. Someone knows that."

Connors shook his head. His whole manner suggested that he really did not know that Jim was embezzling money. "I don't understand," he said finally. "I don't know about this bank business, but I don't believe that Jim would steal."

"He did in Vietnam," I pointed out.

Connors's head snapped up at that.

"You and he stole supplies for the orphanage. I know all about that."

"That was different," Wheeler said. "We done that to help the kids. The army didn't need that stuff. They just ordered more. But those kids didn't have nothing; some didn't even have blankets."

"You did it for a good cause, but it was still stealing. Maybe he's found another good cause."

Connors shook his head. "That's not why he left."

"You tell me that, but the bank tells me a different story. If he's not involved in robbing the bank, how do you explain the man who shot Peter and spied on Suzanne?"

"I honestly can't," Connors said. "But I know you're wrong about the bank."

"Maybe it would help if you told me why Jim really left," I suggested.

"I'd help you if I could," Connors said, and he seemed to mean it. "But I promised Jim I wouldn't tell, and I won't. Now we got to get back to work. You want us to replace that window?"

"Later," I said.

I stopped at a Denny's to get a cup of tea and try to figure out what was going on with Connors and Wheeler. I asked for Earl Grey and was told that they didn't have herbal teas. It felt a lot like my discussions with Sam Connors.

I was fairly sure he was not involved in the bank scam. He really did not seem to take the whole thing seriously. On the other hand, he was clearly worried about something connected with Jim Mendoza and had strong reasons for hiding his whereabouts.

Whatever Mendoza had told Connors had convinced his friend of the need for absolute secrecy. Connors was afraid of something—whether he was afraid for Mendoza or of him, I couldn't tell. If Colonel Westin was right, the murder of Luis Ramirez in Vietnam gave each man a powerful hold over the other and made them both potentially dangerous.

Connors wouldn't talk to me, but Craig Worth might. I paid for my tea and went in search of a liquor store. I found one in the next block, bought bourbon and beer, and headed for Craig Worth's place.

24

CRAIG WORTH ANSWERED the door wearing only a pair of jeans and a dazed expression. His hair was mussed from sleep, and it was a good bet he'd just awakened.

I held out the booze and smiled. "Hi again. Can I come in?"

He frowned, and I wasn't sure he remembered who I was.

"I was here yesterday with my friend."

He nodded. "Yeah, I know."

"Can I come in?" I asked.

He shrugged. "Sure."

The living room looked the same; the pile on the chair was the same, or maybe it was new; you couldn't tell. I moved it again and sat down as Worth collapsed on the sofa.

He eyed me warily. "You damn near broke my arm."

"I'm sorry. You scared me. I don't like knives."

"What the hell was that you did? Karate? I never seen a woman do nothing like that."

"It's called aikido, sort of like karate but without the chops."

He opened two beers and passed one to me. I hoped that meant he was feeling more friendly. "Man, I was on my ass before I knew what hit me," he said, more in surprise than anger. "You're damn good."

"Thanks. I'm sorry I hurt you."

He shrugged. "I been hurt worse. I'm sorry I scared you. It was dumb. Sometimes I get an idea, and I get all juiced up and do stuff I don't mean to. Sam says it's 'cause I done so many drugs, but my old man was the same way, and the only drug he done was booze."

Worth began rummaging around for his stash box. He found it and extracted a joint. He lit the joint and took a drag. "Where's your friend?" he asked as he passed it to me. I took a small drag and held the smoke in my mouth for what seemed the right amount of time.

"That's why I came," I said. "Something really weird happened." I told him about the outside player and what had happened in the park.

"I can't figure out who this dude is," I said. "I thought maybe you could help. It's gotta be someone connected with Jim, and you know more about him and his friends."

"Shit, I don't know," he said. He passed me the joint again, and I faked another drag and passed it back. The room was filling with the sweet, acrid smell of sinsemilla. "Like, you know, Sam and Terry don't tell me what's really going down. They treat me like a little kid. I don't know nothing about where Jim went or why. Just know they're worried about you asking about him."

"Were there any guys with your group in 'Nam who were trained for Special Forces?" I asked.

"Yeah, I knew several of them Special Forces dudes. They were bad news."

"Were any from Modesto?"

He took another drag and tried to remember. "Well, maybe John. He reupped, did another tour, and I think he went into Special Forces."

"John Langer?"

He nodded.

"Tell me about him," I asked, shaking my head when he offered me the joint.

"I don' know. He was a regular guy, I guess. He didn't hang out with us much. Sam didn't really trust him, never told him about the orphanage. He was kind of mean, I think. He liked to fight. I think he even enjoyed the fuckin' war."

"Where is he now?"

"Ain't seen him in a couple of years. Last time he was through, he got in a fight in a bar and nearly killed a guy. Come to think of it, he was always a mean son of a bitch."

Worth's voice had lost its hazy, stoned quality and taken on an edge of bitterness.

"Where does he live now?"

Worth shrugged. "Drifts, I think. He talks about all kinds of places when he comes through, but I've never heard him refer to any place as home. Last couple of times he talked about being in the jungle someplace, sounded Spanish, I think. Maybe he's smuggling dope."

We talked some more, and I finally asked a question that had been troubling me. "How did you find me and my car? You never saw me before, did you?"

Worth smiled. "Sam described you so I'd know you if you came to see me. He's so into cars, he told me about yours. I called around the motels and found you. Yours was the only blue Volvo in the lot."

"You're a pretty good detective yourself," I said.

"I hang out a lot, and I watch people. Sometimes I even follow them, sort of as a game. It's something to do."

I'd stayed as long as I could stand to in the smoggy room. Worth urged me to have another beer, but I told him I had to get back to see Peter in the hospital.

"Tell him I'm sorry he got shot up," he said. "And he should come on back when he's well, and we'll smoke some dope together."

The day seemed bright after the cavelike darkness of Worth's cottage, so I put on my dark glasses as I walked to the car. The sun was high in the sky, but the day had the same diffuse haziness as the day before. In San Francisco, where the air is relatively dry, winter light is always a bit stark in its whiteness, but here the moisture in the air softened and diluted it.

I was having trouble keeping my bearings. The land was so flat that there were no points to steer by. The horizon looked the same in all directions, and there was nothing to give an indication of how far away it was. It was like being on a plate covered by a high silver dome.

I realized with a shock that I was stoned. I must have gotten too interested in what Worth was saying and inhaled a couple of times, or maybe the smoke in the room, helped along by too little sleep and too much nervous energy, had gotten to me. Whatever the cause, not only was I having trouble keeping my mind focused on business; I reeked of marijuana. I could probably be arrested just for smelling the way I did.

I drove back to the motel very carefully, glancing at the speedometer frequently to figure out whether I was going as slowly as it seemed. Back at my room, I called the hospital to check on Peter. His condition was still stable, and he was sleeping. The nurse suggested that I wait an hour or so before visiting.

I showered and changed clothes; then, torn between the hungry munchies and exhaustion, I crawled under the covers and went to sleep.

I awoke around four with a stiff neck and a headache. I was no longer stoned, but I was still tired. My stomach was complaining loudly about missing lunch. I remembered that there was something Worth had said that I wanted to check on, but I couldn't figure out what it was.

Finally, as I was brushing my teeth, my brain kicked in, and I recalled that I wanted to know more about John Langer. I reached for the phone to call the office and realized just in time that it was still bugged. It was a real drag to have to hunt up a public phone every time I needed to make a call of importance, but the portable phone in my car wasn't secure, and I wanted to keep the bug on the phone in my room. It might still prove useful.

What I ate didn't much matter to me anymore, so I hit a Jack-In-The-Box for a very late lunch and found that the phone there was reasonably private. Eileen was at the office. I gave her the status report and suggested that she come to see Peter tomorrow. "He's sleeping most of the time now. It's when he's feeling better that he'll really need company," I explained. We discussed which books she should bring, though I had little faith that reading would keep Peter occupied once he felt able to get out of bed.

She was handling Peter's injury better than I'd expected. In the year and a half since she'd begun working for him, she'd grown a great deal. She was still idealistic and optimistic, a significant accomplishment, given the type of cases Peter got involved in, but she'd had enough experience to learn that things don't always turn out as they should.

"Any word from Chris?"

"She's checked three towns in Humboldt County. Nothing yet."

"I want you to check on someone," I said. "His name is John Langer. He's a vet from Modesto, and I think he reenlisted after his first tour of duty. See if you can find out if he reenlisted and where he was assigned. It's possible he was in Special Forces. I want to know what kind of training he had and his general description, especially height and hair color. Try to get Colonel Westin to help on it."

"You think he's involved?"

"I don't know. But I keep bumping into the Vietnam connection, and I have a gut feeling there's something there," I replied, wishing that I had something a whole lot more substantial than a gut feeling to go on.

Peter was still asleep when I got to the hospital, and he still looked dreadful. The nurse tried to reassure me that he was progressing very well, but the grayish cast to his skin wasn't comforting. I sat beside him, and after a while another nurse arrived to check his vital signs.

He didn't seem thrilled to be awake, and when he asked about pain pills, I understood why. The nurse told him he'd have to wait an hour, and he groaned.

"Just like a damn hospital, wake you up so you can suffer for an extra hour."

We sat quietly because he obviously didn't feel like talking. I'd have done anything to help him, and there wasn't a thing I could do.

Finally, I got up and went to hassle the nurse to get her to part with the pain pills ahead of schedule. I wasn't any more successful than I'd expected to be. She was a real by-the-book lady, and the book said an hour. I'd have cheerfully strangled her.

It was getting to be a long hour for both of us. Peter became more restless and uncomfortable as the time passed. Whenever he moved to relieve the restlessness, it set off a spasm of pain that made him clench his teeth. After about twenty minutes, he turned to me and said wanly, "I'm not much company now; why don't you come back after dinner."

"I'm not here for the entertainment," I said.

"Don't be a damn masochist. We don't both need to suffer. Besides, the strain of pretending that it doesn't really hurt is killing me."

"The high price of being a tough guy."

He tried to smile but winced instead. I got up and kissed him on the forehead. His skin was salty with sweat. "I'll be back later, champ," I said.

I realized as I left the hospital that I hadn't checked in with Bert and Ernie since Peter was shot. I'd equipped them each with cellular phones and told them to call only on my cellular phone or leave a message at the desk but not to call the room.

With the window on my car broken, I kept my phone in the trunk of my car. It was still there along with the walkie-talkies and Peter's gun. Al must have told me he'd put the gun there. It bothered me that I'd forgotten. This was no time to get careless.

I called Bert and Ernie and filled them in on what had happened. Ernie sounded quite agitated, and I offered him the chance to pull out, but he decided to stick with us. Bert had found a young woman at the phone company who was willing to get the record of Sam Connors's phone calls, and he expected to see her tonight.

"Will you pay for me to take her to dinner?" he asked.

"Sure," I said. "Let me know if you find someplace decent to eat."

                    * * *

Langer was not a common name. I found a phone booth with an intact directory and looked it up. There was one listing, for P. Langer on Fairmont.

P. Langer turned out to be John Langer's aunt. She was a large woman with at least three chins and an expression that suggested chronic constipation. She didn't invite me in and greeted my question about her nephew with "What's he done now?"

I gave her a line about locating witnesses to an accident. She looked as if she'd heard that one before and didn't believe it then or now. "I'm not responsible for anything that boy does," she announced. "He's not even my own, and he's a grown man now."

I assured her that there wasn't any question of liability, that I just needed to locate her nephew and find out how reliable a witness he'd be. "I don't want to put him on the stand and have him swear to something, then have the other attorney come up with a bunch of skeletons from his closet," I explained.

She gave a short laugh. "Then you'd best not call on him," she said. "He's got plenty of skeletons, I'd bet."

With a little prompting, she told me that he'd been in trouble since he was a kid. She ascribed his misbehavior to his mother's lax discipline after his father's death. "Joe'd have taken a strap to his butt and straightened him out plenty quick, but Martha just couldn't bring herself to lay a finger on her darling boy. I thought the army'd straighten him out, but he came back worse than he left."

She recounted a series of jobs lost because he couldn't get along with supervisors, drunken binges, and tavern fights during the years after he returned from Vietnam. She hadn't seen him for over four years. When I asked where he'd been, she gave a harsh laugh. "You think he'd tell me?" She shook her head. "But I think he did get a job somewhere. He was working for some man the last time he came through. Wouldn't tell me a thing about it, real secretive and superior, but I haven't had any desperate requests for money since then, so he's found some way to feed himself.''

"Any idea what he was doing that was so secret?'' I asked.

She shook her head emphatically. "I couldn't count on it being absolutely honest,'' she said. "On the other hand, he might be one of them soldiers of fortune, guys who hire out to fight in any war that comes along. When he was living with me for a while, he subscribed to some soldier-of-fortune magazines. He used to say that's what he wanted to be.'' She paused to consider what she'd said, then added, "But that was a long time ago. Probably he's just driving a truck somewhere.''

I asked if she had a picture of John, and she retreated into the house and came back with a fuzzy snapshot that showed a younger, less heavy version of herself with her arm around a lean young man whose long dark hair was held back in a ponytail. He was several inches taller than her, probably around five nine or ten. Close enough to kick my heart into fast gear.

'It's not recent,'' she said, "was taken ten, twelve years ago.''

I forced myself to keep my voice steady as I asked about John's army buddies. She didn't know much except that he used to hang out with a guy who ran a garage or something. "You might ask him. Maybe he's seen John. Last time he was here, we got in a real screaming fight, and I told him not to come back till he got himself together.''

I'd have liked to know what caused the fight, but when I asked, her mouth snapped shut and she shook her head. At that point she decided that she'd told me all I needed to know, and the interview was over.

Peter was asleep when I got back to the hospital, so I couldn't tell him what I'd learned about Langer. As I thought about it, I had to admit that it was a long shot. After all, our description could fit thousands of men. Just because Langer was the only one remotely connected with the case who physically resembled our outside player didn't mean that it was him.

It was after nine when I left the ICU, and I was feeling the lack of sleep of the night before. The pain in my head was slowly coalescing around a spot above my right eye. The fluorescent light in the lobby seemed far too bright, and as I squinted under the glare, I realized I was in the early stages of a migraine.

I groped through my purse and came up with my portable pharmacy. I selected a blue-and-yellow capsule from the as-sortment of aspirin, decongestant, and several other pills that I no longer recognized. There was one of those metal water fountains with ice-cold water near the elevator, and I went through the gymnastics necessary to swallow a large capsule with a single mouthful of water.

Migraines tend to focus attention on themselves, but after the experience of the last forty-eight hours, there was no excuse for my carelessness as I walked into the darkness of the parking lot.

THE LIGHTS IN the parking lot made bright pools on the pavement, and I was glad I hadn't parked under one of them. I kept my eyes on the ground to avoid the brightness and skirted the cones of light. My stomach was starting to get jumpy, stage two of the migraine; and I was anxious to get home and crawl into bed.

As I approached my car, a noise ahead of me made me look up just in time to see the bright flash of a gun firing. I hit the ground, knowing I didn't have a prayer if the gunman was accurate. Behind me I heard a cry and a thud like something hitting a car. A woman screamed, and there was the sound of high heels running on cement.

I turned and saw a body on the ground two rows behind me. I crawled backward, got to my feet behind the cars, and staying low, ran for the hospital door.

The woman I'd heard scream had gotten there before me and was tearfully telling a security guard that someone was hurt in the parking lot. She thought maybe he'd been hit by a car. She'd seen his body fly backward and hit a parked car; then he crumpled to the ground.

"He was shot," I announced, and they all looked at me as if I were the one with the gun. "I don't know if the gunman is still out there, but I think you'd better be careful."

Having people shot in the parking lot didn't seem to be one of the eventualities covered in the manual, and it took a few minutes for them to get organized. I pointed out that the victim might be bleeding to death, and a nurse called for an ambulance and medics. The receptionist called the police, and the security guard suggested that the woman and I sit down. She was sobbing; I felt as if I might throw up.

I replayed the events in the parking lot in my mind's eye. The flash probably hadn't been as close as I'd thought, but it was close enough that it was amazing I'd survived. My body started what was becoming an all-too-familiar set of responses to near death, and the migraine grew like a firestorm.

But even the pain of the migraine couldn't blot out the realization that an innocent person had been hit by a bullet that must have been meant for me. Peter had warned me, but I'd been so sure of my version of the case that I'd ignored him. In my carelessness and bull-headedness, I was responsible for this. For the second time in as many days I prayed to a god I wasn't even sure I believed in.

I went to the rest room and vomited. I should have felt better, but I didn't.

By the time I got back to the lobby, the nurse had gotten

the news that the victim in the parking lot was dead. The police were on their way.

I forced myself to walk up to the nurse and ask, "What do you know about the victim?"

"A white male in his thirties," she answered.

The spot of pain above my right eye was growing, and all I wanted to do was crawl into a hole, but something else drove me outside to see the man whose death I'd caused.

A group had gathered around the body, and the ambulance attendants were keeping people back. I moved to the edge of the group and gently worked my way forward. When I reached the front, I was looking down into the face of Craig Worth.

He lay crumpled on the ground behind a silver Datsun. His eyes were open, staring up into the darkness, and the expression on his face didn't reflect the violence of his death. But below his chin there wasn't much left of his neck.

The bullet must have hit him in the middle of the throat, and even a quick glance showed that it'd done massive damage. My stomach wasn't up to the sight, and I turned away quickly.

"Shouldn't we cover him?" one of the attendants asked.

"Don't do anything until the cops get here," the other said.

A man whose manner and tone of voice suggested that he was either a doctor or an administrator hurried up to one of the attendants and demanded to know why the body hadn't been brought to Emergency. The attendant explained the exact nature of the wound. "There's nothing you guys could do for him."

The doctor mumbled a bit before retreating to the hospital. "I suppose he thinks he could've sewed the guy's head back on," the attendant quipped to his partner.

"They all think they're God," the other replied.

I took a last look at Worth's face and wondered why on earth he'd been behind me and if perhaps he and not I was the target. That would explain how a gunman who had hit

Peter twice while he was moving could have missed me at such close range.

It was dark, but from where the gunman stood, I would have been backlit. Worth, too, would have been backlit. Both of us were easy targets. And there'd been only one shot. If the gunman had been after me, he would certainly have fired a second and third shot into the space where I'd ducked. The more I looked at the setup, the more sure I became that I was not the target. That left me with the question of why anyone would want to kill Craig Worth.

The fact that Worth's death was not an accident was no comfort. I looked away from the body. It wasn't the attack in the park or the trashing of my car that I remembered but his smiling face, as I left that afternoon, telling me to bring Peter back when he got well.

My face was wet with tears as I stepped back out of the group of curious onlookers. I wanted to be alone, to go home and have a good cry, but I realized, as a police car pulled up, that I couldn't do that.

The arrival of the black-and-white raised a new problem. The cops weren't going to buy random chance the second time they found me involved in a violent crime. I watched the uniforms go through the procedure of sealing the crime scene and wondered if I could just disappear. The risk was too great. They'd be looking for witnesses soon, and too many people had seen me in the lobby.

There was a good chance they wouldn't connect me with the shooting the day before, at least not for a while. They might not even ask if I knew the deceased. I could probably get through tonight by simply describing what had happened and not offering any further information.

Of course, they'd figure it out eventually, and then they'd land on me like a ton of bricks. But I might have as much as twenty-four hours before that happened. I decided it was worth the risk.

I watched the crime-scene investigation unfold. The routine was similar to the one used by the San Francisco police. My ex-husband was a homicide inspector with the SFPD, and I'd watched from the car a couple of times when he was called to a crime scene. I could pick out the sergeant who was supervising the uniforms. Two of them were questioning the crowd to locate witnesses. It wouldn't be long before they got to me.

A couple of guys in green jumpsuits arrived in an unmarked car, and one began to draw diagrams while the other searched for physical evidence. A few minutes later a third man arrived, pulled a bunch of camera equipment from the trunk of his car, and began setting up to take pictures.

A middle-aged man in a gray tweed sport coat and tan slacks climbed out of an unmarked car. He was about medium height and on the heavy side, and his head seemed small for his body. I watched him as he talked with the uniforms and decided he was probably the homicide inspector.

The officer who was looking for witnesses finally reached me. He was an older guy with a face that said life held few surprises anymore, and his response to the news that I'd witnessed the murder was no more than a nod. He asked me to follow him and led me into the lobby, where he seated me next to the woman who'd reported the crime.

My companion was in her early fifties. She wore a fair amount of makeup, and her mascara had settled into great black smudges under her tear-reddened eyes. She wanted to talk to me about "this awful thing," but I told her I wasn't feeling well and leaned back in the chair and closed my eyes.

I wasn't feeling well, not on any level. The Fiorinal with Codeine I'd taken for the headache might as well have been a sugar tablet for all the good it'd done. The entire upper right quarter of my head seemed to be squeezing down on my eye, the light in the lobby had become unbearably bright, and I was ready to throw up again.

At that auspicious moment, the homicide inspector arrived. He introduced himself as Lieutenant Cardina and explained that he needed to ask a few questions. I mumbled something about the migraine. He was apologetic and solicitous, but he wanted to get a few answers before

I left. I'd have agreed to anything to get somewhere dark and quiet.

We were almost finished with my statement when I heard a familiar voice behind me. It was Larsen, the older cop who'd interviewed me yesterday. I kept my back to him and hoped he'd leave. He told Cardina that someone named Beemer was out sick, so he'd been assigned to assist. Cardina asked him to wait while he finished taking my statement. I knew I was in deep trouble.

Cardina read back to me what I'd said just before we were interrupted, and I resumed the narrative in a low voice that I hoped wasn't too familiar to Larsen. My luck had been lousy all day, and it remained consistent. Larsen moved around to the side so he could see my face and said with surprise, "Mrs. Harman?"

Cardina's head jerked up. "I thought your name was Sayler."

I explained that I used my maiden name but hadn't bothered to correct people yesterday when they called me Mrs. Harman because it didn't seem very important. Both men were looking at me very suspiciously.

Larsen explained that my husband had been shot the day before in Tuolemne River Regional Park. "They both said they had no idea who the shooter was, that it was a random act of violence, but he's a PI from San Francisco," he added.

"Let me see your identification, please," Cardina said.

I took out my wallet and started to remove the driver's license, but he motioned for me to pass the whole thing over. My investigator's license was right behind the driver's license. He frowned when he found it and passed it to Larsen. "She tell you about that?"

"He didn't ask," I pointed out.

Cardina's face had a nasty frown, and he made no effort to hide the anger in his voice when he said, "Have someone take her downtown and hold her till we're through here."

They turned me over to a uniformed officer who put me

in a black-and-white for the trip downtown. It was one of those with heavy wire mesh behind the front seat, and the smell was more than my stomach could take. I managed to catch the cop before he slammed the door. I leaned out and dumped the last of my dinner on his shoes.

He swore, and I apologized. Cardina was only a few feet away, and he came over to see what was going on. He just shook his head. Maybe he thought I was faking.

THE POLICE DEPARTMENT was downtown, in a low two-story building in the middle of an area that rivaled St. Louis for urban blight. The officer led me in through a back door and settled me in a small room with a table, two chairs, and much too bright a light.

"Could I have a glass of water?" I asked.

The cop nodded and came back with a Styrofoam cup of lukewarm water. I dug around my purse and took a second capsule. It hadn't been four hours, but I figured that the first one didn't count since it didn't do any good. I leaned forward and put my head down on the table like a kindergartner at nap time.

At some point I awoke to the wonderful discovery that the second pill had worked. I was exhausted, and my stomach was still rocky, but the pain had receded from behind my eye. I savored the absence of pain as I retreated back into sleep.

I was drifting somewhere on the edges of consciousness when a loud voice startled me. "You have a lot of explaining to do, Ms. Sayler. And I don't want to hear any shit about how this is a random act of violence. I want to know exactly what you and Harman were working on, all of it, understand.''

I didn't know the law on withholding evidence, but I had a strong suspicion that I'd probably already violated it. It's not a good idea to lie to the police; I'd listened to both my dad and my ex-husband recount stories of catching uncooperative citizens in damaging falsehoods. They had special contempt for private investigators who held out on the authorities.

I took a bit too long trying to decide how to avoid revealing the bank's identity or the reason for wanting to find Mendoza, and Cardina was short on patience.

''Don't fuck with me, lady. I could bust you right now. You cooperate fast or I'll throw you in a cell.''

When you've lived around cops most of your life, you learn to size them up pretty fast. I didn't like Cardina, and I suspected my father wouldn't have liked him much, either. I gave him the look my mother used to give me when I got out of line and said, ''I'd appreciate it if you wouldn't use that kind of language.''

He looked absolutely astonished. Score one.

''I have every intention of cooperating with you. I was simply gathering my thoughts so that I could present the information as clearly as possible.

''First, I honestly believed at the time of the attack on my associate that it was an act of random violence. In light of Craig Worth's death, I have to reassess that assumption. I will tell you everything I can about the case I'm working on, but I'm afraid I can't disclose the name of my employer or the reason I was hired.''

I told him just about everything; that James Mendoza had disappeared and I was looking for him, that someone had been watching his house and monitoring his phone calls, and that his disappearance might possibly have something to do with the death of Luis Ramirez in Vietnam almost twenty years ago. I told him who I'd interviewed and about Worth's attack on me and his rambling revelations. I also told him about Raoul's suspicions of his brother's former comrades.

It took quite a while, and Cardina managed to keep that cynical you-don't-fool-me smirk on his face the whole time. He hassled me a bit about my client, but I stonewalled, and finally, he said something like "We'll see" and walked out of the room.

I sat and waited. I guess I was supposed to be sweating it out, tormenting myself with visions of life in prison, but I was too tired for that.

After what seemed like hours, Cardina returned. "You were married to Dan Walker, San Francisco Homicide?" he asked.

I nodded and groaned inwardly. My refusal to give up what Dan considered a dangerous occupation was one of the main causes of our divorce. Now, in addition to worrying about my getting hurt, he could worry about my getting busted.

"You ought to know better than to play these kinds of games with the police," he said, but he'd dropped his intimidating manner. I had been restored to a measure of respectability.

About twenty minutes later he sent me back to the motel with the warning that I could be in substantial danger and an admonition to let the police handle the case.

I was asleep almost as soon as my head hit the pillow—and awake moments after that. Only the last scene of the dream remained with me, but it was enough. Craig Worth's bloody corpse and a dark faceless figure pursued me across rough, rock-studded ground, and a huge stone wall loomed up just before me.

My heart was pounding, and my back was sticky with sweat. I got a drink of water and did some yoga stretches to calm myself, then took a second chance on sleep.

I woke up a couple of more times with similar ugly scenes before I finally managed to stay asleep. I was dead to the world at nine the next morning and would happily have stayed that way if the phone hadn't awakened me. I knew before I picked it up who it'd be.

"Catherine, it's Dan, are you all right?"

"I'm fine, Dan. How are you?"

"Donnely got a call from the Modesto police earlier today inquiring about you, said you were involved in a murder case."

"He seems to have given me a good character reference. Please thank him for me."

"Catherine, what's going on? What's Harman gotten you into this time?"

I gave a mirthless laugh. "It's *my* case, Dan. Peter was working with me on it and damn near got killed trying to help me."

"Donnely tells me that there's a homicide."

"That's right," I said.

His next comment should have been about the dangers I was facing and the folly of a woman getting involved in this type of case, but to my surprise, Dan had learned something from our numerous rehashes of that argument. He asked, "You need some help?"

"It's good of you to ask, but I think I can handle it. I don't think the killer is after me."

"If you get close to him, he'll be after you," Dan said. I thought that, ironically, this was one point that Peter and Dan could finally agree on. "I've got some time off coming."

"No," I said. "I appreciate it, I really do; but I can handle this."

Dan sighed loudly. He probably thought I resented his intrusion, but the truth was that two people had already been shot because of me, and I didn't want to add Dan to the list.

"The guy would have shot me last night if I was the one he was after," I said. "I am not going after him, so he won't have any reason to go after me."

I could tell that Dan wasn't convinced, but he accepted the fact that I wasn't going to give in, and we ended the conversation with my promise to call if I needed help.

* * *

I felt I could use another eight hours of sleep, but instead I stood under a shower for a bit, made myself a cup of coffee, and climbed into my only clean pair of jeans. My stomach refused to accept the idea of skipping breakfast, so I bought a doughnut on my way to the hospital to see Peter.

Eileen was already there when I arrived, and Peter was awake and trying to reassure her that he didn't feel as bad as he looked.

"I hear you had quite a night," he said.

"The police been here?"

He nodded. "I'm sorry to hear about Craig. I liked the guy."

"So did I," I said. "I'm beginning to feel like a Judas goat."

"Hey, I don't think you can claim credit for this," he said, pointing to his chest. "Any idea why Craig was following you?"

That was a question I'd been asking myself. "Did they tell you he was carrying a gun?" I asked.

"No, you mean he was?"

"Yep, a government Colt. It was stuck in his belt back of his hip, same way you carry yours. He never had a chance to reach for it."

Peter frowned and considered the information. "You think he was after you?"

"I don't like to think so, but it's a possibility. The other explanation is that he was there to protect me. I went to see him earlier in the day and I told him that someone had shot you. Maybe he thought that I needed protection."

Peter nodded. "What kind of mood was he in?"

"He was friendly; I thought we'd made it up. But he also admitted that sometimes he gets tanked up and does things he doesn't mean to. I left him with a fifth of bourbon and some beer, which was obviously a bad idea."

Peter shook his head. "No, I think he was protecting you, the same way he tried to drive you out of town to protect his buddies."

I thought so, too, though I knew it might be because that was what I wanted to think. "He told me he liked to follow people just to watch them without them noticing him," I said.

"Only this time someone noticed."

"Yeah," I said. "Which leads us to the second big question, why did our man shoot Worth?"

"Maybe Worth had seen him when he was following you?" Peter suggested.

"Or maybe he thought Worth was after you and shot him to protect you," Eileen suggested.

We both looked at her with surprise.

"Well, if he was following you, he knew that Worth had slashed your seats and that he tried to stab you," she said.

"He heard the scene in the motel room where Worth admitted both those things," I said. "And he didn't hear Worth and me patch things up."

"There's a third possibility," Peter put in. "He could have been after Worth."

I considered that. "But why kill him in front of the hospital? It would have been much easier at home."

"Maybe, but maybe Worth saw him and got scared. Maybe he was coming to you for help rather than the other way around. Did Worth say anything new when you saw him?"

"The only thing was that he thought one of the vets, John Langer, had reupped and might have joined Special Forces."

"He did," Eileen said. "I got hold of Westin, and he called back to confirm that Langer did two tours in the Special Forces. He's an excellent marksman, and he's been trained in unarmed combat. Westin's very interested in Mendoza. He asked you to keep him informed on the investigation."

Peter was looking tired, though he wouldn't admit it, so I made the excuse of wanting breakfast and invited Eileen to join me.

* * *

We found the hospital cafeteria and got coffee and sweet rolls that looked as if they came from the people who supply airline food. As we talked about the case, Eileen became suddenly grave.

"What's up?" I asked. "Something's bothering you."

"You said Worth thought Langer had been in the jungle someplace, maybe South America. You know who's in the jungle down there—dope dealers and the CIA." I must have looked skeptical, because she hurried on. "No, I mean it. That's how they fund those 'covert' operations. It all came out during the Iran-Contra scandal, but nobody wanted to pay attention."

I'd followed Iran-Contra with the same avid attention as all the other aging liberals, and it was clear to me, if not to the Establishment press, that drug money was buying guns. But I've never been big on conspiracy theories, and that's where Eileen seemed headed.

"During the Vietnam War, the dope came from the Golden Triangle; now we're in Latin America, and it comes from there. It's not unrelated."

"I accept that. It doesn't even surprise me, which is pretty sad in itself, but I don't see what that has to do with this case."

"Langer could be working for the CIA," she said. "He'd be a natural—former Special Forces, loved to fight, a misfit back home. See what I mean?"

I did, and I didn't like it. This case was thorny enough without the possibility that it could involve the CIA or anyone associated with the CIA.

"What are Mendoza's politics?" I asked Eileen.

"Liberal to radical, a Jackson Democrat."

"Doesn't sound like someone who'd get mixed up with the CIA."

"Not knowingly, but maybe someone who'd help an old friend."

"Oh, shit," I said. "I don't need this."

27

T HE BODY SHOP was closed. Connors was no doubt at
home or making arrangements for the funeral. Good
taste and sensitivity would dictate leaving him to his grief,
but we didn't have time for that. I headed for his house.

He answered the door, and his immediate reaction was
fury. "What're you doing here?" he yelled. "It's your fault.
You did this. He'd be alive if it wasn't for you." He slammed
the door.

At some level he was probably right, which didn't do anything for my peace of mind. But he was equally to blame. If
he'd just leveled with me in the first place, maybe Worth
wouldn't have been killed. And what about his promise to
look after Worth, to keep him out of trouble? There was
plenty of guilt to go around on this one.

I went back and sat in my car and brooded. I hated this
damn case. I just couldn't get my hands on it. I didn't know
why Worth had been following me. I didn't know why he'd
been shot. I didn't even know why I was being followed.
Was the outside player following me to get to Mendoza, or
was he there to make sure I didn't find my quarry? And now
I had to worry about the damn CIA.

Connors and Wheeler didn't trust me. I doubted that there
was anything that I could do to change that. In fact, I suspected that they didn't trust most people. Maybe they'd been
raised that way, or maybe it was the legacy of the war. Vietnam had been a bitter lesson for all of us—superpatriots and
antiwar protesters alike; we'd all learned to distrust our government and, to some extent, ourselves.

Many of us, whether in the jungles of Asia or on the streets of Chicago, had discovered that noble causes can lead to ignoble actions and that we were capable of sacrificing honor to a sense of efficacy.

My thoughts were interrupted when a woman emerged from the house and got into Connors's gray Chevy. She was small, not much over five feet, and delicately built. Her dark hair was short and curly, and she wore jeans and a bulky sweater. She matched the description Ernie had given me of Connors's wife, Carol. I decided to follow her.

As I followed Carol Connors down the street, it seemed to me that she represented my best chance of getting through to Sam. It was no longer just a matter of Jim Mendoza or the bank's money. Sam and Terry and possibly George Davis were also in jeopardy; and the only way I could protect them was to find out what was really going on.

Mrs. Connors pulled into a Safeway parking lot and got out. I followed her into the store. When I caught up to her, she was studying the roasts in the meat section.

''Mrs. Connors?'' I said.

She looked up; her face registered surprise and discomfort. She probably wasn't used to being addressed by a stranger with a black eye.

''I need to talk to you,'' I said. ''I was with Craig Worth when he was killed last night, and I believe that your husband may be in serious danger.''

My warning had the effect I'd hoped for. She was shocked and frightened and ready to pay attention. ''Can we go someplace to talk?'' I asked. ''It's important.''

She nodded, but in her distress she couldn't seem to think of a place to go. The meat section of Safeway wasn't what I'd had in mind, so I suggested that we go to her car.

By the time we'd climbed into the Chevy, she'd collected herself enough to ask who I was and why I thought Sam was in danger. I decided it was time for the truth.

I told her the whole story, even the part about the bank. I had to find a way to convince her to trust me, and I didn't think anything less would do.

When I finished, she sat for a few minutes. Then she nodded as if to herself and said, "I don't know what's going on, but I know Sam isn't involved in anything dishonest. I'll talk to him for you and try to get him to see you."

I gave her the number of my car phone, warning her that it could be bugged; and she agreed to call me as soon as she'd talked with him. I knew she'd taken me seriously when she drove home instead of going back into the market to finish her shopping.

I didn't really have anyplace to go, and I figured I'd be lousy company for Peter right now, so I followed Carol Connors back to her house, got the cellular phone out of the trunk, and waited up the street.

As time dragged on, I felt my chances of getting Connors to talk slipping away. The lack of sleep of the last two nights was getting to me, and by the time the phone rang, I'd drifted into an uneasy sleep.

It was Eileen. She'd just called Annlyn to check in and learned that Suzanne Mendoza had been ordered to bed.

"The doctor put her in the hospital because he's afraid she'll go into premature labor. It's too early for the baby; they probably couldn't save it. They don't know what's causing it, but I think it's all the tension over Jim's disappearance."

"You haven't told her about the shootings here?"

"No, of course not," Eileen said, "but I told Annlyn so she'd be on her guard. It's not knowing where Jim is and feeling that he could be in danger that's taking a toll."

I thanked Eileen and told her to keep me posted, then hung up to wait for Carol's call. With the threat of Suzanne's premature delivery, one more life was now at risk, and there seemed to be nothing I could do but wait and hope that Carol could convince her husband to trust me.

It had been almost two hours. Too long. The waiting and my growing sense of helplessness was getting to me. I understood why men sometimes broke down and tried to beat information out of each other with their fists.

The phone finally rang, and I was so tense that it nearly sent me through the roof of the car. It was Carol. Sam was willing to see me. He wanted to hear what I had to say for himself; then he'd decide whether or not he had anything to tell me.

Connors was sitting in the living room in a leather recliner when I came in. He didn't get up to greet me. I sat down on the couch across from him.

"Carol says you have something to tell me," he said tonelessly.

I told him what I'd told her. That's one advantage of the truth; you don't have to worry about getting it right the second time. He stared at the carpet as he listened, never once looking up. There was a long pause when I finished. Then he reached for a pack of Camels on the table beside him.

His hand shook as he lit the cigarette. His fingers had taken on the yellowish tinge of a heavy smoker. I didn't remember seeing it when I'd first met him.

"So, you think Jim's robbing the bank and that's somehow connected to Luis's death. You're wrong." His eyes remained on the cigarette, never meeting mine. I waited.

He let the silence stretch as long as he could. "There's stuff I can't tell you, but I can swear to you that Jim did not kill Luis; none of us did."

"Not good enough," I said. "Craig Worth is dead, and there's every reason to assume that the killer will strike again. This is no time to play 'I've Got a Secret.' "

Connors rolled the cigarette between his fingers. "Luis isn't dead," he announced, and for the first time looked up at my face to see the impact of his words. "He didn't die in 'Nam, but he would have if Jim hadn't gotten him out. He was on the edge, ready to blow his own brains out 'cause he couldn't take any more."

"What do you mean, 'got him out'?" I asked.

"Got him home. Switched his tags with a guy who was blown apart by a booby trap and bribed some guys to smuggle him out."

My incredulity must have been written all over my face, because Connors sighed and began all over.

"Look, we were getting short, near time to go home, when our CO got killed and we got this spit-and-polish horse's ass, this new CO, who was a real gung-ho prick. He knew that the way to move up fast was to have a real aggressive record in the field, and he didn't give a damn about how many of our guys he got blown away pinning medals on his chest.

"On top of that he wasn't real smart, didn't know a lot about conditions in the field, so he was all the time sending us into situations where we should never have been. Stand downs got shorter; the casualty rate skyrocketed. And what really pissed everyone off was that while we were on the ground getting cut to pieces, he was flying around in a chopper above it all."

Connors paused to take a long drag from his cigarette and tapped the ash into an ashtray. "Our first CO wasn't a prize, but he had guts. He stayed on the ground and took his chances with the rest of us, and we respected that. But this guy was up there flying around watching us die.

"Everyone hated him, and pretty soon word got around that there was a bounty on him—anyone who liked the idea chipped in a few bucks, and it didn't take long before the bounty was fifteen hundred dollars." He looked up at me, waiting for some response.

"I'd heard that kind of thing happened," I said.

"Yeah, well, about a week later we were in the middle of another of his crazy patrols, and suddenly there's ground fire that hits his chopper and damn near knocks it down. Just after that, three Vietnamese guys run by us and dive into a hooch. Our lieutenant, who's this college kid who's only been in 'Nam a few weeks, orders us to surround the hooch and yells at the guys to surrender. They come out with their hands up. They're all of about twelve years old, and when we search the hooch, there are no guns.

"So now the lieutenant is shitting bricks because he knows that someone's shooting at the chopper and if it wasn't the kids it must have been one of his own guys. So he grabs my rifle, announces that we just found it in the hooch, and orders some guys to take the kids and gun into the base to turn them over to Intelligence.''

Carol looked stricken. She hadn't heard much about this side of war, and it bothered her. But her husband continued, oblivious to her distress.

"So the lieutenant knows one of his guys is trying to kill the CO, but he doesn't know who. He questions everybody and decides that Luis is the one he can break, or maybe he just chose Luis because he was a real cracker and hated Mexicans. Anyway, he decides that Luis knows something, and he starts leaning on him—giving him every shitty job, questioning him for hours, volunteering him for ambush patrol; he even took away his R and R.

"Then, when the CO was fragged, the lieutenant really went after Luis. Luis was already shaky. His nerves weren't good, and he was doing a lot of drugs. He was just getting by before the lieutenant started in on him. One night he got drunk and started saying good-bye to all of us, saying he couldn't stand it anymore and he was going to blow his brains out. We got him through that, but he kept talking about it, and on patrol he started doing crazy things, like he wanted to get killed.

"It was just a matter of time before he got himself blown away, and maybe the rest of us with him. So one night on patrol Jim and Luis and this new guy and I got separated from the other guys. We were trying to find them without Charlie finding us, and the new guy blundered onto a booby trap. Luis just broke down. He couldn't even go on. He was moaning about how he wished that was him laying on the ground. We had to shut him up, so Jim hit him and knocked him out. When morning came and Luis had come to, he was still moaning about wanting to die.

"Jim says, 'The new guy was about your size, and there isn't much left of him. He could be you.'

"So we sat there figuring out how to hide Luis and how we'd get him home without anyone finding out. It was simple to switch the tags, and there wasn't enough of the guy's uniform left to worry about. But getting Luis to someplace we could hide him was the hard part.

"Fortunately, we were in an area not too far from the orphanage. So Luis hid in the bush, and we went scouting to figure out where we were. When we hit the road, we knew we were only about five miles from the orphanage. Jim took Luis there.

"After that it was pretty easy, except that the lieutenant was suspicious as hell of our story. He got this idea that Luis was about to tell him who fragged the CO and that we'd killed him." Connors gave a snort that might have been a dry laugh.

"The funny thing was we figured they'd go nuts about not finding the new guy; that was what worried us. But when they couldn't find him, they assumed he'd been captured and listed him as missing in action; it was Luis's 'death' that they kept hassling about."

"And you shipped Luis home, just like that?" I asked with some incredulity.

"Well, it wasn't that easy. But Jim had friends, and with his connections in Supply, he could do people favors. Vietnam was really wide open; there wasn't anything you couldn't buy if you had money and knew the right people. Jim knew guys who knew guys—you know what I mean."

I didn't, but I believed his story. "Who killed the CO?" I asked.

Connors shook his head. "Oh, no. That's not something anyone needs to know."

"It could be. After all, we're looking for a killer here, and it seems to me that your man is an excellent candidate."

" 'Cause he killed the CO? No. That wasn't murder, that was self-defense and protecting your buddies. Like if there was a mad dog in the neighborhood and you knew he was going to bite someone you loved, you'd have to shoot him. Guys were dying all the time because of this guy; he had to be stopped. It wasn't murder like you think of it. Besides, it wasn't any of us."

"None of the group from Modesto?"

"No, it was someone else."

"What happened to Luis when he got home?"

"He went to Colorado, to my uncle. I wrote and told him a buddy was coming through and asked my uncle to look out for him. I guess they hit it off. Luis stayed there."

"And Jim's there with him now?"

Connors nodded.

"Then why all the mystery?"

"Because we couldn't have anyone know he was there. Luis has started having these nightmares, and they've been getting worse, so he called me and begged me to get Jim to come see him. He's cracking up; he's ready to turn himself in."

"Why Jim? Why not you or Terry?" I asked.

"Because that's what Luis wanted. He wanted Jim, no one else, I suppose because they were so close before. Or maybe because it was Jim who arranged to get him home. He was real determined that it had to be Jim."

"Letting him turn himself in might be a good idea," I suggested. "Then he could come home to his family, and he could get the counseling help he obviously needs."

"He's a deserter." Connors voice made clear his irritation at my naïveté.

"Yes, but the military isn't going to court-martial him at this point. They're only too anxious to avoid any publicity that reminds the public of the seamier side of the war. He'd just get a quiet discharge."

"No, you don't see at all!" shouted Connors. He jumped up in agitation and began pacing the floor. "The lieutenant is still pissed about the sniper and Luis's death. Jim met him in an airport last year, and the guy said something like he knew what we'd done even if he couldn't prove it.

"If the military ever found out Luis was alive, the whole thing would be opened up again, and it wouldn't be Luis's ass they'd be after, it'd be ours. They'd claim we killed the new guy to get his tags. And Luis is crazy enough now that there's no telling what the shrinks could get him to admit to.''

I saw what he meant and didn't want to. "So Luis has become a real liability to everyone involved in smuggling him out. Was anyone else involved besides you and Jim?''

Connors wasn't following too closely, or if he was, he didn't let on. ''Just Terry and John. We needed their help to pull it off.''

It was too much information to assimilate that quickly. I wasn't sure what it all meant, but it was looking increasingly possible that the veterans were in serious danger from one of their own.

I ASKED CAROL if I could have a cup of coffee and followed her to the kitchen to give myself time to think. The kitchen was a cheery yellow, warm and inviting. Beyond it, a porch had been glassed in to form a family room. The floor was strewn with children's toys, and an unfinished chess game waited on a low table.

I walked to the sliding-glass door and stood and looked out into the Connors's backyard. The grass was green, but the beds around the lawn were empty. The black soil lay turned and broken up; it reminded me of the way earth mounds up over a grave.

If Sam was telling the truth, and I was fairly sure he was, Jim Mendoza had not left town because he was about to rob First Central. I should have felt relief, but I didn't. We still had a killer out there and no idea of why he'd killed or who his next target would be. Instead of solving the riddle, Connors had just added another set of questions.

"Do you know who killed Craig now?" Carol asked as she handed me a steaming mug.

I shook my head. "It's still a bunch of pieces that don't connect," I said.

"Is Sam in danger?"

"I wish I could tell you," I replied. "I don't honestly know, but I think we'd better assume that he is until we know differently."

She bit her lip and folded her arms as if to hug herself. I walked back into the living room. Connors hadn't moved except to light another cigarette. "Who do you think killed Craig Worth?" I asked.

He shook his head. "I don't know. I only know that there wasn't any trouble till you arrived."

I nodded. "It's likely the killer followed me here. He's probably the same person who was watching Suzanne Mendoza just after Jim left."

"I don't see why anyone would be watching Suzanne," Connors said, his voice sharp with irritation.

"Had Jim been in contact with John Langer?"

Connors looked surprised. "No, I don't think so. He'd have said something if he'd seen him. No one's seen John for a couple of years."

"Craig saw him about a year ago."

"Did he? It seems like it's been longer than that."

"Langer was a part of the scheme to smuggle Ramirez out of Vietnam, wasn't he?"

"Yeah, we needed him to arrange some stuff. I didn't like to get him involved, never really trusted him, but Jim said we needed him. What's he got to do with this?"

I asked if he knew about Langer's assignment to Special Forces and his training in marksmanship and other deadly skills.

"You think *he's* the killer?" he asked, suddenly animated. "Naw, why? What reason would he have to hurt Craig?"

"If he knew Luis was falling apart, he might be afraid of having the whole story come out."

"Yeah, but Craig didn't know about Luis. Besides, how would Langer have known?"

"Maybe from Jim."

Connors was skeptical. He didn't believe that Jim would have gotten mixed up with Langer.

"Are you sure that Jim is in Colorado?" I asked.

"Yeah, there's no phone at Luis's cabin, but Jim called from my uncle's Sunday night. He wanted me to check on his wife."

"Did you tell him about me?"

"It was a week ago Sunday, before you came."

Two things were clear—I had to get to Jim Mendoza and bring him home, and I had to do that without any of us getting killed. I told Connors I was going to Colorado to bring Jim home.

"He can't leave Luis," he protested.

I told him about Suzanne. He accused me of making it up so that I could bring Jim back to the bank. "You're just interested in covering for the bank."

I wasn't in any mood to defend myself to Sam Connors. I did want to solve the First Central case. That's what I'd been hired to do, and I take my work seriously. But I also cared for the Mendozas, and in some strange way for Connors and Wheeler, too. I didn't tell him any of that. I just asked, "You want to call the hospital to check my story?"

Carol spoke up from the doorway. "Sam, you've got to help. Remember what it was like when I started spotting before Lila was born."

Connors smashed out his cigarette in the ashtray. "All right, but I'll have to go with you. Someone has to stay there to take care of Luis."

I wasn't sure how I felt about having Sam Connors along, but he clearly wasn't going to give me any choice.

I reminded him that we still needed to find a way to get to Colorado without the killer following us and warned him that the man who had bugged my phone had almost certainly bugged his as well. He promised not to try to contact Jim, and there wasn't much I could do but hope he'd keep his word.

I spent the next several hours working out a plan, then went to the hospital to run it by Peter. As I'd expected, he didn't like it.

"It's too dangerous," he said.

My plan was that Connors and I would make reservations for San Francisco to Phoenix and Phoenix to the western Colorado town of Grand Junction. In Phoenix, we'd go to the Grand Junction gate and appear to board the plane but slip away instead and board a plane for Pueblo, sixty-six miles from La Veta, the town where Ramirez lived. The police in Grand Junction would be alerted to pick up anyone matching the description of our outside player. The town was small enough so that both commercial and private planes used the same airfield, making it easy to monitor all incoming flights. It seemed to me that there was really very little danger; even if we didn't catch the killer, Connors and I would elude him.

Peter grumped about every detail, but I knew it was because he wasn't going to be part of it. Finally, he said, "What makes you think the police will go along with this scheme?"

"Commonality of interest. They want the killer; I want them to have him. The plan gives them a way to catch him. I think they'll go along."

"And you're flying through Phoenix instead of Denver because you don't want your father to know about it," Peter suggested.

"I didn't think it would do anything for his blood pressure to know that I was working a case like this."

"It'd do a lot to his blood pressure," Peter said. "Mine, too. Didn't you ever learn that you shouldn't get involved in anything you couldn't tell your parents about?"

"I wouldn't have hooked up with you if I had," I replied.

He gave me a crooked grin. "All this depends on the police agreeing to go along with you. No point in us arguing till you see them. Maybe they'll have more sense than you do."

I bent over to give him a kiss and discovered that he was feeling better. "Hmm," I murmured appreciatively. "Signs of recovery. I'd better warn the nurses."

"Nurses are safe," he declared. "You will be the first to know on the recovery front."

I met Dr. Berger on the way out. He was wearing chinos and a T-shirt that said "Berkwood Bombers," and if he hadn't also been wearing his little black badge that said "Steven Berger, M.D." and a stethoscope, I might not have recognized him.

"My son's soccer team's playing today," he said, pointing at the shirt. "Your husband's doing remarkably well. Living testimony to the virtue of staying in shape."

"His skin looks so gray," I said.

"That's from the blood loss. He'll look that way for a while. But he's recovering nicely. We'll probably take the drain out today, and if he promises to stay quiet, he can go home tomorrow or the next day."

"He won't stay quiet," I said. "You should keep him here as long as you can, because I can guarantee you that once he's out, no one will be able to keep him in bed."

He laughed. "This time I don't think he'll have a lot of choice. He's going to be very weak for quite a while."

"Just don't let him out on promises of good behavior," I warned.

Cardina didn't like my plan any better than Peter had, but he was anxious to close the files on the Craig Worth case, so he was willing to consider it.

He demanded that I tell him why I was following Mendoza and hassled me some more about the connection between the missing man and the shooter. I stuck to my story that I was looking for Mendoza because his wife was worried about his disappearance and that I didn't know anything about why the shooter was following me. It was closer to the truth than I'd have liked.

"And Jim Mendoza is in Colorado," he said. "Why?"

"I don't know," I lied. "I don't need to know why, only where."

"Why should I get involved in this?" he asked.

"Because the killer is on my trail," I pointed out. "Once I leave Modesto, he leaves; and your chances of catching him goes to just above zero."

He made noises about detaining me in Modesto; I made noises about calling my lawyer. The way he fussed you'd think I'd asked *him* to play decoy to help *me* catch the shooter. It took a lot more patience than I normally possess, but he finally agreed to go along with my plan.

We spent the rest of the afternoon making the plane reservations and arrangements. US West Airlines wasn't thrilled to have a walking target as a passenger; they complained long and hard about the additional security measures we suggested. As I listened to Cardina reassure and cajole an endless succession of bureaucrats, I discovered a new side to the man. Unfortunately, the benign good humor he lavished on airline officials disappeared as soon as he hung up the phone. After four hours with him, I'd used up my quota of good behavior for the next six months.

I called Jesse to fill him in on my plans. He fussed like a mother hen, and I assured him several times that I'd be careful. I had to tease him about losing his cool to get him off my back. He retaliated by reminding me that I'd promised to keep Daniel Martin informed of our progress and a phone call was in order.

"How's he holding up?" I asked. "He was looking fairly haggard on Monday."

"Mr. Martin does not deal well with anxiety," Jesse informed me. "Makes him real testy, which makes him even more difficult to deal with than usual. Better you should ask how I'm doing."

"You have my deepest sympathy, which will be reflected in a fat bonus if we pull this thing off," I said, then asked, "How much do you know about how Mendoza's going to get the money?"

"Not enough."

"Can you tell if he's going to do it? I mean, is there any unusual activity that would signal the theft?"

"Martin won't tell me that, but from what I can tell, there are indications. Problem is, they aren't definitive. It's like when A, B, and C happen, it could mean that the theft is about to take place. However, it could also mean that there's unusual but perfectly legitimate activity in the system."

"Have A, B, and C happened?"

"I think so. Again, I can't get Martin to confirm that, so I'm guessing based on things I've been able to learn here and from the computer security people in Sunnyvale."

"You've been able to get them to help without bringing them on board officially?" I was impressed.

"Let's just say that we've had some productive exchanges of information," Jesse replied.

"Very nice," I said. "At this rate you'll soon be sneaky enough to run for public office."

"No need to get insulting," he informed me. "Don't forget to call Mr. Martin."

29

FOR ONCE I was looking forward to calling Daniel Martin. "I've located Jim Mendoza," I announced.

"Thank God," he said, "I was afraid—But you've found him. Where is he?"

"He's in a little town in Colorado, and as far as I can tell, his reason for being there has nothing to do with the bank."

"I beg your pardon. I'm afraid I don't understand."

"It appears that he went there to help a friend."

"Help a friend?" he said incredulously. "Help a friend to five million dollars?"

"It's certainly possible that he's planning to embezzle the money," I said, "but there is another explanation for his actions. Does the computer give you any way of knowing whether he's preparing to steal the money?"

"Nothing conclusive, but, yes, there are indications. Actually, I should think that the fact someone has been shooting at you proves that he's not off on an innocent trip. Where exactly is he?"

"A place called La Veta. It's a small town in southern Colorado."

"How soon can you go get him?"

Martin must have thought he'd hired the Northwest Mounted Police or a subsidiary of the FBI. I pointed out that (a) I had no authority to compel Jim Mendoza to do anything and (b) he had not yet violated any law; therefore, even the police had no power to force him to return to San Francisco.

There was a long silence. Finally, he asked, "Well, what do you recommend? We can't just allow him to steal five million dollars."

"My usual approach would be to convince him to confess and resign quietly in exchange for the bank's promise not to prosecute. We're in a particularly good position to do that because the actual theft hasn't taken place yet. I need your assurance that if he makes no attempt to withdraw the money and resigns quietly, the bank won't take legal action."

"I hate to see him get away with it, but keeping this thing quiet is our top priority."

"There's something else involved here." I told him about the killing of Craig Worth. "I've told the police I was looking for Mendoza. I haven't told them why. If it turns out that there's a connection between the murder and the plan to rob First Central, there'll be no way to shield the bank from publicity."

"Is there a connection?" he asked.

"I don't know. I can't find any reason why Mendoza would have wanted Craig Worth dead, but I don't know why anyone else would have killed him, either."

"But you're going to Colorado to talk with Mendoza?" he asked.

"Yes."

"Isn't that risky? What about the gunman?"

"I expect he'll try to follow me," I said. "But he won't get a chance. I'm working with the police to trap him before I leave."

"It all sounds so dangerous," he said. "How will you do it?"

I explained our plan, and it seemed to reassure him. I also promised to call as soon as I'd talked with Mendoza.

"I can't tell you what a relief this is," Martin said. "I really appreciate what you and your associates have done. I know it's been difficult and dangerous. You've really done a fine job."

It's not done till it's done, I thought, but there was no point in sharing my qualms with Martin.

When I went back to the hospital that evening, Peter was feeling well enough to have become a problem for the nurses. I found him in the corridor, leaning against the wall. A young black man in pajamalike green shirt and pants was trying to cajole him into going back to bed.

"Hey, man, the doctor said for you to try walking for a *short* time. He didn't say marathon. You keep this up, you're going to burst your stitches."

Peter still didn't look like he belonged standing up, but he was slightly less gray. My relief at his recovery was quickly replaced by irritation as I realized what a hassle it was going to be to keep him in bed. "You want his attention, you better hit him in the head with a board," I suggested, not hiding the exasperation in my tone.

The nurse looked shocked, but Peter gave me a guilty grin. "Just trying to get my strength back," he said.

"Iron man strikes again. Let me help you back to bed."

"Ah, don't I wish," he said, giving the nurse a broad wink. He leaned against me as we walked back to his room.

I delivered the obligatory don't-be-a-jerk-and-do-as-the-doctor-says speech, knowing he'd ignore it, then told him of my visit to Cardina.

Peter was not overjoyed to hear of my success. "Catherine," he said seriously, "if you're going to do this, I want you to take a gun."

"No," I said. "Absolutely not."

"I mean it. What if you don't manage to shake our mystery man? And even if you do, there could be someone else out there. How do you know Mendoza is harmless? There are too damn many loose ends in this thing. I want you to carry a gun."

Peter knew how I disliked guns. I only owned one because

my ex-husband had bought me a Smith & Wesson Chief Special and insisted on teaching me to shoot it. "Look," I said, trying to be patient, "a gun isn't the answer to every problem. I'm safer relying on my aikido, which is a lot better than my marksmanship."

"Aikido won't save you if the other guy has a gun and is some distance away," Peter said.

I argued that I couldn't carry a gun on an airplane; he countered that I could put it in my suitcase. I explained that I didn't have a permit; he dismissed that as no problem as long as I didn't wave the gun in a cop's face. I pointed out that I didn't have a gun with me, and he told me to take his or have Eileen bring mine to the airport. Finally, I said, "I'll think about it."

"No," he exploded. "Catherine, please. I'm lying here in the goddamn hospital, and there's not a thing I can do to help you. Please take the gun."

There was real anguish in his voice, so I conceded. "Okay," I said, "I'll take the gun."

"And wear it. Don't leave it in your suitcase or your purse."

"I suppose you want me to stick it in my belt, the way you do. That's going to do great things for the line of my clothes."

Peter swore; he was losing patience. "Wear jeans and a jacket. And put it on as soon as you get to Pueblo, in a john at the airport."

I groaned. The thought of driving all the way from Pueblo to La Veta with a gun pressed just behind my hip was not pleasant. But I looked at the concern etched on his face and softened. I nodded and agreed.

"You don't even trust Connors?" I asked.

"Mostly I trust him, but like I said, there are too many loose ends. Right now I don't think you should trust anybody, especially not Mendoza, and that means not his friends."

We went over the plan a couple of times so that Peter could

spot any weak points. He grumbled some more, then gave me a long good-bye kiss.

"And Catherine," he called as I reached the door, "load the gun."

I gave him the finger and left.

THE FLIGHT TO Phoenix was uneventful. The problem I'd most feared, the discovery of the gun in my suitcase, never materialized. When we arrived at the Phoenix airport, a stewardess took me aside and handed me a long note. It seemed that after their original resistance, someone at US West had really gotten into the spirit of things.

Grand Junction and Pueblo are served by what they call commuter lines, small planes that carry up to thirty-seven people. You board these minijets by walking right out on the tarmac, just the way you used to board all planes. I've always liked that; it's comforting to get a chance to look your plane over up close before you climb aboard.

The note directed us to walk all the way out to the plane for Grand Junction, staying at the end of the line. As the passengers were boarding, a large catering truck would pull up; we were to climb into it, and it would take us to the gate for the Pueblo flight. Very cloak and dagger. I'll bet they loved it in the front office.

We followed instructions. I watched for the shooter, but no one matching his description was on the flight. I hoped he was either a makeup artist or charting a private plane.

* * *

The plane to Pueblo was small and noisy, the aerial version of a compact car. Connors and I had gotten the seat in the back, which was really only big enough for one and a half adults. Made me glad I'd drawn Connors rather than Wheeler for a sidekick.

I struggled to get comfortable in the tiny seat, gave up, and resigned myself to looking out the window. We were flying above heavy clouds, so all I could see was a dense carpet of white. I actually like small planes when they fly low enough so I can enjoy the scenery, but a jet VW is the worst of both worlds.

By the time we began the descent for Pueblo, I was deaf, stiff, and slightly nauseous. The clouds were still a thick layer beneath us, and I considered for the first time that it might well be snowing below. Driving snowy mountain roads ranks right up there with swimming among sharks for thrills and challenges.

The Pueblo airport isn't much more than a squat building with a tower. It matched the plane in elegance and comfort. We scrabbled down the metal staircase from the plane in gale-force winds that carried the first snow crystals. I'd forgotten how cold it gets in Colorado in the winter.

It didn't take long to get our bags. There were only ten of us getting off in Pueblo. I picked up my bag and headed for the rest room.

They hadn't heard of wheelchair accessible in Pueblo, and the toilet cubicles were not much bigger than your standard coffin. It was a real trick to get my suitcase open and my gun and parka out without dropping everything else in the toilet.

I stuck the .38 in my belt just behind my right hip. The damn thing was like an ice cube, a heavy metal ice cube. It was just as uncomfortable as I'd expected it to be. At least it wasn't too big. I'd teased Dan when he gave it to me because it seemed so small. Now I was grateful. I pulled my parka on to cover it and felt fairly smug until I realized that I needed to pee.

By the time I emerged from the rest room, Connors probably figured I'd drowned. I was painfully aware of the gun pressing against my back as I walked across the room, but no one was staring or backing away, so I assumed that it didn't show. I had my belt so tight it was cutting me in half, and I still felt like my pants might fall down.

We rented a Chevy Corsica. There weren't any four-wheel-drive vehicles available, or I'd have gone for one of those. The girl at the counter confirmed that the weathermen were predicting snow. I hoped they weren't any more reliable in Colorado than they were in California.

Pueblo is not a pretty town, not even in the summer, when the lawns are green and the trees have leaves, but especially not in the middle of winter, when the lawns are dun colored, the trees all look dead, and there are patches of dirty black ice everywhere.

It is a company town, and the company is CFI, Colorado Fuel and Iron. Their huge steel mill dominates the plains and fouls the air. It is a Faustian landscape. The mill juts up from the surrounding prairie like a demonic castle with blast furnaces and coke ovens belching fire and smoke, and slag heaps stretch out from it like great black fingers.

I'd first seen that mill as a child when we drove through Pueblo on our way to New Mexico. My dad had tried to explain the steel-making process to my sister and me, but while he talked of ore and the extracting process, I dreamed fantasies to fit this man-made version of hell. It was even more eerie at night, when railroad cars shuttled out across the top of the red-black hills and dumped their cargo of still-burning slag, setting the hills afire so that they glowed like great mounds of lava.

Say "Colorado" and people think of mountains, but southeast Colorado is flat and arid, miles of rocky, hard ground broken by an occasional butte. The only plants that grow there are small, compact, and tough, adapted through time to live with hot sun and little water. It is beautiful in the way the sea is beautiful, vast and untamed. And, like the sea, it forms half a landscape, with the sky its complement. Today both halves were dark with the impending storm.

"This is sure godforsaken land," Connors commented as we drove south through the countryside. "Never understood why anyone would want to live on the prairie."

I smiled. "It grows on you," I said.

The snow was falling steadily by the time we spotted the Spanish Peaks, and it was getting dark. The Indians called the twin peaks Huahatoya, or the breasts of the land, but white men, who were busy raping the land, had conferred a less suggestive name on them.

Connors played navigator and steered us toward La Veta. I remembered that it was in the mountains west of the Spanish Peaks, but that was as far as memory would take me. A half hour later, we passed through La Veta and took a small side road without a name.

"My uncle's place is off that way," Connors said, pointing in the opposite direction. "He got the cabin for my cousin Dale, who's sort of a loner, but Dale didn't like it, so Luis's been living there." Four miles farther, we turned up a dirt road marked only by two rusty mailboxes.

"We can't drive all the way there," Connors said as we came to a dead end where the earth fell away to a streambed. Only a footbridge crossed the ravine, and the path that continued from it turned and led into the woods. Above the trees I could see smoke from a cabin.

"It's just about fifty yards up the trail," Connors said. "I don't know what kind of shape Luis is in. Maybe I'd best go get Jim and send him down to you."

I wasn't about to let Connors out of my sight at that point, so I said, "No, I'll go up with you. You can tell Ramirez that I'm your wife or a friend or whatever you want."

"It could spook him," he protested. "He was real clear that he only wanted Jim."

"I'm going with you," I said firmly. "It's up to you to

handle Ramirez. I have only a couple of hours to get Jim back to Pueblo for the flight home, so we need to hustle.''

Connors didn't like it, but he nodded, and we got out and walked up the trail. The cabin was larger than I'd expected, more the size of a house but made from logs. I stayed a little behind him as we approached it.

We climbed the stairs to the porch. The cabin looked rustic, but it was in excellent condition. The elements are hard on structures in the mountains, and they deteriorate fast without adequate attention. Luis Ramirez might be in bad shape psychologically, but he'd still managed to take good care of his cabin.

James Mendoza answered the door. I recognized him immediately from his photo. He was wearing jeans and boots and a heavy red flannel shirt, and the expression on his face said that he wasn't expecting us. His large dark eyes were worried as he ushered us in.

The cabin looked neater than Craig Worth's bungalow, but it had that same single-man feel to it. The furniture was basic—an old couch and a couple of chairs and tables, lamps, shelves of bricks and boards, a cheap stereo system, and a kitchen table and three chairs. The large L-shaped room we'd entered had a fireplace against the left side wall. In the back on the right side, I could see a sink piled with dishes and a stove that looked older than me.

There were two doors in the wall opposite us, and a man I assumed to be Luis Ramirez emerged from the one on the right. He was shorter than Mendoza and stocky, with broad shoulders and muscular arms. His face was a rich brown, with the leathery texture that comes from life under the sun, and a scar ran along the cheekbone under his right eye. He looked anxious and unsure of what to do. His eyes flicked from Connors to me and back again.

Connors greeted him heartily and introduced me as his sister. ''She came along to visit Uncle Ralph,'' he explained. ''Always was his favorite.'' Mendoza was watching me closely. ''Isn't that black eye a beaut? Don't let her tell you I gave it to her.'' He laughed, and they joined in.

I gave him a playful punch and said, "Don't let him tell you he didn't want to." They laughed at that, too, and Ramirez seemed to relax some.

"Ralph tells me you bought that little sorrel off him," Connors said to Ramirez.

Ramirez nodded. "Yeah, she's a good little horse. Gets skittish sometimes, but mostly she's fine."

"Where you keeping her?" Connors asked. "You got a place here?"

"Out back. I built a corral and a shed big enough for three, four horses. Got me a real nice quarter mare out there, too."

"Well, hey, I gotta see that. Let's go see that." He moved toward the back of the cabin.

Ramirez looked uncertain. "You wanta come, Jim?" he asked.

"I have news from Suzanne," I said, putting my hand on Mendoza's arm. "Can he come after we talk?"

Ramirez didn't look happy, but he pulled on a jacket and moved toward the back door with Connors at his heels.

As soon as the door closed, I told Mendoza that Suzanne had been hospitalized because of the danger of premature delivery. He looked absolutely stricken.

"Oh, my God," he cried. "I've got to get to her. What happened? Is the baby okay?"

"They baby's fine now, but if she were to deliver, the chances of the baby surviving wouldn't be good," I told him.

"She was doing fine. There was no sign of trouble at the last checkup. What went wrong?"

"They don't know, but the fact that she's worried sick about you can't have helped."

"I didn't realize . . . I've got to pack. Can you drive me to town?"

"I've got reservations on the seven o'clock plane from Pueblo to Denver, then on to San Francisco," I said. "While you pack, maybe you can tell me about the man who bugged your phone, watched your house, and started following me when I went looking for you."

That was a real showstopper; he just stared at me with an incredulous look on his face.

"It wouldn't have anything to do with the bank's five million dollars would it?" I asked.

Not a flicker of recognition. I was getting tired of this game. I was also getting very hot in my parka, but I couldn't take it off without revealing my gun, so I just stood there and steamed, which didn't improve my patience. Finally, I said, "I'm here because Daniel Martin sent me."

"But why?' he asked.

"To stop you from withdrawing the five million," I said.

Mendoza looked thoroughly confused, and it was catching. "Why would he suspect me of stealing money?" he asked.

"Maybe because you disappeared rather mysteriously," I suggested.

"But I told him I'd be gone. He approved a three-week leave."

Now it was my turn to be silent. The pieces were finally falling together, and I didn't like the picture they made.

31

I HAD JUST enough time to figure out that our outside player must be Daniel Martin's hired gun when the door burst open. He looked just as he'd been described—white male, thirties, medium height, straight brown, longish hair. He didn't look particularly impressive, but the automatic in his hand made up for that.

He stepped in and kicked the door shut. "Put your hands

on your heads," he ordered in a voice that was surprisingly high. I'd seen what he'd done to Peter and Craig, so I had no illusions about his abilities. I put my hands on my head.

Mendoza was frozen. One too many surprises had left him dazed and slow to react. "Do as he says," I urged. He did.

The hit man looked around the room quickly. There was a rifle leaning against the wall near him. He moved over in front of it.

"Where's the other guy?" he asked.

Jim was too stunned to reply. I kept silent. The gunman was in a tough spot. Having Connors unaccounted for presented a problem. If he shot us now, he'd alert the missing man and lose the advantage of surprise. Connors could run, or he could fight. Neither would be good for the gunman.

"Where is he? Answer me."

"In the bedroom," I said.

"Get him out."

"You get him," I said, not feeling nearly as brave or cocky as I sounded. Our only chance lay in playing for time, time for Connors and Ramirez to come back to the house. I prayed that I was right in my assumption that the gunman would wait until he had us all together.

"Call him," he ordered Jim.

"Don't," I said. "He's only waiting for Sam so he can shoot us all together."

Jim looked confused, disoriented. The gunman's face was an expressionless mask. With his left hand, he pulled a pair of handcuffs from his jacket pocket. He tossed them on the floor in front of Jim and ordered him to put them on. "Don't screw around or I'll shoot the lady," he said in that soft, high voice.

"Don't put them on," I warned Jim. "He doesn't want to kill you here. He needs to take you someplace else so that when they find Sam and me, they'll think you shot us."

The gunman's lips curled a fraction in what might have been a smile. "No reason not to shoot you, sweetie," he said, raising the gun slightly. "Put on those cuffs quick or I'll do her."

"And warn our friend? I don't think so," I said, trying to put more conviction into my voice than I felt. "Besides, you'll shoot me either way."

"Yeah," he said. "But get this. You can die from a gut shot same as one in the head. It just takes a lot longer. Your choice."

Jim bent and picked up the handcuffs. He snapped one on his left wrist, then began fumbling with the other one. It's not real easy to cuff yourself, but it's nowhere near as hard as Jim made it look. I hoped it was an act to stall.

"Hurry it up, or she gets it," the gunman warned.

Time to play my last card. "Wait," I said. "I'll call him. He'd already be here if he weren't deaf as a post. Sam," I yelled at the top of my lungs, with my face turned toward the bedroom door. I yelled a couple of more times.

The hit man was watching the bedroom door when Sam threw open the back door and yelled, "Somebody calling me?" It startled him enough to draw his attention away from me for a few seconds. I grabbed my gun, dropped to one knee, and fired.

I'm not a great shot, and I missed the first time. By the time I got the second shot off, he had turned back to me. As I saw the gun swing toward me, I fired again, then reacted as I would in the dojo. I rolled backward to get out of the way.

I heard his shot, but I was alive as I came up. I probably wouldn't have stayed that way long if he'd had another shot, but before he or I could fire, another gun barked.

The bullet hit him in the middle of the chest and knocked him backward against the wall. The gun fell to the floor, and he slid down the wall just the way they do in the movies. No one moved; we all stared at the body.

Finally, when I was sure he was really out and wouldn't grab his gun, I turned to see who'd fired the fatal shot. Luis Ramirez stood by the back door with a rifle in his hand. He looked like he was in a state of shock.

I went to the hit man and kicked the gun away, then felt for a pulse in his neck. There was none, and at the rate he was bleeding, we couldn't have saved him if there was. Luis must have hit him right in the heart. But he was also bleeding from an arm wound, so I wasn't as bad a shot as I'd thought.

I turned back to Luis. After what Connors had told me, I was afraid that this would send him over the edge. When he exploded with "Who the fuck was that?" we all relaxed.

Now attention shifted to me. "What's going on?" Jim demanded, speaking for all three of them.

I told them what I'd figured out in the moments before the hit man burst in on us. Much of it was speculation, but it was the only story that fit the facts. Daniel Martin must have been planning to use the computer flaw to rob First Central before Jim Mendoza called to ask for a leave. When Jim refused to explain where he was going, Martin may have suspected that he, too, was about to rob the bank. Or he may simply have seen an opportunity to frame Jim for his own crime.

He realized that if Jim were to disappear, everyone would assume that he had embezzled the missing funds. But for the plan to work, Jim had to disappear permanently, and that was why Martin had hired me. My role was to find Jim and lead the hit man to him. Had the scheme succeeded, the hit man would probably have killed me and left my body where it would be found easily. He'd have taken Jim to some remote spot to kill him and disposed of his body down an old mine shaft or some other place where it wouldn't be found. The police would assume that Jim had killed me, embezzled the money, and gone into hiding. All their efforts would concentrate on finding him while Martin lived the good life back in San Francisco.

It was a very tidy plan, and I felt like a damn fool for not suspecting Daniel Martin. It was a bit of consolation that Jim found it difficult to believe his boss was capable of such machinations.

"But why'd he shoot Craig?" Connors asked.

I explained to Jim and Luis what had happened in Modesto. They were both shocked and saddened, but after what we'd been through, they were still a bit numb.

"Craig must have followed me after I left him. He wasn't too fond of me, but I think he liked Peter, and he probably decided to be my protector while Peter was in the hospital. The gunman saw him. He knew that Craig had attacked me once, so he got worried that he might be after me again. He needed me alive to find Jim."

"So he shot Craig to protect you?" Connors asked.

"That's my guess," I said.

Connors shook his head and stared at the floor so we wouldn't see the tears in his eyes. "Just a big fucking mistake."

We sat silent witness to his pain until Luis pulled out a bottle of bourbon and poured healthy glasses for all three of us. As I picked mine up, my hand was shaking. I don't drink straight whiskey, and it burned my mouth, but I needed something to slow my heart down before it banged a hole in my chest.

I sank into a chair and tried to breathe deeply. My mind was numb, but my entire body was reacting to the fact that it had narrowly escaped death. My muscles had turned to Jell-O, and I couldn't seem to catch my breath.

I knew it would pass, but I also knew what would follow—nights of replaying those few minutes in vivid detail, waking soaked in sweat with my heart pounding, being afraid to go back to sleep because the whole thing would start over again.

Finally, my body began to calm down. I looked at Sam, Jim, and Luis. They didn't look any better than I felt. All three were pale and shaky, but no one was falling apart.

I noticed the handcuff dangling from Jim's wrist. The key must be in the gunman's pocket, but I didn't want to look for it. Dan always said that there was no legitimate reason for anyone to carry a set of lock picks, but I'd just found one. I dug the picks from my purse and freed Jim's wrist.

"How was that for stalling?" Jim asked proudly.

He described for the others what had happened while they were out at the barn, making me sound a lot braver than I'd been and giving a comical repeat performance of his struggle with the cuffs.

"Good thing you stalled," Connors said. "We just barely heard you as we were coming back toward the cabin."

I congratulated Luis on his quick thinking and good marksmanship, and Sam and Jim joined in enthusiastically.

Luis acted embarrassed but pleased. "Good thing I keep that gun by the door," he said. "Foxes kept going after my chickens, so I put it there so I could nail them."

Jokes about foxes and hit men, with a lot more laughter than they warranted, and another round of bourbon—stage two of the recovery process. Finally, I pointed out that we were going to have to call the police. "Are you in the city limits here, or is this county land?"

"County," Ramirez replied. "I think the sheriff's down in Walsenburg."

"Can you handle talking to cops?" Jim asked him. "We could drop you off at Ralph's and say you weren't here when it happened."

"I could say it was me shot him," Connors offered. "It's self-defense, anyway."

Luis considered. "Might be best. I can handle the cops, but there'd be fingerprints probably."

"Were you ever arrested and fingerprinted?" I asked.

He shook his head.

"Then you don't have to worry. They'll take your prints, but they won't find a match. Military prints aren't in the search," I said. "It's usually safest to tell the truth. That way you don't have to worry about being caught in a lie. You can tell them that Jim just came for a visit, which is true, and you don't have to tell them why."

We discussed it some, and Luis decided he could handle telling things as they'd happened. The bourbon had warmed my stomach and taken care of the shakes. Luis offered me another glass, but I wanted to be close to sober when I talked with the sheriff. Jim and I went out to find a phone.

There was a green Ford parked behind the Chevy, and the Chevy wouldn't start. I figured the problem went beyond the cold, and a quick check of the engine confirmed my fear. The distributor cap was missing. The hit man had made sure we couldn't make a run for it.

I wasn't anxious to go through a dead man's pockets to find his keys or our distributor cap. Besides, we needed the cops firmly on our side, and I knew that messing up the crime scene wouldn't endear us to them, so we went back to the house to see if there was any other way to reach a phone.

Luis volunteered to ride to the ranch over the hill where there was a phone, and Connors offered to go along. That left Jim and me and the bottle of bourbon. We made some coffee and put a couple of more logs on the fire, then sat near it with our backs to the dead man.

"Will Luis really be okay?" I asked.

"I think so. He's calmed down a lot since I got here," Jim said. "Hasn't had nightmares for a couple of nights. I think he just needed to talk, about the war. The rest of us got to talk it out when we came home, but Luis had to keep it all inside. He got real confused, especially about that night on patrol. He half-believed he'd killed the new guy so he could get home."

"You think he can handle the police, then? They could put a lot of pressure on him if they don't accept what we tell them."

Jim nodded. "I know, but what's messing him up is that he can't talk about 'Nam; he sure doesn't need another thing he can't talk about."

"Good point. Tell me one more thing, why didn't you tell Suzanne where you were going?"

Jim's coffee cup was empty. He rolled it between his hands. "Well, in the beginning I didn't tell her because I'd promised the others I wouldn't. Before we put Luis on the plane, we swore that we'd never tell anyone, not even family; and we made Luis promise that he would never contact his family. His mother was dead, and he wasn't close to his father, but it was real hard for him to know he wouldn't see his sisters and brother again. We promised we'd be his family.

"Once we were back and I met Suzanne and settled down, I began to realize the seriousness of what we'd done. In 'Nam, we just did what had to be done without too much thought of the future, but suddenly I realized that I could go to jail for a very long time.

"Then, a year or so ago, I met the guy who was our commanding officer in 'Nam at the airport and found out he's still after us. It scared me to death, but I figured if I just stayed away from Luis, I'd be okay."

"But you couldn't stay away when he called Connors," I put in.

"No, I had to come. But I couldn't tell Suzanne. It would have upset her too much. We've waited a long time for this baby; I didn't want her worrying that someone was going to come along and drag me off to jail. I've gone off like this for years. I didn't think it'd cause a problem."

"What about John Langer? Is he involved in this?"

Mendoza looked surprised. "No, I haven't seen John in years."

"He was one of our suspects. He fit the description of the man who was watching your house. We even thought he might be working for the CIA."

Mendoza laughed. "I doubt that even the CIA would take John. He was working on serious alcoholism last time I saw him. Trying to forget Vietnam. He's a mean drunk."

We sat quietly for a few moments. I watched the man whom I'd thought about day and night for the last two weeks. I knew more about him than I knew about most of my friends. I'd assembled information, examined his character under a microscope, and struggled to understand what made him the man he was. From all that, I'd constructed a scenario that was rational, logical, and on the one point that mattered, totally wrong.

We go through life getting only part of the story, and from that part we construct meaning. If it "makes sense," we believe it. Our meaning becomes our reality. Truth doesn't have a whole lot to do with anything.

Mendoza got up and poked at the fire, and I brought my thoughts back to the case, and to Daniel Martin. There was a very good chance that while Martin wouldn't get the money, he'd never be charged with Craig's death or Peter's shooting. With the hit man dead, we had no way of connecting him to Martin.

I wanted Martin to answer for his crimes. I also wanted Jim Mendoza cleared of any question of wrongdoing. There had to be some way to trap Martin.

Sam and Luis got back about a half hour later, and it was another hour before the sheriff and his deputy arrived. The sheriff was about forty-five, short and squarish, with an ample belly that strained the buttons of his sport shirt. With his cowboy hat and boots and his string tie, he looked very much like the Hollywood version of a small-town western sheriff. His deputy looked about fifteen and stood extra straight to make himself look taller and more official.

The older man introduced himself as Sheriff Valardi, and his speech had a Hispanic cadence. He looked around the room, puffed out his lips and sucked them in a couple of times, then squatted by the corpse. Finally, he turned to us and said, "Tell me about it."

I offered him and the deputy a seat, and Luis brought coffee while I spun out the story. He listened without interrupting, his face absolutely expressionless. It's a real trick to keep your face that neutral and unnerving as hell to the person doing the talking. The cabin felt uncomfortably warm by the time I finished.

He puffed out his lips a couple more times. "You know this fella?" he asked.

I shook my head. "I never saw the man who was following me, but this guy fits the description of two witnesses. From the way he operated, I assume he was a pro."

"You say the Modesto police are involved in this. Any officer come along with you?"

"No, we didn't want to make him suspicious."

"So you're out here on your own."

I nodded. "Lieutenant Cardina in Modesto can confirm what I've told you."

The sheriff looked at each of us with his impassive expression and nodded to himself, then announced, "I'm going to have to ask you people to come down to the courthouse in Walsenburg." He turned to the deputy, whose face was far from impassive, and said, "Jimmy, you wait here and secure the crime scene; don't let anyone mess with it till the boys from the state police get here."

"Yessir," the deputy barked. He looked as if this was the biggest assignment he'd ever gotten and was standing at attention to convey his professional competence. That boy was headed for back trouble when he got older.

The ride to the courthouse was silent. I got in the front seat with the sheriff, and the men squeezed into the back. The snow had stopped, which was a good thing, since Sheriff Valardi drove like he was trying out for the Indy 500.

THE HUERFANO COUNTY Courthouse is a two-story sandstone governmental Gothic on the main street of Walsenburg. I remember hearing that Mother Jones was once imprisoned in the basement there. In most places, public buildings of the last century started out as the biggest, grandest edifices in town, only to be dwarfed as newer commercial buildings sprouted. But the flush of prosperity that produces ever-larger buildings has passed Walsenburg by, and the courthouse was still the most impressive structure on the main street.

Inside it was high ceilings and dark wood. The sheriff's office was on the ground floor at the end of a short corridor. It had a frosted window with Huerfano County Sheriff's Office emblazoned on it in heavy black letters and inside a little wooden rail with a swinging gate that separated the room into two sections. Looked like it had been designed in Hollywood.

Another fifteen-year-old deputy sat at an old oak desk that an antique dealer would have snapped up in a minute. He had bright red hair and freckles, and the sheriff called him Luke. Valardi had him take the three men into one room while he took me into another. He brought in a portable tape recorder and had me go through the whole story again.

So far he hadn't given me a clue as to whether he believed a word I said. If I couldn't convince him to trust me, I was going to end up spending the next forty-eight hours in Walsenburg while Daniel Martin collected his five million dollars and disappeared into the sunset.

I tried to explain that to Valardi. Still no reaction. He simply thanked me for my cooperation and left the room. I waited, then waited some more. There wasn't a damn thing in the room to distract me, not even a magazine. I was into some serious pacing by the time Valardi returned.

"Lieutenant Cardina in Modesto confirms your story, and Lieutenant Donnely in San Francisco says nice things about you. Tells me you were married to a police officer."

I admitted that I had been married to Lt. Dan Walker of Homicide and tried not to think about how Dan would react to the news that his ex-wife was in trouble again.

"Then you probably understand that I have a problem here," he said. "You want to leave right away to get back to California, but you're a witness to a homicide here, and actually a bit more than a witness, since you admit to having shot the dead man, too. It'll be some time, probably days, before we can make a judgment on this, and then there's still the coroner's jury that'll want to hear from you.

"Now if you lived over in the next county, I could probably let you go home till I needed you, but California's a long ways. It's another jurisdiction, not easy to get people back who don't want to come. The district attorney, he'd be real upset if I let you go at this point."

"But the Modesto police have confirmed my story."

"Well, now, they've told me what you told them. They don't really have any proof that that's what happened. You see, for them this isn't such a problem; there's no evidence you're involved in their homicide. But here, you're involved. If we find that this isn't self-defense, you'd be an accessory. So while it's no big deal for them to let you go, for me it could mean a major blunder."

He took out a pack of chewing gum and offered me a piece. I accepted, and we each concentrated on extracting the gum from its wrapper and inserting it in our mouths. Finally, after he'd taken a few chews, Valardi continued. "And then there's the matter of the gun, the one you shot the deceased with."

"It's mine; it's not registered in Colorado, and I don't have a carry permit," I volunteered.

He nodded and made a clicking sound. "Well, you were on private property, and you don't need a permit to have a gun on your person on private property, so that's not a problem, assuming you didn't carry it as a concealed weapon on public property, say, the freeway."

His manner told me he wasn't looking for a confession, so I kept my mouth shut and just nodded.

"Possession of an unlicensed weapon is not a serious offense so long as you don't commit a crime with it," he commented. "Probably be a fine and a lecture from the judge."

"Does that mean you're going to release me?"

"Oh, no, I can't do that. I expect you get a lot of murders in San Francisco, but out here we don't have many, and the ones we have are usually pretty straightforward. This case is going to cause a good bit of excitement; newspapers are going to love it. I screw up and I'm going to look real bad. That's not going to happen.''

''But this story is much bigger than a guy getting shot in a cabin in La Veta,'' I pointed out. ''It involves a major bank and five million dollars. You could be part of an interstate effort that catches the thief and saves the money. That ought to make impressive headlines.''

He puffed his lips and considered. ''Well, now, I only have your word for that. From what you tell me, there isn't anyone at the bank that can confirm it for you.''

It was true; I couldn't very well have him call Daniel Martin for confirmation, and I didn't know if Martin had told his superiors at the bank about hiring me. Then, suddenly, I saw the way out.

''But you *can* call the bank for confirmation,'' I declared. ''Suppose you were to call the bank official who hired the dead man at the cabin and tell him that you'd found my body. If what I've told you about him is true, he'll give you a story about how Jim Mendoza is embezzling money from the bank, and he'll suggest that Jim probably killed me when I found him. He'll admit that he hired me, and that should confirm my story.''

Valardi shook his head. ''Now, I'm just a country boy, but I do know that when things get this complicated, it's best to go slow.''

I was getting desperate. It looked like I might have to call my dad in Denver and get him to post a bond. He was not going to be at all happy to hear what I was mixed up in. In fact, he might just suggest that Valardi throw me in a cell for a few days to teach me a lesson. We'd both be a lot happier if I could avoid waking him up in the middle of the night to tell him I'd almost gotten myself killed and needed to get back to San Francisco so I could have a second try at it.

I had one last idea. ''Maybe you should accompany me to San Francisco. You could keep an eye on me, and you could also be part of the investigation of the banker. I think it's technically the Modesto department's case, but San Francisco will have to be involved, and Huerfano County should be, too."

He smiled. I don't know which appealed to him, the possible glory of a major bust or a short vacation in California, but it looked like things were finally going my way.

"What makes you think you can catch this banker?" Valardi asked. He pointed out that if the man at the cabin was a professional, we'd probably never find out much about him, and he wouldn't have anything identifying his employer.

"It'll be up to Lieutenant Cardina," I said. "But I'd be willing to wear a wire and confront Martin. I could pretend to want a cut of the five million to stay quiet, and he'd probably incriminate himself."

"Or he'd try to kill you," Valardi said.

"I don't think he's got the guts to kill me himself. Hiring someone else to do the dirty work is more his style. Anyway, I assume the police would be close enough to step in."

We discussed it a bit more. The sheriff was as sharp as I'd suspected he was. Like many lawmen, he had a feral intelligence that would have made him a wealthy man had he chosen the other side of the law.

"I'll have to talk to the district attorney, of course," he said finally, "but I think we can arrange it."

This time when we went out, he asked if I wanted some coffee, which I took as a sign that he'd decided we were on the same side. I'd had enough police coffee to know better; I asked for tea.

It took a good part of the night to work out the details. The snowy roads caused several accidents, and a man was seriously wounded in a knife fight at a roadside bar. The sheriff's office filled up with angry, loud people who wanted immediate attention. Valardi and his deputies took statements, issued warnings and advice, and tried to keep the crowd moving.

It was late, but I knew Peter wouldn't be able to sleep until he heard from me, so I called the hospital. The nurse informed me that he had been released that afternoon and was presumably at home now. I'd known this would happen, but it irritated me, anyway.

"But he just had the tube taken out of his chest," I said.

"I wasn't on duty, Mrs. Harman, but I understand that he was most anxious to get home. We don't hold patients prisoner here. I believe he was released against medical advice."

"Will he be all right?" I asked.

My anxiety softened her response. "They wouldn't have let him go home if they thought it posed a serious risk," she said. "The danger is that if he moves around too much, he could reopen the wound. As long as he stays quiet, he should be all right."

Peter stay quiet? Fat chance. I thanked her and hung up. Peter answered on the first ring.

"I see you went over the wall," I observed dryly.

"Never mind that, what happened to you?"

"I found Mendoza," I said. "The hit man found us. He's dead, and we're alive, so you can relax." Peter wanted all the details. He was as surprised as I was by Martin's scheme, and he had the same chagrined reaction to the fact that we'd fallen for it. Peter was in amazingly good shape for a man who'd been shot twice in the chest, but I was fading, so I made him promise to go to bed and stay there and said good-night.

Next I called Jesse. He was incredulous when I revealed Martin's role in the case. "I wouldn't have guessed he had it in him," he said. "Never seemed to have either the guts or the imagination."

"Greed does amazing things. Besides, it doesn't take a lot of guts to hire someone to kill for you," I said.

I explained that Martin must believe that his plan had worked until I was ready to confront him. Jesse offered to call Martin the next morning and pretend to be worried because he hadn't heard from me.

My biggest concern was time. Monday was the fourteenth day, the day that the funds would be wired. That left me a little under twenty-four hours to get back to San Francisco and maneuver Martin into admitting his guilt. If it had just been a matter of getting my own team organized, it wouldn't be so bad, but I despaired when I thought of trying to get the Modesto and San Francisco police departments to agree on a plan and coordinate their efforts in less than a day.

If anyone could make all that happen, it was my ex-husband, Dan Walker. So I pulled out my credit card and made yet another call to San Francisco.

It was one o'clock in California, and Dan's voice was fuzzy with sleep. I started slowly to give him a chance to wake up. By the time I got to the hit man's appearance at the cabin, he was awake. It was like going through interrogation all over again, except that Dan asked even more questions than Valardi had.

When I told him my plan, there was a long silence. "We don't have jurisdiction," he said. "Modesto would have to request our assistance before we could do anything."

"But if they did, you could participate?"

"Yes, sure."

"Dan, this has to happen by tomorrow night; Monday morning he'll have the five million dollars."

"I'd say we have enough justification to pick him up for questioning if Modesto requests it. Even if they don't, we can pick him up on suspicion of embezzlement so he won't get away with the bank's money."

"But you'd have to find the money to prove anything, and we may not be able to figure out how to trace it. Even if we can find it, I don't know that we can tie it to Martin."

"He could walk, it's true," Dan said. "It'd be a lot better to get him to implicate himself."

"Which leads us back to: Can you cut enough red tape to pull this off in the next twenty-four hours?"

"I'll call Cardina in Modesto and see what I can do," he promised. He couldn't resist hassling me over the danger of confronting Martin, and he was sure there must be a safer way than the one I'd devised, but I let that all pass and figured we could argue over it when I was back home.

33

VALARDI, MENDOZA, AND I left Walsenburg sometime before the crack of dawn with too little sleep and too much adrenaline. We caught the eight o'clock plane out of Pueblo for Denver, ran from the end of one concourse to the end of another, feeling the effects of the altitude every step of the way, and arrived in Oakland at 11:40 A.M. It was a trip I hope never to repeat.

Since Jim and I were supposed to be dead, I chose the Oakland airport over San Francisco to avoid meeting anyone we knew. Oakland, San Francisco's poor cousin across the Bay, still suffers from Gertrude Stein's judgment that "there is no there there." Like Rodney Dangerfield, it just can't get no respect.

Its airport is modern and efficient and has about one-tenth the number of people per square foot as San Francisco's. It was enough to make me weep over the hours I'd wasted trying to park at S.F. International and the hassles I'd put up with there.

Amy met us at the baggage carousel. She recognized Jim from his picture and greeted him with the good news that the doctor had sent Suzanne home because she was doing better and that she was anxiously awaiting his return.

"Annlyn will intercept any calls or visitors," she told me,

"because Mrs. Mendoza is too upset by her husband's disappearance to see anyone."

I smiled my approval and introduced Sheriff Valardi. He was still wearing boots and a cowboy hat, but he'd donned a tweed sport coat and substituted a real tie for the string tie he'd worn in Colorado.

I was glad to see that Amy had brought my Volvo instead of her little Japanese car. Her car was fuel efficient as hell, but we'd never have gotten ourselves and our luggage into it.

"You got the seats fixed," I exclaimed in delight.

"Peter said you'd like that done," she replied. "Poor Alfonse was horrified."

Poor Alfonse would be perfecting his lecture on the responsibilities of car ownership. I'd have preferred slashed seats.

I gave Sheriff Valardi the front seat, since he was the tourist, and Amy turned into an instant tour guide, yet another side to her multifaceted personality that I hadn't known about. The Nimitz Freeway doesn't have a lot of tourist attractions, so she managed to find time to tell me that our crew was at the office and that Dan and Cardina would meet me there at one.

I walked into my office and found Jesse, Eileen, and Chris huddled around my desk and Peter lying on the couch. His skin was still grayish, and he looked like the before part of an ad for embalming fluid.

"You look like a vampire who's been on a diet," I said.

"That's about the way I feel," he replied.

"This, I suppose, is bed rest."

"Might as well be. I'm just a spectator. We're all waiting for the full scoop on what happened in Colorado."

I introduced Jim Mendoza and Sheriff Valardi. Jim was in a hurry to get home, so I sent him off with Amy while I recounted, for what seemed the hundredth time, my adventures in La Veta. I also filled them in on my plan to get Martin to confess to hiring the hit man.

When I finished, they all looked to Peter. He cleared his throat and said, "There's another way this could be done."

It didn't take a rocket scientist to figure out that they'd already worked out the other way. "Oh?" I said.

Jesse spoke up. "If you confront him, he'll know the jig's up, and he'll probably suspect you're trying to entrap him. But if I call and tell him I've figured out how to catch Mendoza when he withdraws the money tomorrow, what do you think he'll do?"

"Probably try to kill you."

"Right, and if we set it up right, we'll get him."

"And if we set it up wrong," I said, "you'll be dead."

Jesse didn't look like he thought that was a serious problem, which worried me. He explained that they'd figured out how to set things up so he'd be safe. I reminded him that I'd done that when I went to Colorado and things hadn't worked exactly as planned. We argued for a while, and finally I said, "No, it's too dangerous."

Jesse's face grew tight with anger. "You're saying you don't trust me not to screw up."

"No, I'm saying I don't want to risk your getting hurt."

"You can't do that, Catherine," Peter said quietly. "You won't let anyone smother you in the name of protection. You can't do that to him."

"I'm not smothering him," I said. "I just don't want to see him hurt." I could hear the echoes of my parents and my ex-husband in those words, and it made me uncomfortable to the point of irritation.

"I'll have to quit, Catherine," Jesse said. "I can't stay with you if you're never going to let me take the initiative."

"Oh, shit," I said. I hate being wrong, and I especially hate being wrong in front of a roomful of people. "All right, all right. If you want to risk it, I'll go along."

Everyone in the room seemed to sigh with relief, and I realized that they'd all known exactly how the argument would go; they'd probably even practiced it. I'd been out-gunned.

Dan and Cardina arrived exactly at one. Both were surprised to see Peter there. Dan and Peter are never comfortable in the same room together. They were so stiffly polite to each other that they made everybody else uncomfortable, too.

I let Jesse describe the plan, since he was the one who was putting his neck on the line. Dan was enthusiastic in his response. I'd known he would be.

Jesse'd drawn a plan of the inside of the bank. He'd been working in a room with several workstations. None of the other employees would be in on a Sunday, so he planned to ask Martin to meet him there. The great virtue of the room was that it had an alcove with the copying machine in it; two men could stand at the back of the alcove and be out of sight. We could put another man across the hall, where he could come in behind Martin if need be.

"What if he decides to take Jesse hostage?" I asked.

"If he threatened Jesse, we'd have to shoot him," Dan said calmly.

"I think Jesse should wear a bullet-proof vest," I said.

Jesse started to object. "Be a good idea," Peter put in, and Jesse acquiesced.

"We'll use a wire so the men across the hall can hear what's going on," Dan said. Cardina and Valardi both nodded.

"I think you want a backup plan just in case you do get into a hostage situation," Valardi said. Cardina shrugged, as if to say that wasn't necessary, but he looked to Dan. It may have been Modesto's case, but it was clear who was in charge.

"Always good to be careful," Dan said, and we started working out the backup plan. Valardi may have been a small-town sheriff, but his instincts were good, and he more than kept up with the big-city boys.

Dan wanted to put sharpshooters at both ends of the

hall. Valardi puffed his lips a couple of times, then said, "I always wondered what'd happen if you greased the floor, made it real hard for a fellow to keep his footing."

"The Crisco method of hostage rescue," Cardina said. He looked disgusted, but Dan and Peter were intrigued. We played with the idea until one of us realized that Martin might shoot when he slipped. We ended up relying on the sharpshooters, and backup units outside.

The final step was deciding who went where. Dan and Cardina took the alcove. Valardi and Dan's partner, Jerry, drew the room across the hall. I asked to join them. Dan agreed, but only because he couldn't face the hassle he knew I'd put up if he tried to freeze me out of my own case.

Peter didn't ask; he just announced that he'd come with me.

"Oh, no," I said. "You can hardly stand up. You'll do more for Jesse by staying here."

He didn't like it, but he knew it was true, and he grudgingly agreed.

It was three o'clock. Dan called Jerry and arranged for the sharpshooters and backup units. We were ready to head for First Central.

I sent the others on ahead and came back to Peter. "My gun's in Colorado," I said. "Lend me yours?"

He raised an eyebrow, but he didn't say anything. He just reached under the jacket folded on the floor at the side of the couch and pulled out the Colt.

"You know how to use an automatic?"

"Well enough," I said.

34

THE ROOM ACROSS from Jesse's office was small and hot, and putting three of us in it just made it smaller and hotter. There was a desk but no chair. Dan's partner, Jerry, put the recording equipment on the desk and then leaned against the wall. Valardi and I leaned against the opposite wall.

Dan had replaced the security guards downstairs with his men, and the sharpshooters were in place at both ends of the hall. We listened as Jesse made his call to Martin. Beyond his original announcement that he'd found a way to catch Mendoza when he pulled the money out of the system, all we heard was a series of grunts and murmurs ending in "Right, 'bye."

After he hung up, we heard Jesse announce, "He bit. He'll be right down."

I tried to look cool leaning against my wall, but it got old fast. Finally, I slid down and sat on the floor. There was barely room to stretch out my legs. Valardi took my lead and sat down next to me, and a few minutes later Jerry joined us.

For the first twenty minutes I was jumpy and nervous, for the next twenty I was bored, and by the time Jerry's walkie-talkie crackled to life with the announcement that our man was on his way up, I was dozing. We scrambled to our feet, and I could tell by the grimace on Valardi's face that his legs had stiffened up just as mine had.

The sheriff drew his gun from his shoulder holster and moved up next to the door. Jerry stayed by the desk with the tape machine. I pulled Peter's automatic from my purse and took my place behind Valardi.

Jerry had one set of headphones. I picked up the second set and held it between Valardi and me so we could hear what was happening across the hall. Jesse's microphone was a good one. I could hear the door open as Martin entered. My heart started to pound, and my mouth got dry. Waiting it out while Jesse faced Martin was going to be infinitely harder than facing him myself.

Jesse went through the rap he'd worked out with the guys at Computer Security. It sounded like gobbledygook to me; I hoped it fooled Martin. There was a long pause when he finished, during which I imagined Martin pulling a knife or gun. Finally, he said, "You really think it'll work?"

"Absolutely."

"Good work, very good work," Martin said. The recording distorted his voice just enough so I couldn't be sure of the tone. "This is a great relief. A great relief. I've underestimated your abilities. I believe this calls for a drink. Will you join me?"

"Gee, I'd like to," Jesse said, "but I was just starting the process I told you about, and I need to finish it before I do anything else."

"You've already started?" Martin asked, and I thought I could hear the strain in his voice. Little lines of sweat trickled down the side of Valardi's face. The room felt like an oven, and the air was stale. I had trouble breathing.

"Well, I just started, but if I turn the machine off now, the work I've done will be lost."

"Don't worry about that," Martin suggested. "You can start it again later. I'll help you, but I'm ready for a drink now, and I'll bet you could use one, too."

"No, I think I better finish this now."

There was another pause and then Jesse's voice, an octave higher than usual, "What the hell? What's that for?"

I reached past Valardi to grab the doorknob, opened the door, and shut it loudly. A reminder to Martin that he wasn't alone in the building.

We heard Martin's voice. "Shut the computer off and come with me."

"You're the one," Jesse charged. "It isn't Mendoza; it's you that's about to rob the bank, isn't it?"

"Just shut off the computer."

"Where's Catherine? Oh, my God, that's why she hasn't called, isn't it? What did you do to her?" Jesse was giving an all-out, Oscar-quality performance, but Martin was muffing his lines. He didn't seem to understand that this was the point where the villain tells all.

"The man who was following her, was he working for you?"

"Shut it off," Martin said.

"Hey, man, you don't have to kill *me*," Jesse argued. "I can keep a secret. Matter of fact, if Catherine's dead, I take over the firm. You arrange for the bank to throw some cash my way as compensation for her death, we both be ahead. I can cover for you if anything comes up."

"We'll talk about it in the car."

" 'Course, Catherine gotta be dead for this to work," Jesse said, subtly shifting into street language.

"She's dead," Martin announced.

"How you be so sure?" Jesse asked. "She's one tough lady, wouldn't kill easy."

"The man I hired is a pro. They'll find her body in a few days."

"But not Mendoza's, I bet."

"Of course not. He escaped after he killed her."

Jesse gave a high laugh. "Damn good," he exclaimed. "Hey, man, we could do some shit together."

Just as I was wondering what Dan was waiting for, I heard his voice. "Freeze, police."

I shouted, "Go," and Valardi was out the door and across the hall faster than I'd have thought he could move. He kicked the door open and leveled his gun at Martin. I was right behind him.

Martin froze, not because he was ordered to as much as from shock. He stared at the guns pointed at his chest, then slowly lowered his weapon. It took him a few seconds to register the fact that I was standing in the hall. When he did, comprehension replaced confusion.

"Jesse's right," I said. "I'm not easy to kill."

35

THE MENDOZAS HAD their baby in April, a beautiful little girl they named Annlyn. Peter hooked Sam Connors up with a counselor in Pueblo who worked with veterans suffering from posttraumatic stress and who, having been an antiwar activist, was only too happy to keep Luis Ramirez's secret. Luis recently took a job in Walsenburg in the auto-parts store and has been talking a lot about a girl he met there. I've gotten a couple of calls from Lieutenant Colonel Westin but never managed to return them.

Peter recovered from the bullet wound despite the fact that he refused to stay in bed. We finally admitted to ourselves that we were living together, and Peter's housekeeping abilities immediately went to hell. He still cooks, but he no longer picks up his clothes, papers, or dishes. I shudder to think what would happen if we got married.

My parents' visit went remarkably smoothly. My father was torn between pride that his daughter had foiled a major bank-embezzlement scheme and distress that corporate security was no safer than police work. Peter managed to charm my mother on our trip through the wine country. She's now dropping broad hints about his potential as a husband.

Daniel Martin is in jail in Modesto awaiting trial on a murder-for-hire charge and can expect to spend a long time as a guest of the state. His trial is still months away, but the DA has already carved another notch on his law book.

And the fees and bonus? Well, Stephen Chin is still talking to First Central about that one. They have about fifteen lawyers trying to prove that they don't have to honor the contract Martin signed, but they're no match for Stephen. I knew we were fine when he offered to take the case for a percentage of the settlement.

Jesse's near brush with death hasn't reduced his enthusiasm for this kind of work. In fact, it seems to have given him an extra boost of self-confidence, and he is harder to live with than ever. Last month I decided it was finally time to take a step I'd put off for too long, and I offered him a partnership in the firm.

Several people have asked why I chose Jesse instead of Peter if I wanted a partner. I try to explain that it's one thing to trust a man with your life and quite another to trust him with your agency.

About the Author

LINDA GRANT lives in Berkeley, California, with her husband, two daughters, two cats, and miscellaneous rodents and fish.